CATSKILL MONSTERS

BOX SET

ANDIE FENICHEL

CONTENTS

THE MANTICORE'S MATE

THE
MANTICORE'S
MATE
ANDIE FENICHEL

THE MANTICORE'S MATE

CATSKILL MONSTERS

LEONA

I thought I could handle it, but I was wrong. My ex just married my sister at a fancy hotel in upstate New York. The party is just getting going when I reach the last of my strength. I can't take it anymore. With no idea where to go, I run into the woods, hoping to catch my breath. In my panicked state, I get off the hiking trail and lose my way. The music is so far away, I'm not even sure what direction it's coming from. That's when I see a lion. I must have lost my mind because there are no lions in New York. My instinct says to run, but there's something in his eyes that's almost human. I see pain and hopelessness, and in that moment, I can relate to this beast. Thinking he must be injured, I carefully draw close enough to see there's an injection dart protruding from his chest. I might lose an arm for my troubles, but I move in and pull the needle.

CADE

At first, I imagined the beautiful brunette running toward me was a woodland sprite. I've been stuck in my manticore form for too long. Soon I'll lose my humanity completely. I don't know who shot me, but with the poison still pumping in from the syringe, I can't turn back. Then she speaks, telling me to please not bite her. Her voice is sweet and soothing. She pulls the damned needle. I immediately shift into a man, wanting to know more about the angel who saved me. So, when she runs, I chase her. Why she's more scared of a naked man than the monster? I don't know, but I'm willing to spend the rest of my life trying to find out.

Trigger Warning: There is some violence against women from the villain in this story.

CHAPTER ONE

LEONA

$\mathcal{M}$y bridesmaid's gown catches on the brush along the hiking trail. I pull it free with a satisfying tearing of the material. I should care about the gown and the wedding, but I only care about finding enough air to breathe. I had to leave the crowded tent where my sister and her new husband were celebrating their wedding reception. I should get a medal for gutting it out as long as I did. I stood up with my younger sister and watched her exchange vows with the man *I* was supposed to marry one year ago. A better person might have just smiled and sucked it up for the entire horrible night. I'm not that girl.

Making it through the toasts was a monumental feat. The twinkle lights covering everything at the outdoor reception by the lake were starting to make me feel claustrophobic. No one will notice that I'm not there.

My heel catches on a root and I stumble, but catch myself

on a tree. My palm scrapes on the rough bark. The pain is slight, but my emotions bubble to the top and the tears start. I can't stop them. I wander down the hiking path through the woods of Upstate New York.

A whimper that's not mine makes me stop running. Did someone come after me? Why would they?

"Hello?"

The sound changes to a growl.

Narrowing my gaze, the light of the full moon is bright enough to illuminate a figure several yards away. "Who's there?"

Maybe it's a bear and I'm an idiot from the city who's about to get mauled and eaten. I inch closer. After my fiancé dumped me and two months later announced he was going to marry my little sister, getting eaten by a wild animal sounds pretty good. "Who's there?"

The noise stops. The silence is so thick my heart pounds.

The growl starts low and grows into a roar.

"There are no lions in New York," I whisper to myself. "If you're trying to scare me, you've succeeded, but I'm still coming through these trees." There's no way I'm going back to the hotel and having nightmares about this. Whoever is in there is probably a person playing a bad joke.

I push through a row of trees and underbrush. The stupid gown gets tangled and I lose my balance falling forward. My knees hit the ground as do my hands. Grateful for the layers of leaves, I stand and brush myself off.

My heart leaps into my throat. It's a lion, but there are wings and a tail with a stinger at the end. It's been a few years since I studied mythology, but I'm pretty sure this is a manticore in the New York woods. What does one say to a monster who shouldn't exist? "Um, don't kill me?" I step back.

Growling, it leaps forward on all fours but stops short and cocks its head. It sniffs, then looks at me as if I'm something new and curious. Its eyes are golden and intelligent.

Unable to help myself, I reach out a hand and comb my fingers through the soft hair at the side of its cheek. "What are you doing here?"

It leans into my touch and whimpers. The sound is like an injured cat.

I scan its face. "Are you hurt?" Stepping to the side, I scan its body and quickly realize this is a male beast and my cheeks heat. I'm definitely losing what's left of my mind.

His tail looks venomous, like a scorpion's, and it curves up, hovering over me.

"I won't hurt you. I don't think I could if I wanted to." The beast is magnificent and I run my hand along his side. I graze the edge of his bat-like wings and then feel the softness of tiny feathers. I want to explore every inch of him, but I pull my hand back to his side, looking for whatever ails him.

Muscles flexing under my palm, he growls and backs away.

"I want to help you, but I don't know how." Frustrated, I step back to the edge of the small clearing. "Maybe I should go back to the hotel and call a veterinarian." Even as I say it, it sounds ridiculous. Who would believe me?

The manticore faces me and lifts onto his hind legs, exposing his massive underbelly, some parts that look far too human and make me blush yet again, and a broad chest. He's not as furry underneath and a red feathered dart sticks out of him just below his heart.

He bats at the needle with his large paw but to no avail.

"Oh no. Who did this to you?" I start forward and then stop as the beast towers over me by more than two feet. "If you kill me, you won't get that injection dart out of you."

The way his expression softens is almost human and the sound he makes is more purr than growl. Easing back on his haunches, he watches me.

Swallowing down my fear and pushing aside how foolish this is, I move closer. Of course, none of this is possible. I've probably fallen and banged my head. Maybe I'm dying somewhere in these woods. Well, if that's the case, the least I can do is save the creature in my fantasy from whatever liquid is still in the syringe poking from his chest.

His breath is warm and as I reach him, his front leg wraps around my back. Touching me as gently as if he were a house cat looking for affection, he dips his nose to the crook of my neck.

My skin prickles at how close he is and how sensual this all feels with the moon shining down on us. Unable to resist, I run my fingers through the silky fur of his chest until I reach the dart. "I hope this won't hurt too much."

Gripping my waist tighter, his sound is like a human groan of pleasure.

I have to hold back similar sounds. Being in the breadth of his body, standing so close, the warm, musty scent of him fills me, and I'm the most turned-on I've ever been.

I've either lost my mind or am lying unconscious somewhere and my imagination is going wild. Manticores only exist in mythology. The only thing is, I've never had this good of an imagination. I mean, if I could conjure up a sexy monster at will, I'd do it every day.

"I'm going to pull it out." I close my eyes, expecting that

once I remove the needle, this monster is going to devour me. It's lodged deep, and I have to give it a hard yank, but the projectile slides free.

His roar fills the woods, and I try to push away, but he holds me tightly to him. His body is warm and soft fur tickles my face, neck, and chest to the edge of the low neckline of my gown. When he stops the terrifying noise, he caresses my back from my shoulders to the swell of my ass and purrs along my throat.

His cock grows larger and hard against my thigh.

My skin prickles with desire and I grind my hips against him, needing him to satisfy my desire. The want is more than I've ever felt before. Nothing and no one has ever made me out of control until now. I grip his shoulders and run my fingers through the thick fur. Unable to stop the moan that makes its way to my throat, my body aches for release.

I want to climb him and find satisfaction. The need is terrifying. This is absurd. I drop the dart and press harder on his chest.

Releasing me, he stares with longing in his eyes.

"I'm not going to lie. I can see, and I felt how aroused you are, and I felt the attraction too. But I'm a human woman and whatever you are…is too much to comprehend." I inch toward the trees. Wrapping my hand around a yearling, I'm going to need its support to walk away from the beast who in a moment stole my heart. "I hope you'll be alright now."

His face contorts.

"Oh no."

There must be something else wrong. He's in pain again.

The crunch of bone echoes in the woods as his entire body shifts and shrinks. He's distorted, and I feel as if my mind is lost.

I can't move or I would run, but I just stare, the way people can't look away from an accident on the highway. He changes from a magnificent manticore into the most beautiful man I've ever seen. His hair is golden and hangs to his shoulders. His jaw is strong with several days of growth. The cat's eyes are now the most stunning amber but human as they search my face. The rest of him is pure perfection and his shaft, still hard, stands out at attention from his toned body.

My skin prickles with goosebumps. This is any woman's dream. Not mine though. I am terrible with men and the wedding of my ex and my sister is only the most recent evidence. Still, I can't move. I'm mesmerized by his perfection and the way he looks at me like I'm something special.

Opening his mouth as if he's going to speak, he closes it again and shifts his jaw from side to side. "I…argh… A…"

Clouds dim the moon and I blink to see better. I've got to get out of here. "You clearly have some things to deal with. I'm certainly out of my mind." Turning, I run back to the hiking path. My heels are making me stumble, so I stop long enough to kick them off, then run as fast as I can.

His hard footfall and strange noises follow me.

Oh god, he's chasing me. I can't decide if I want him to catch me or not, but I keep running away. The beast was amazing. I have no idea why I helped him, but the man is more than I can bear.

When I reach the hotel, I make a wide arc around the wedding tent and run into the lobby.

"Miss DeRosa, are you alright?" The concierge stands up from behind his desk, concern etched on his narrow face.

Putting on my best all-is-well expression, I attempt a smile. "I'm fine."

He stares at the torn bottom of my gown and my bare feet. "Are you sure?"

I can only imagine what the rest of me looks like. "I took a walk in the woods and lost my shoes." I fake a laugh. "All I need is a hot bath and some sleep."

"If there's anything the hotel can do for you, please call."

"Thank you." I turn and go to the elevators. Waiting for the doors to open, I peer around in case a naked manticore man strides through the lobby to whisk me away. My lady parts tingle at the idea.

The doors open and I rush inside, pressing the button for the twelfth floor. Once I'm in my room, I lock the bolt and flop on the bed.

It was some kind of hallucination. That's all. Maybe someone slipped me something in my champagne. That creepy friend of Derek's, Toby, has never seemed right to me. That's it. I managed to get through the worst night of my life, had a crazy adventure that almost made the wedding worth it, and now I'll go to sleep. Everything will be fine in the morning.

CHAPTER TWO

CADE

She was like a goddess who had come to save me by the light of the full moon. Only she isn't magical or a monster like me. She's a human. Maybe I shouldn't have chased her, but my beast couldn't help himself.

I wish I could have spoken to her, found out her name, and told her mine. I'd been in my manticore form too long. Whatever that poison was, it meant to keep me a beast. Whoever shot me must want to expose what I am. If I'd remained a monster much longer, my humanity might have left me for good. It's never safe to be shifted for more than a day, and I was going on three when my angel found me.

Standing in the shadow of the thick trees and cover of darkness, I stare up at her window. Once my ability to speak returns, I'll introduce myself. The scent of her fills me with desire and more. I want to protect her, though I don't know what from. All I know for sure is the brown-haired beauty who saved me is mine and I have to make sure she knows it, too.

Movement inside her window catches my attention. She leans on the windowsill with her chin in her palm and stares at the moon. Is she thinking about me? Have I made her look so wistful?

My long keen can't be stopped as my beast calls to her.

Wide-eyed, she looks toward the ground, but her gaze never stops when it passes my hiding place. She can't see me, even though I think she knows I'm here. She moves away from the window and a moment later, the light goes out.

There's no hope of seeing her again tonight, so I head through the woods toward my home. Maybe I can get a few hours' sleep and, in the morning, I'll be able to speak to her.

The Greentree Resort has been here since a few years after I moved into these woods eighty years ago. I was a young manticore then, with plans to find my mate and raise a dozen beasts in the wilds of New York State. Foolish idea to think there was a shifter who would happen into my woods and identify herself as my fated mate.

All these years later, it never happened. Well, until last night when I was hours from losing my humanity, the one woman meant for me finally arrived. The problem is, she's no shifter. She's human and does not know anything about monsters. Still, she didn't run away from my beast. No, my angel didn't run until I was in my human form. Curious, she was more afraid of a man than a manticore.

Pulling up in front of the Greentree's main building, I park and draw in a long breath. I'm far too excited. I need to be calm and keep her calm when I see her. I need to be a gentleman, though all I want is to drag her back to my house and claim her.

I catch the scent of her, and I'm out of the car in an instant. Sniffing the air, I head toward the lake. She's alone, her wavy brown hair gleaming in the sunlight and catching the breeze as she strolls along the edge of the water.

Instincts are pulling me to run, but I force myself to walk only fast enough to catch up with her. I don't want her to feel chased.

Another woman with similar hair color calls out, "Leona, where are you going?" She's standing with a large group having a picnic at the nearer side of the lake.

"Just taking a walk, Mom. I'll be back in a little while," my angel responds with a wave.

Leona. Her name rolls through my mind as if it's a sign from above. I walk a bit faster.

"You'll miss brunch," her mother scolds.

Another woman, younger, wearing a white sundress, puts her hands on her hips. "Just let her go, Mom. She's in a mood again."

I get on the path that's been maintained to keep strollers from accidentally walking too close to the edge and falling into the lake. Hopefully, I look like a guest out for a walk.

As I draw closer, I'm able to hear Leona whisper, "I have every right to be in a mood. Why did I ever agree to come here for the farce of a wedding? Now I'm a crazy person who sees monsters and talks to herself."

The path winds into a stand of trees at the farthest end of the lake. As soon as I'm shaded by the trees, I find Leona leaning against a tree with tears running down her cheeks.

My heart breaks. "You're not crazy if that's any consolation."

She gasps and covers her mouth with her hand as if she's holding back screams. "You."

Holding out my hands palms out, I hope I don't look threatening. "I'm not going to hurt you, Leona."

"How do you know my name?" She skirts around the tree, putting it between her and me.

"Your mother bellowed it across the lake." I love the way her eyes scan down my body, and I long to know what she's thinking.

Shifting her gaze toward where her mother and sister are having brunch under a white tent with about fifty other people, she laughs. The sound is intoxicating. "You're real."

"Of course, I'm real. I wanted to thank you for saving my life last night." I risk a step closer.

Gripping the oak tree, she holds her place. She's just as beautiful as I remember and those blue eyes are mesmerizing. Her little white sneakers crunch the old leaves and her matching shorts now have a smudge of dirt on the left thigh.

I love the way her curves are perfectly contained in those shorts and how her pink top dips low across her breasts, which makes my mouth water.

She brushes the dirt from her shorts. "I think that's a bit dramatic. I just pulled the dart out. Anyone could have done that."

One more step closer and I'm only an arm's length away from everything I've always dreamed of having. "But no one else found me in the three days since I was in that state. If I'd stayed in that form much longer, I wouldn't have been able to shift back. I was losing my humanity. You saved my life. I don't know why someone poisoned me or even how they knew about me, but I shudder to think about what might have happened if they'd been able to keep me a manticore forever."

"Why would anyone want that?" She steps away from the protection of the tree, which brings her even closer.

I shrug. "My kind live a long time. Maybe they wanted to kill me and prove my existence."

"What's your name?"

I hold out my hand. "Cade Petroyan. I'm forever in your debt."

After a short hesitation, she shakes my hand and her cheeks pink. "Leona DeRosa. There's no debt. I'm glad I could help."

"May I at least buy you lunch?" My heart is pounding with worry that she'll turn me down. I'm already thinking of other ways to be in her company.

She glances back toward the tent, then at me. "Can you get me away from this fucking place for a few hours and do you promise not to turn into a beast and kill me?"

"Man or beast, the last thing I want to do is kill you, Leona."

Her mother's fake laughter carries across the lake. Her sister and a male voice talk above the din of the group about how glad they are their friends and family could join them for the start of their married life, and wishing everyone a safe journey home.

Looking through the tree's canopy, she looks at the sky. "I just need to be somewhere else for a while. Maybe I can borrow Mr. Baker's car." She says the last to herself.

Suddenly, my good friend Brian is on my not-so-friendly list. Has he been flirting with my Leona?

I take a deep breath. "Brian is a nice enough guy and I'm sure if I asked him, he'd loan you his car. He and I have been friends for ten years. However, I'd be honored if you'd allow me to assist you in running away for a few hours." I offer my arm.

It's adorable the way she sets her jaw before she threads her hand through my elbow. "No killing me or eating me or stabbing me with that tail."

"I will only do what you allow, Leona, and never will I harm you in any way. I promise you that on the graves of my parents and their parents." I caress her fingers with my other hand and have to close my eyes for a moment as a wave of purposiveness floods me.

"You're kind of formal, Cade. I like it." She takes a deep breath, which lifts her breasts high, and her shirt stretches to contain them. When she lets it out, she nods and we walk.

My cock thinks the top and shorts should go altogether, and the woods were a good private place to remove them. My monster agrees. I quell both and enjoy walking her to my car.

She keeps her gaze straight ahead and never looks over at her family.

"You don't want to tell them where you're going? Won't they worry?" I open the passenger door.

"They won't even notice as long as Melony is the center of attention and Derek is making money selling his vitamins. If anything goes wrong, they'll regret I'm not there to blame it on." She sits and buckles her seatbelt before crossing her arms over her chest and staring blankly out the windshield.

Gently closing the door, I'm quickly growing to dislike the picnickers. I round the car and get in. "I know a great place for burgers unless you want something fancier."

"No. I'm not dressed for fancy. I love a good burger and fries."

I get on the road toward town and call Brian.

"Hi, Cade. Where have you been?" Brian's chipper voice asks through my car's speakers.

Leona's shapely brows pull together, and she opens her mouth as if to scold me. She points her finger at me.

I wrap my hand around her finger and bring it to my lips.

She gasps at the touch but doesn't pull away.

"I had a bit of a cold, but I'm fine now. I'm taking one of your guests, Miss DeRosa, to lunch and a tour of the area. Just wanted to let you know in case her family asks about her. I wouldn't want you sending the police looking for her when we're at the Burger Barn."

Brian laughs. "Have fun. I think they're planning to play games on the back lawn until the bulk of the guests leave. They've booked a formal dinner for the immediate family before the show tonight."

Leona says, "I'll be back by dinner or maybe the show, Mr. Baker." The way her cheeks darken, I wonder what she thinks might delay her past a couple of hours. I'm in favor of whatever it is.

"Have a good time, Miss DeRosa." Brian disconnects the call.

With her hand still in mine I lower both to her thigh. "Is this okay, Leona?"

Shifting her hand, she threads her fingers through mine. "Yes."

"You'll tell me if I do anything you don't like?" My cock is already responding just to the sweet touch of her hand in mine. I never want to let her go.

"I'll tell you."

CHAPTER THREE

LEONA

Cade didn't lie. The Burger Barn had amazing food and now, standing at an overlook with his strong body only an inch behind mine, all I want is to feel his touch. Well, I also want to know exactly what he is. There are a slew of questions floating around in my head.

He skims a hand over my shoulder and the electricity shoots between us as if we're both charged by lightning.

I lean back against his chest and he wraps his arms around me. "Why am I so attracted to you?"

"I'm very good-looking." He laughs.

I can't help joining in the amusement. "That's true, but not exactly what I meant."

Nuzzling my neck, he kisses where it meets my shoulder. "I know. I don't know how to answer."

Turning to look him in the eye, I study him. "But there *is* an answer?"

He shrugs and tucks my hair behind my ear. "Maybe."

The sky is bright over the rolling mountains of green where he brought me to a gorgeous overlook. It won't be dark for several hours. I'm supposed to be back at the hotel for dinner at eight. "I don't have my phone. What time is it?"

"Almost one." He takes my hand from where I've got it tightly wrapped around my waist. "I could show you another beautiful view of these mountains."

"Where do you live?" The first of my questions. "I found you last night and you were maybe a mile from the resort. Do you have a home or den somewhere nearby?"

"I have a *house* about twenty miles from where we met." He studies my face as if he can read my mind. "Do you want to see my home?"

My cheeks are on fire. I hate that I blush at the drop of a hat. "I want to go somewhere we can talk. I want you to explain what I saw last night. I want to know why I want you so fiercely. What are you? Who are you? Why would someone want to hurt you? Why are you here with me instead of finding out who attacked you?"

His massive shoulders rise and fall with a sigh. "Lots of questions. Are you sure you want all those answers?"

No, is the truth, but I nod. I'm not sure of anything except that I don't want him to take me back to the resort and never see him again.

Without a word, he leads me to his shiny black high-end car and opens the door for me. I'm embarrassed that at thirty years old, he's the first man who's ever held a car door for me. As soon as we're on the road, he takes my hand and kisses my knuckles, then rests our hands on my leg as if we've been riding together for years and this is perfectly natural.

"Since once we arrive at my house, I need to respond to all those thoughts rolling around in your mind, may I ask you a question?" He gives my hand a gentle squeeze.

"Go ahead." My life is not a secret.

"Why are you so keen to be away from your sister's wedding party, Leona? Why did you escape to the woods last night?" His voice is gentle and the sound fills me as he speaks.

I could listen to that sound for a hundred years. The way he pronounces every syllable with equal importance. He says my name with so much reverence. I'm doomed if I stay near him, yet I can't pull away. "My sister married the man I was engaged to for three years."

While he still holds my hand gently and caresses my palm with his thumb, his other hand tightens to white knuckles on the wheel. His voice is tight. "When did you end the engagement?"

I pull my hand from his. "Derek ended it by telling me he'd met someone else. A short time later my sister announced that they were getting married. Then she told me it was better this way. That if I loved him, I would have set a date. Then he told me he was sorry he hadn't said something sooner, but he didn't want to hurt me."

The same growl he'd made when he was a beast in the woods rumbles through the car as he pulls into a driveway that takes us up a mountain. When the trees clear, a beautiful two-story home with stone columns and a wraparound porch fills the space. The sun gleams off large front windows.

He throws the car into Park and growls as he exits.

Not sure what to do, I stay in the car.

Cade stands in front of the hood with his back to me and

his fists at his sides. His broad back stretches the material of his shirt as he breathes.

After a long minute, I get out of the car and walk to him. "I'm sorry I made you angry." Half expecting him to transform into a manticore, I touch his arm gently.

In an instant, he pulls me into his arms, wraps himself around me, and holds me against his body. "You never need to apologize to me. I know she is your sister, but her behavior is abhorrent. The man is a pig. How is it that your mother has sided with this marriage?"

Loving the feel of him all around me, I relax against him. "Mom goes with the flow. She likes Derek because he's very wealthy. My father was less supportive, but eventually decided he may as well go along."

"Why did you go to their wedding?" He cups my cheek and bends his knees so he can see my eyes.

"I don't know. Maybe to prove that I could, that I'm over him and her. To be the bigger person. Then I got here and it was too horrible and all I've done is run away and hide." My laugh sounds as sad as it feels.

Even in the short time that I've known Cade, it's easy to see that he wants to say something more.

"It's okay. I know I'm a loser for being here and letting them walk all over me." I walk to the porch, step up, and give the rocking chair a push. It makes the most wonderful sound on the wood deck and I wonder what it's like to sit here and have coffee in the morning.

"That's not what I was thinking, Leona. They should treat you with more respect, but I'm glad you're here with me, regardless of the circumstances." He slips his hand into mine.

My tears start, and I throw myself against him and sob. "I'm sorry. I never cry."

He cups the back of my head and caresses my back. "Maybe it's just what you need." Lifting me as if I weigh nothing, he carries me inside and sits with me in his lap on one of three long gray couches with red and black throw pillows.

I hate crying at all, but crying in front of someone is the worst. I sniffle and pull myself together. The house is a mix of rustic and modern with a cathedral ceiling and steps at the back wall. Behind the couch, the kitchen stretches along one full wall, with an island and stools. A dining table stands in the front portion of the house, and a large hand-hewn post at the corner separates the kitchen from the dining room. The cabinets are natural oak with glass fronts on the very top ones.

I sniffle again. "Nice house."

His smile is everything and goes right to my heart.

"May I use your bathroom?" I badly need to wash my face and blow my nose.

Nodding, he points to the stairs. "Under the steps, you'll see a door to the powder room. If you need more space, there are two bathrooms upstairs."

I wiggle from his lap, completely turned-on by how good he feels, no matter where we're touching. "The powder room will do."

It takes me a few minutes to get myself calm enough so that my eyes aren't red and my nose has stopped running. Any makeup I applied this morning is gone, but at least the cold water helped with my swollen nose and eyes.

He's still sitting on the couch, but now he's at one end. His gaze never strays from me as I make my way around the coffee table and sit on the other end of the same couch.

I like the way he's grouped three large couches around

the table to fill the extremely large room. "Tell me everything."

There's a slight twitch in his lips. "Let me see if I can remember all that you asked. First, you want to know what you saw last night. Well, you saw my manticore form. I was born this way to a mother and father who were also shifters. We lived in a community of monsters in the Rocky Mountains. My mother became ill about eighty years ago and wanted to come back here to the place where she was born. She died here and soon after, my father also died. That's often the case with mates, when one dies, the other doesn't last long. I could have gone back west, but I like it here so I stayed. Four days ago, while in my manticore form, I was hunting a deer and someone shot me with a dart. I wasn't able to shift back to human. If you hadn't pulled the dart, I would never have been able to shift back, as I was losing my humanity.

"That covers what I am and what you saw. I don't know why anyone would want to hurt me, but it's not the first time someone has found out about monsters and thought they might gain something by capturing us. I'm not interesting in my human form, so keeping me a manticore would be beneficial to a circus or something like that. I can't say for sure, because I don't know who shot me."

When he doesn't continue, I draw a long breath. "That leaves why you're with me instead of finding out who did that to you."

He grins and slowly crawls toward me on the couch. "You forgot about why you want me so fiercely."

Swallowing my sudden trepidation and wishing I had kept my big mouth shut, I say, "I didn't forget. I guess I was hoping you had."

Running his nose along my throat and down my chest to the crease between my tits, he breathes me in. "I won't forget any of this." His eyes glow gold like the manticore's. "I'm with you because I want you as much as you want me. More maybe."

I shift so that I can look him in the eyes. "Impossible."

"I'm over a hundred years old, Leona, and I've never wanted anyone like this. Do you want to know my theory about why that is?" He skims his hand down my waist then touches the exposed skin between my shorts and my shirt.

His touch sets me on fire with need, and I lift my hips trying to get some friction. Any small satisfaction would help this fire roasting inside me. "Tell me your theory."

"I think you're my mate. I think after all these years, you are the one woman who can complete me." He kisses my neck and his tongue touches my pulse.

Gasping, I wrap one leg around his and press my center against the bulge in his pants. My moan fills the room. I'm breathless, but I say, "I don't believe in soul mates or that there's only one person meant for each of us. I'm not even a manticore. So how can your theory be true?"

Cade cups my ass with his hand, squeezes, and rubs his shaft against me. "Soul mates are something different. I can't say if they exist or not. Even love is something else, though not mutually exclusive. A fated mate is nature's way of bonding two people for life. I can't give you scientific proof or even explain how it works. Last night I was a monster. I might have killed a human who came close to me. I was starved and barely aware of who I was. When I saw you, that changed." He suddenly stands and rubs the back of his neck.

"I knew the moment I caught your scent that you are my

mate, Leona. Don't ask me how, the beast inside me just knows."

Lying on his couch, probably looking wanton and disheveled, I should be embarrassed, but I've never wanted anyone more. "I don't know what any of that means. I only know that I feel like I'll die if you don't make love to me."

CHAPTER FOUR

CADE

*H*er admission should make me take a step back and give her time, but I need to feel all of her and have her feel all of me. It's primal, and I can't push it away. I kneel so that we're eye-to-eye and run my knuckles along her jaw. "I don't want you to regret anything between us."

Leaning into my touch, she bites her bottom lip. "Will you promise me something?"

"Anything." I would give her the world if it were mine to give. There's nothing she can ask of me that I wouldn't move mountains to make hers.

"Promise me that you'll never lie to me. Even if you think the truth will hurt me. Even if you're sure no good can come from me knowing. I know it's possible this is a weird expression of my insane year and maybe none of this is real.

Maybe I just need to be good and laid." She laughs, but her eyes shine with unshed tears.

"I promise you there will only ever be truth between us." I lift her from the couch, stand, and carry her upstairs to my bedroom. Laying her gently on my bed, I have to take a moment to calm the beast inside me. He is jostling for position and perhaps one day, I'll let him have his way, but not today. I don't want to scare her. I want to worship her.

She sits up and scrambles to the middle of the mattress. "Um, I have a concern."

With one knee on the bed, I freeze. "Tell me."

Her face is bright red and the flush goes all the way down to where it disappears beneath her pink top.

Stretching out with my head on the pillow, I open my arm for her to lie back with me.

Kicking off her little white sneakers, she eases in beside me and presses her cheek to my chest. Using her delicate fingers to toy with the buttons of my golf shirt, her manicured nails lightly scratch my chest. "I'm not a kid."

"I'm aware." I caress the strip of skin that gets exposed between her shorts and top every time she reaches her hand up. She's soft and smells of jasmine and moss. I'm drunk on her as I kiss the top of her head.

"Well normally, there's time in a relationship where I get to know a person before I've seen them naked and, um, well, aroused." She buries her head against me.

"Not the case with us as I was already hard when I shifted yesterday." I try my best not to laugh at her obvious embarrassment. "What concerns you, Leona?"

"I'm not a virgin, but um…"

Changing our positions so she's on her back and I can

look into her eyes, I wait for more, but she blushes impossibly darker and closes her eyes.

"And now the siren from the living room is shy?" I kiss her cheek, her jaw, her earlobe.

She moans softly. "You're very big, Cade. I'm concerned that you'll be disappointed."

It takes a lot of willpower not to chuckle, but I can hear in the shake of her voice that she's serious. "I promise you, nothing between us could disappoint me. There's a lot to do before we get to that, sweet little lioness. I need to make you come at least three times before I bury my cock deep inside you."

"Three times." She lets out a short loud laugh. "I never orgasm more than once."

It sounds like a challenge to my beast and I have to agree. "Today you will."

Biting her lip, she says, "I trust you, but…"

I kiss a path down her shoulder and across her chest to the edge of her top. "I don't like the 'but' so tell me what other concerns you have." Unable to resist, I take her ass in my hand and massage the soft flesh, letting my thumb slide against the soft skin of her inner thigh.

"Oh god. That feels good. Will you turn into the other you?" There's no fear in her voice.

When I look at her face, her pupils are dilated and her breath is quick. I can't tell if she longs for my beast or is worried he'll take over. "Do you want the manticore, Leona?"

"No lies between us?"

"Never." I kneel between her legs.

Easing up onto her elbows, she meets my gaze. "I want you both, or are you the same? I don't know how to explain it. I want you, and I want the beast, but I'm a little afraid of both of you."

My cock jumps to fully erect. I grab it through my trousers and massage it while she watches. "Neither man nor beast will ever harm you, but for today, I will remain a man if that's alright with you."

Her smile is everything. "It's good to know what to expect. Well, sometimes."

She's cute, beautiful, and cheeky. She's everything a man or beast could want.

I reach for the button at the top of her shorts and undo it with one hand before sliding the zipper down.

Pulling her top over her head, she stares at me. The rouge of her areolae shows through the pink lace bra, making my mouth water.

Gripping the sides of her shorts, I pull them over her ass and down her legs. In just the lace bra and panties, she's a vision in my bed. "You're beautiful."

Unhooking the front of her bra, she tosses it away. "Do I get to see you?"

Leaning in, I press my lips to hers and taste her for the first time. She's sweet and her mouth moves softly and sensually against mine. Her tongue seeks mine with shy urgency. Kissing her is like a melding of souls. She calms the beast more effectively than anything or anyone has in my life. Reluctant to break the kiss, I don't want to deny her anything, but I need to taste more of her.

I press my lips to her nipple and lave my tongue over it before stepping from the bed and stripping out of my clothes.

"I don't know if I can ever get used to how perfect you

are." She traces the pads of her fingers along my ribs as she rolls toward me.

My beast purrs, but I need more. I need to give her pleasure. Wrapping my arm around her thighs, I drag her around, kneel on the floor, then pull her to the edge of the bed. Placing her knees over each of my shoulders, the scent of her arousal fills me.

"Cade?"

"I want to taste you." I blow a puff of air against her wet center.

"Yes." She grips the bedding and arches her hips.

Taking the first taste, it's like a drug addiction. She's sweet and I want everything she is. I press my tongue inside her.

She rises and falls with the pressure of my tongue.

I lick her from bottom to top. "You taste like heaven." I suckle her clit.

Grabbing fists full of my hair, she calls my name and rides my face.

I feel her need and suck harder. Skimming my hand over her abdomen and ribs, I find her breast and mold it to my hand then pinch her nipple.

She screams and comes apart, drenching my face with her nectar.

Lapping up every drop until she pushes me away with her feet on my shoulders, I take her in my arms and pull her against me on the bed. "You're gorgeous when you come."

"I think I may have alerted your neighbors with my screams." She giggles.

"There's no one within ten miles of here. Scream all you want, as long as it's with pleasure, Leona." I run my hand down the curve of her spine. She's so strong and soft at the same time. I cup her ass cheek and kneed the flesh.

She arches against me and makes the most delectable sounds in her throat.

The cat in me purrs against her ear and she must like it because she nibbles my earlobe, then my throat while rubbing her pelvis against my cock. She's so wet her juices coat my shaft and thigh. I reach between her soft inner thighs and press my finger inside her wetness.

"Yes. Oh, Cade. Yes." As she rides my thigh rubbing her clit against my muscle, I press a second finger inside her tight pussy. "I can't. Oh fuuuck!"

Her body pulses around my fingers and my cock jerks with the feelings of being cheated of being inside her and feeling her pleasure erupt.

Lifting my fingers to my mouth, I taste her for the second time. "I promised one more."

"You make it sound like a dare." She presses her lips to my chest, finds my nipple and sucks.

My cock jerks between us. "A promise is a promise, sweet little lioness." I grip her hips and lift her so she's straddling my face.

Her gasp makes me smile as she settles her spread slit over my hungry mouth and rides my face hard and fast.

Screaming my name, she rocks faster.

I grip her hips and keep her where I can suck her tight little clit while sliding my thumb, wet with her juices, over her puckered little back entrance.

Jerking hard and fast, she comes on a long scream. She rolls to the side and collapses on the mattress. "You're a wicked beast."

I might be offended, except I can hear the delight in her voice. "You're the most spectacular woman I've ever met."

"I still don't think your massive cock is going to fit inside me." She snuggles her ass back against me and moans.

Wrapping my arm around her, I pull her tight. "You can decide how much, how far, how fast, mate."

With a glance over her shoulder, she smiles. "Does that mean I'm in charge?"

"You will always be in control unless you don't want to be, Leona." I caress from her tits down to her abdomen, dipping a finger in her belly button.

My reward is a gasp and she rolls her hips against my straining cock. "I still want you, even after three orgasms, I still want more. Is this what it's like to have a mate?"

"I've never had one before, so I can only guess. I can tell you one thing—I'm yours for the taking." I roll onto my back.

CHAPTER FIVE

LEONA

*M*ine. Yes, I can feel that this perfect man is mine. Nothing before him can compare. My engagement to Derek had been a terrible mistake and now I know why. I shudder at the possibility that I might have married him and never met Cade.

Facing him, I skim my hand over his broad chest. Every inch of him is perfection and I make my way along his ribs, loving the way his breath catches. His alarmingly big cock draws me like a magnet, and I wrap my fingers around him. Teasing, I gently slide up and down the soft turgid flesh, eliciting a satiating groan.

"You can't know how good that feels or how much I want you to take me inside you." He combs his fingers through my hair.

I love the feel of his hands on me no matter where, but I need to give him some of the pleasure he gifted me. I lick the precum from the tip of his cock, grip the base, and suck him as deep as I can.

His hips rise to meet my mouth each time I suck him in, and his hold on my hair tightens enough to make my scalp tingle. It's so erotic I might come again just from giving him a blow job. Everything about him, about us, is exquisite.

"I don't think I can hold off much longer if you keep sucking my cock like that. If this is what you want, I'm not going to stop you, but I'd love to be inside that luscious pussy." His voice is rough.

I love the idea of him coming in my mouth, but maybe that's for another time. My pussy aches to have him inside me. I lick him like an ice pop on a hot summer day and meet his gaze. "I want more."

Straddling his hips, I align my slick folds with his thick shaft. I'm still not convinced I can handle his size, but I trust him as I've never trusted anyone. Letting gravity take over, I take in an inch of him and the stretch is wonderful. "Oh god. You feel…"

He rests his hands on my hips. "You're perfect, Leona."

Rising, my clit pulses and I cry his name as I lower, taking more of him and stretching to accommodate his girth. "So good." I want to say more but the waves of sensation are making me incoherent.

Again, I rise, then take more and more. My body pulses around him and my screams of pleasure fill the room. I collapse on his chest, trying to catch my breath while the waves ebb but don't stop completely.

Petting my hair, he kisses the top of my head. Strain tightens his voice. "You're driving me crazy. I knew feeling you come around me would be fantastic, but nothing could have prepared me for how good that feels."

I should be sated, but I can't get enough of him. I tilt my pelvis, changing the angle and creating more delight. "I can't. So good."

He holds my hips and fucks me from below. His moans mix with mine.

Sitting up, I throw my head back and ride him hard and fast until my body convulses with pleasure and he empties himself deep inside me, taking the orgasm to another level. I collapse and roll to the side.

Cade pulls me into the circle of his arms and holds me close. "You are everything, little lioness."

"I don't know anything about you," I whisper, wondering if I should keep my mouth shut and keep all of this the dream it is.

"Don't you?" His lips press to the back of my neck.

I sigh. "You live in the woods in a beautiful home. What do you do for a living, or don't people like you work?"

"I have investments left to me by my parents and I live extremely comfortably from those. I have a broker's license and do some advising to a select group of clients. I pay my taxes and stay out of trouble." His voice is soft and strong and even after the marathon sex, it stirs me to want him all over again.

"How do you explain your age on paper?" It's another question that's been nagging at me. "Are there other creatures like you?" I'm trying to figure out how this dream goes beyond a weekend and into real life. Emotions bloom inside me and I have to bite my lip to keep from crying.

Rolling me over so that I'm on my back and he's leaning over me, he meets my gaze. "On paper, I have to die every so often and then become a new person, but it's easy enough to make that happen. Why do you look ready to sob?"

My chin quivers, and I can't get it to stop no matter how hard I bite my lip. "How do I fit into this life?"

"Any way you want to, Leona." He says it so softly, sweetly, that his emotions show, too. "I don't know much about how you live, but I will do whatever you need to see you beyond this weekend." He sighs and kisses my forehead. "There are other monsters in various places. Some live in secret and there are a few towns where they live in the open."

Gulping in air helps the well of worry from brimming over. "I'm a technical consultant for digital marketing. I live in Brooklyn in a tiny apartment. I refuse to take money from my parents, so it's all I can afford at the moment."

Cade leans his back on the headboard, opening his arms for me to sit with him.

Pulling the sheet with me as if he hasn't already seen every inch of me, I cuddle against his chest. "I'm having a hard time seeing how this thing between us works. I mean after I go home." I'm jumping to a lot of conclusions and making assumptions about his feelings, which is not like me.

His arms tighten around me. "Let's get dressed and get you back to the resort for your family dinner."

That's it then. He'll drop me off, and I'll never see him again. I know he said he wants more, but men say things to gain what they want. Look at all the lies Derek told me and I knew him for years. I've only known Cade for a fraction of that time. At least I have this afternoon as the best memory of my life. I wipe away a rogue tear and get out of bed. Gathering my clothes, I dash into the bathroom. I slide the black barn door closed before the waterworks start.

Dropping my clothes on the black granite vanity between two copper sinks, I take a deep breath, hoping it will push aside my emotions. It turns into more of a shudder and I cover my mouth to keep the sob from being audible.

Get a grip, Leona. You just met this guy. He's a monster. Well, a monster who happens to seem like the best man I've ever known. How was this ever going to end well? It wasn't, so pull yourself together.

The shower is glass with one end open. The tile has flecks of copper that catch the light. I turn on the water and hope the sound covers my inability to stop crying. As soon as it's warm, I step under the spray and sob.

The wheels of the barn door roll against its track. Rather than turn around, I keep my back to the door and pray he won't notice I'm a wreck!

Cade steps under the water and the heat of his body engulfs me before he wraps his arms around me. "Are you having regrets about today?"

I shake my head. How could I ever regret a single minute with him? No. I'll never regret today, only that I'm ruined for life because this will be what any relationship is compared to and nothing can live up to perfection.

"What is it?" He turns me in his arms and uses his body to block the water from spraying in my face. Everything about him is kind and considerate.

"I don't know how I became so attached, but I'm sad about what happens when you drop me off today." Why was I so honest? I'm pathetic.

Kissing my forehead, then my cheek, he pulls me tight against his body. "I'm not giving up on you or us. I don't know how this works out, but somehow, we'll find a way. If you agree, I'd like to meet your family. You could bring me to dinner tonight."

My emotions turn from sorrow to panic. My family is a nightmare. "Why would you want to meet them?"

"Because they are a part of your life. If you don't want them to meet me, I understand." He pulls back and the water sprays between us.

This is a crazy conversation to have naked in the shower, but he has to know. "It's not them meeting you that I'm worried about, Cade. They can be a bit much. Once you meet them, you'll find out that…"

"What will I find out?" He smiles as he uses two fingers under my chin to tip my gaze to his.

My heart is pounding, and my mouth is dry despite the water flowing over us. "That no woman is worth being associated with a family so dysfunctional."

His full laugh calms me. "I don't want to be with them, Leona. I want you."

Cade waits in the hotel lobby while I go up to my room to change for dinner. When I return, he's leaning on the concierge desk, chatting with Brian. In a black suit with a white shirt and no tie, he looks every bit the casual businessman. No one would believe a beast lives within that elegant form and easy smile.

With his top two buttons undone, just a hint of blond hair shows, and my mouth waters at the sight. I'm not at all sure why he wants me, but I shouldn't overthink it.

As if sensing me, he turns and studies me from head to

toe. I was going to wear black pants and a peach blouse but decided on the red slip dress. I bought it on a whim and never dared to wear it before.

Without looking back, he says something to Brian, who laughs. Cade makes his way to me like a lion stalking his prey. "You're stunning." He leans close and kisses my cheek. "I want to take that dress off of you right now. It's going to be a long evening."

My cheeks heat but before I can respond, my mother bellows my name from across the lobby.

Every head in the room turns toward Patty DeRosa with her perfectly dyed and styled hair, wearing a bubblegum-pink pencil skirt and matching blazer. "Where have you been all day, Leona Jane DeRosa?"

She pulled out the middle name. I must be in trouble. Taking a deep breath, I face her. "I made a new friend, Mom. We went to lunch and he took me for a tour of the area." Not all of the truth, but not a lie either. I'm good with Mom not knowing Cade was giving me the best sex of my life for the last few hours.

Mom's attention shifts to Cade. She gives his suit a long stare and then his watch. I can practically see the calculator ticking off dollar signs in her head.

Wearing the most charming smile, he holds out his hand. "Mrs. DeRosa, it's a pleasure to meet you. I'm Cade Petroyan."

Completely out of character, my mother blushes as she gives him the tips of her fingers, and giggles when he kisses the back of her hand. "Do you live in the area, Mr. Petroyan?"

"Cade, please. I live about twenty miles from here." He keeps her hand in his when she makes no move to take it back.

"You must call me Patty. Will you stay for dinner and the show? We'll have an extra setting made. We'd love to get to know Leona's new friend." Mom's voice is like syrup.

His smile could light the entire resort. "It would be my pleasure, and I confess, Patty, I'm in no hurry to leave your daughter's side."

Slipping her arm through the crook of his arm, Mom says, "We should go before we're late."

He looks about to burst out laughing when he takes my hand and draws me along with them. "See, this is going to be fine."

My stomach swims with butterflies.

CHAPTER SIX

CADE

$\mathcal{I}$ want to be the bigger man and not react to the sister who betrayed Leona or the ex who hurt her. Just not sure I can pull it off. Plastering a smile on my face, I offer my hand when Patty introduces me.

John DeRosa stands and shakes my hand. "How do you know our little Leona?"

"We met while she was walking the path through the woods. I needed some help and Leona was gracious enough to assist." It's mostly the truth.

Her sister, Melony, makes a scoffing sound. "What on earth could she do to help a man like you?" She looks at me as if she might like to have me for dinner, instead of whatever's on the menu.

Melony has been married for one day and her husband's frown says it all. He sits as straight as the back of his chair will allow and scratches his five o'clock shadow. His gaze narrows on me. "I'm sure Leona was happy to help. Would you care to share what service she provided you, Mr. Petroyan?"

There's no way to tell the truth, but I struggle for a believable lie.

Clearing her throat, Leona smiles. "Cade is exaggerating. He had his foot caught under a root and I just helped him work free. It was nothing. Like Melony said, what could I do? I'm not an outdoorsy woman."

"I might still be out there if it hadn't been for you." I hate that she accepts the disrespect from her sister, and I get the impression it's a common occurrence.

Derek mutters something under his breath.

Giggling, Melony glances at her husband, then as soon as I sit, she faces me. "Cade, what do you do for a living? You look as if you might be a professional weightlifter."

"Hardly." I force a smile. "I'm a financial adviser."

Melony raises her eyebrows and gives Leona a knowing grin.

I suppose esthetically, Melony is pretty. She has blond hair with the tips dyed dark brown and her face is heart-shaped. However, her blue eyes shine with deception.

When I look at her, my gut tightens, inspiring caution.

The rest of dinner is filled with small talk. Even between family members, there is no substance to the conversation.

"It's unusual to stay after the marriage. Are you two going anywhere besides the Catskills for your honeymoon?" I wave off the waiter filling wine glasses. I've already had two glasses, and I don't want to assume Leona will invite me to her room tonight.

The way Melony's mouth pulls into a tight line and her eyes narrow before she plasters a smile on her face shows her annoyance. "We wanted some time with our family." She exaggerates the last word. "We'll go somewhere when Derek's work is less busy."

He wraps his arm around her and kisses her cheek. "I promise in a couple of months, things will wrap up on this project and I'll take you wherever you want to go."

Leona's shoulders stiffen, and she too waves off the waiter serving wine, as well as the one coming around with chocolate mousse. "I need to get some air. I'm not used to two glasses of wine with dinner."

Derek stands as I do. "Are you alright?"

Tugging his jacket, Melony frowns. "She's fine."

"You'll be at the show, won't you?" Patty asks, but her attention is locked on the newlyweds.

"Yes. Just a short walk in the fresh mountain air and I'll be fine." Leona walks away, and practically runs out of the dining room.

I scan the table and only Derek is looking at anything other than his dessert. However, he's not watching Leona leave. He's staring at me. His jaw ticks and his eyes narrow.

If he still wanted Leona, why had he dumped her and married her sister? Maybe I've got that wrong. I push my chair under the table. "It was nice to meet you all. Thank you. I'm going to check on Leona."

Without waiting for anyone to respond, I head toward the front of the resort.

As I cross the lobby, Brian clears his throat to get my attention, then points toward the back of the main building where the pool and gardens are.

Changing direction, I make my way outside. Since dinner is still being served, there are only a few people in the pool.

I see her red dress at the other end of the pool, heading

for the rose garden. Following, I hope she isn't running from me.

"You probably think I'm a flake," she says as I enter the garden where a rose-lined path circles an English garden. She strolls past the roses.

"No." The moon plus strings of twinkle lights make it easy to see and follow. "If I'm honest, I'm not crazy about your family. But I suppose I should apologize for that."

"Don't. They're horrible. Mom only cares about money and prestige. Dad keeps his mouth shut, so there's no telling what he thinks. Melony, well, you met her. She's insufferable." Leona sighs and leans forward to smell a pink rose.

"Are you still in love with him?" The question is out of my mouth before I can stop it.

Still edging toward the rose, she turns her head to meet my gaze. "I don't think I ever loved him. Not the way I should have if I was going to marry him. Mom loved him. He's an up-and-comer. He and I had fun for a while and then it just became comfortable and what my parents wanted for me." She faces me and her stare is strong and sure. "He proposed at a big corporate party, and I said yes so I wouldn't embarrass him. When he ended our engagement, he told his colleagues that I'd had an affair. That's when I knew I was saved from a lifetime of misery."

The urge to go back inside and beat Derek to a pulp is almost too much. I close my eyes and my fists ache. The beast inside me growls for release.

Leona presses her palm to the side of my face. "What's wrong?"

She should run when she sees me so close to losing

control. She, of all people, knows what I am. Instead, she comes closer and touches me.

Turning into her hand, I kiss the soft flesh, then graze her skin with my descending canines.

She gasps and her pupils dilate. "That feels…"

Reeling in the beast, I say, "I don't like that Derek hurt you or that he continues to cause you pain."

Placing her other hand on my chest, she smiles. "He can't really hurt me. I'll admit, I hadn't been prepared for him to marry my sister and become a permanent member of my family. I had hoped to never see him again after he ended things."

I'm comforted, but I still want to punch him. "I'm glad you don't love him."

"Are you?"

"Yes."

She presses her cheek to my chest. "Why?"

"You are my mate. It would be complicated if you loved another man, even one that isn't available." I cup her head and slide my hand down her back to the swell of her perfect ass. My cock, as well as my beast, think this garden is as good a place as any to strip her naked and pleasure her.

"You're aroused by me even now?" She presses her hips forward, rubbing against my dick and driving me crazy.

"Always, little lioness." I breathe in the floral scent of her hair and kiss her head. "I'm guessing if you don't go to the show tonight, one of your family will come looking for you."

She laughs. "Without a doubt. They want me to toe the line and accept Derek as my brother-in-law. My mother told me that if I wanted him, I should have fought for him. Not a thought to how quickly they were engaged after our breakup."

I lean back to look her in the eye. "Do you think she was the woman he was seeing when you were still engaged, or was there someone else?"

Shrugging, she pulls away, takes my hand, and we stroll through the flowers. "I don't know and it makes no difference now. They're married and since she's my sister. Derek Millar will be a part of my life forever."

Not liking the truth won't change it. "When do you have to go back to Brooklyn?"

"Bored with me already?" She says it like a joke, but I feel her insecurity seeping through.

"Not in the least. I want to know how long I can keep you." My beast grumbles through, making my voice an octave deeper.

She stops and clears her throat. "Do you want to keep me?" Those big blue eyes blink up at me and all I want is to show her how perfect and wonderful she is.

First, I need to find out who wanted to keep me a manticore. I can't afford to put her in danger. "Can I answer that question after I resolve the issue that brought us together?"

Sorrow shadows her gaze and she lowers her chin. "Of course."

I pull her close, ready to tell her to stop worrying. How can I make her feel safe and secure when someone attacked me and nearly destroyed what I am?

Patty's voice cuts through the peace. "Leona, the show is starting in ten minutes. I'm sure you've had enough air. Cade, please join us."

Pressing her forehead against my chest, Leona laughs. Her whisper is only for me. "Sorry. She smells money."

Everything about this woman fills me with joy. With my

hands gently on her shoulders, I look at her mother. "That's very kind, Patty. We'll be right in."

Giving me a wink, Patty turns and heads back inside.

"You don't need to apologize for your family."

"Of course, I do. They'll drive you crazy if you let them. You're too polite. I know that on the inside, you're rolling your eyes." Her chest rises and falls with a resigned breath, and she takes my hand, heading toward the main building.

"They are not relevant beyond what they mean to you. I'm polite because they matter to you. Your sister and Millar, I will tolerate because it's expected. They have a much shorter list of reasons to be polite." Lifting her hand, I kiss her fingers.

"I wonder why Derek took such an interest in you at dinner." She steps through the door.

Holding it until she's safely inside, I follow her in. "Perhaps he regrets his choice."

She shakes her head. "No. I can't imagine that."

"You're spectacular. If I were foolish enough to let you go, I would regret another man showing interest." I don't mention that my beast would likely rip that man to shreds.

I'm saved from saying more when we join her family around a front-facing circular table with a U-shaped booth.

There is a short comedic act to open the night, followed by a female singer with a band. It's entertaining, but I long to have Leona to myself. As if reading my thoughts, she takes my hand.

Across the table, Derek stares for long stretches. I meet his awkward gaze. Maybe Leona is right. There might be some other reason for her new brother-in-law's interest. Though, I can't imagine what it would be.

CHAPTER SEVEN

LEONA

$\mathcal{M}$y parents say good night and go upstairs as soon as the show is over.

Without so much as a look, Melony and Derek head to the bar. It's rude, even for them. But they look like they're arguing and since they only got married yesterday morning, it doesn't bode well for a long, happy marriage.

Hand in hand, Cade and I walk toward the front doors of the resort. "Are you starting to worry about who it was that darted you?"

He tucks my hair behind my ear. "I have been concerned since the event."

"Really? You seem unbothered." How do I ask him to come to my room or take me home with him?

Pressing my palm to the center of his chest, he looks into my eyes, and the swirl of gold that is the monster inside him glows. "Your presence is more important than anything else, but I will need to discover who attacked me."

His heart beats under my fingers, steady and true. My body responds to the man and the beast. "Is that something you're going to work on tonight?"

"Not tonight." His voice is low and gravelly, and he breathes in deeply. "Is there something you want from me tonight, little lioness?"

Asking a man to come to my bed is not something I'm comfortable with. Honestly, I've never done it. I've been invited. It's happened naturally, like it did at Cade's house. I have to swallow several times, then I lean in close. "Do you want to come to my room?"

"More than anything." There's no mistaking the beast in his deep voice.

Lord help me, but I want that monster as much as the man. We go to the elevator and once we're alone inside, I ask the question that's been nagging me since the afternoon. "Will you ever show me the manticore again?"

In an instant, he pins me to the elevator wall. "I want you to see and have all of me, Leona. Though I'm not sure a hotel room is the best place for that."

"I'm here for another full day and night. Maybe tomorrow?" Did I just offer him sex tomorrow after asking him to stay with me tonight? I barely recognize myself. As big as he is, his beast is bigger and stronger, and yet, I have no fear of either of them.

His smile is wicked, and he leans in close.

The bell for the door opening sounds, and he eases back and holds the door from closing again while I step out into the hallway. At the door to my room, I fumble with the key card nervously.

He steadies my hand by wrapping his around mine. "You know, I'll understand if you want me to go home tonight."

Oh god, I've turned him off. "I'm sorry. If you don't want to come in, you should go. I know my nerves can be a turnoff."

He takes the card from my hand and unlocks the door. I step inside, expecting him to say goodnight, but he walks in behind me. "Nothing about you could ever alter my desire, Leona. I only wanted to give you the option of sending me home because you're clearly nervous, though there is no reason to be."

I sit heavily on the bed. "I know. You're wonderful. I don't know why I always expect everyone to disappoint me."

Kneeling in front of me, he takes my hands. "I can think of several reasons why you would be cautious. However, I'm never going to hurt you. Tell me what I can do to convince you of that?"

My mind reels for a response. I have no idea how anyone would prove they won't hurt me. I've had so little experience with anyone being honest and true in my life. When I saw the manticore in the woods, I was afraid, but there was something wholesome in his eyes. Then he turned into a man, and I felt betrayed, strangely. Men have never been trustworthy in my world. "I'd like to see your beast. Something about you in that form was…" I don't know how to explain it to him without offending him. "Vulnerable."

"He and I are the same, you know. I am that monster, and he is me." He kisses my hands.

"It's okay if you don't want to change into the manticore in front of me. I imagine being stuck in that form has made you wary." I think about all the things that Derek kept from me. Secret phone calls and texts. Business deals he couldn't talk about. He never shared anything. "Maybe you could tell me more about your work."

Standing, Cade walks to the sliding door and out onto the small veranda. He looks at the trees and the lake off to the left. Stepping back into my room, he takes off his jacket, and toes off his shoes and waits, staring at me.

"Do you want me to undress?" I stand up.

He shakes his head. "You'll be cold." He unbuttons his crisp white shirt and tugs it off, placing it on top of the jacket on the back of the wingback chair in the corner. "If you want the beast, I can assure you, we are both happy to oblige you. It's hard to speak in that form, so once I shift, get on my back and we'll go out for a while."

"You're going to jump from that railing with me on your back?" My terror at the prospect has my heart pounding. I know I asked for this, but I never expected to jump from the sixth floor.

With his trousers undone, he steps close and cups my cheek. "Maybe you didn't notice, love, but the manticore has wings."

"We're going to fly." It comes out too fast and the words are all jumbled together.

He shrugs. "The beast will not be comfortable in this room. If you want him, we have to leave."

My body pulses with a desire that overrides my fears. I skim the light dusting of hair on his chest and trace a path to his pants hanging low on his hips. "I want you, and I want to trust you."

The sound of the monster's growl rumbles from low in his gut and emerges, heightening how turned-on I am. He steps out of his pants, revealing his thick cock at full attention. He carefully folds his clothes, and looking at me, asks, "Are you ready?"

It takes all my strength to keep my feet in place. I don't know if I want to run to him, or away from the fear of being hurt, but the draw to have him keeps me in place. I nod.

He steps out onto the veranda and gives the area another long look. His body contorts, grows, and stretches. Bones crack and change form. Fir pushes from his skin and grows long around his face as his jaw crunches, extends, and reforms into the lion. Wings sprout from his back and the long scorpion tail grows and forms into the deadly point. The manticore looks over his shoulder toward me.

Unable to look away, I'm drawn to him like a moth to a flame. When he gets low enough, I climb onto his back. My body is on fire, and my pussy pulses needly. Gripping with my thighs around in front of his wings, I dig my hands into the soft fur of his mane. "You're magnificent, Cade."

A purr rumbles through him and he leaps into the air, flapping his wings to take us over the tops of the trees.

Tightening my grip, I take it all in. Not just the amazing view of the tops of trees, a lake in the distance with the moon's reflections shining up at me, but the freedom of flying with the wind whipping my hair and making my eyes tear. His body moves beneath mine in fluidity and grace. Everything about this is sensual and exhilarating at the same time.

He could take me anywhere and leave me, or just as easily devour me with a single bite. No one would know.

Yet, I have no fear as we soar above the Catskill Mountains. This monster is mine. He'll do anything to keep me safe.

Ahead is a clearing in the woods, and he lowers and lands smoothly.

Once we're on the ground, I don't want to let go. He feels so soft and warm. I love that lying across his back seems perfectly normal.

"Cade!" A woman runs into the clearing. She's beautiful with long blond hair and wearing a sheer gown. Her body is perfect, not a dimple or bulge to be seen.

Pulling down my cocktail dress so I don't expose anything, I slide to the ground.

Cade wraps a wing around me, keeping me close, as if he can sense my unease with a practically naked woman running toward him.

Stopping just feet from us, she widens her eyes at the sight of me. "Hello."

"Hi." I've never been more uncomfortable, and that's saying something.

"I'm Astra." She cocks her head, as if her name should mean something to me.

"Leona." Unsure what else to do, I offer my hand. Once she shakes it, I ask, "Are you running away or toward something?"

Her chuckle is musical and annoyingly delightful. "Away, I suppose." She looks at Cade. "My father has arranged a marriage for me."

Cade's growl makes me think I'm intruding on a private conversation. I back away a few steps, but he pulls me in with his wing until I'm pressed against his muscular front leg.

Looking between the two of us, Astra blinks. "I've interrupted something. Forgive me."

Another growl and Cade leaps backward before shifting

into a man. The process looks excruciating, but once he's human again, and completely naked, he smiles. He takes my hand and threads our fingers together. "Who has your father promised you to?"

Neither one of them seems at all bothered by the fact that he's naked and she may as well be. However, I feel very much like a third wheel at my own party. "I can give you two some privacy to talk."

Tightening his hold, Cade shakes his head. "We don't need privacy, Leona. Astra is a nymph. She lives in these woods. Her father is old-fashioned and has promised her to…" He leaves the sentence unfinished.

"A satyr." Astra throws her arms up in the air. Her perfectly round breasts bob up and down. "I haven't met him, but even so. The idea of being forced to marry anyone in this day. What is my father thinking?"

"He's old-fashioned, as I said. Have you tried to reason with your father? I'm sure he values your happiness over making an advantageous match." Cade's voice is comforting and kind. He cares for this woman.

I'm having a hard time disliking her, which is strange since I'm certain this nymph is Cade's lover. Who wouldn't want to have sex with Astra? She's perfect. "I should get back to the resort."

Astra reaches out and touches my cheek. "No. I'll go. I can see I've made you uncomfortable, Leona. It wasn't my intention. Cade has always lent me his ear when I needed it. If I had known he was busy, I would have…" She laughs. "I don't know what I would have done."

She turns and runs toward the woods. "I'll try reason, but if that doesn't work, I may need to hide in your attic."

Laughing, Cade turns toward me. His body is magnificent

and, even while jealous, I can't help my body's reaction to him. "Take me back to my room, please."

As soon as I reach the edge of the trees, I pause, and he stalks toward me. Gently, he unwraps my arms from around my waist. "Astra and I are not lovers and we never have been. She's a nymph. Her gift is she can sense feelings and is attractive to everyone. I'm sure you felt it."

I refuse to say anything. "Then you're attracted to her."

"No. For some reason, my monster is not affected by her nature. Perhaps that's why we became friends. My need to find my true mate may be why I never was lured by her. Don't be jealous, little lioness. I only want you." He reaches around, putting one of my ass cheeks in each of his hands and lifts me.

Instinctively, I wrap my legs around him. "I wanted to hate her, but she's perfect." I curl my arms around his neck. "You *really* are not lovers?"

He shakes his head, then lowers his mouth to kiss my throat. "I only want you, Leona."

"Why does she wear a see-through dress?" I should have asked her, but I was too smitten by her beauty to say much of anything.

"Another bit of the old ways. Nymphs are meant to run naked through woodlands. She's forbidden from owning clothes that will hide her form." He strides across the clearing, and as he walks, his shaft hardens between us.

Every step rubs me perfectly as my dress creeps up my thighs, becoming a band around my waist. "I would be happy to loan her some clothes."

"I think she'd appreciate that." He steps us through the trees where there's a hidden little hut.

"She could have gone now and taken what she wanted

from my room." My breath catches as the thick head of his cock nudges my clit.

He growls and leans me back against the door. "She's telepathic and still nearby. I'm sure she'll be very touched by your offer. Can we stop talking about Astra so I can bury myself deep inside you? I can feel how wet you are through these tiny panties."

"Yes. God, yes." I nibble on his earlobe. "I need you inside me. Your beast is so close to the surface, I can smell the earthiness of him."

Reaching between us, he grips my lace panties, and with one quick jerk tears them off me. Fingering my wet folds, he makes a sound that's both growl and purr. "You are the only woman I will ever want."

Pleasure shoots from his touch and I twist my hips for more. With his cock only a breath away from my slit and his rough fingers rubbing me just right, I'm wild with desire. I kiss him and explore his teeth and tongue. His lips are full and responsive. Gripping his shoulders, I push to get more of him where I need him.

He fucks my mouth with his tongue, spreads my netherlips with his fingers, and lets gravity take me as he fills me with every inch of his thick hard cock.

I scream with pleasure, but the sound is muted by his ravenous mouth.

Giving me time to adjust, he keeps still as he opens the door and moves us inside. Breaking the kiss, he says, "You're perfect. Tell me when it's okay to move. I don't want to hurt you."

Hurt me? Nothing could be further from reality. Every giant centimeter of him is exactly what I need. "Move. I need you, Cade. I need both of you."

Laying me on a mattress, he meets my gaze. The gold swirl of the manticore's eyes looks back at me and his cock thickens as he pulls back and slides home again and again. Still staring into my eyes as if looking for whatever my reaction might be, he gives me exactly what I asked for.

Again and again, he fills me beyond what should be comfortable, but it's pure pleasure. "More, Cade. I want it all."

He roars and pounds harder. Fur grows around his face, thick and golden.

I thread my fingers through the mane, lifting my hips to take more of him.

Gently, his tail traces a path along my leg to my thigh and ass. It skims its point along my backside, breaching that hole.

I shatter into a million pieces as the orgasm erupts with more force than anything I've ever felt.

A long roar falls from Cade's lips and he fills me with hot cum. His cock grows thicker still and he roars again while even more seed pushes me into a second orgasm.

CHAPTER EIGHT

CADE

*N*othing can describe the pleasure of having my mate while in this form. I mean to slide free, but nothing moves. Panicked, I pull away, but Leona cries my name and tightens her grip with her legs.

Half man and half beast, my voice is rough. "Are you hurt?"

"No." She presses her hips against mine and her body jerks as she comes again. "Oh, that's…What is that?"

The milking of her pussy pulls another jet of cum from me and I growl out my pleasure. When it passes, I keep very still and kiss her forehead. This is a first for me, but I suppose that's to be expected. This kind of intimacy is for mates only. "Don't move, my love. It's the knotting."

"What?"

I roll so that she's on top since I don't want to crush her. The movement forces more blood into my shaft and the knot tightens. "Gods, that feels so good. Please tell me I'm not killing you."

"Holy hell. I'm coming again." True to her words, her body pulses with another eruption of pleasure, triggering my own.

"If we remain still, it should pass." I run my fingers along her back, careful of my claws, which are exposed now.

"What's happening, Cade? Why do you sound worried?" Her voice is slightly higher than normal.

"Nothing is wrong. We're knotted and it may take a little while for the bond to loosen. If we lie still, it should be faster." I hope that's true.

Slowly, she lifts her head to meet my gaze. Her pupils are blown and her cheeks are flushed. She's so beautiful, she takes my breath away. "What is knotted?"

This would be easier to explain if the pleasure of being inside her wasn't flowing through me like river rapids. "Knotting is my body linking with yours for procreation. It only happens with mates. It doesn't happen every time. I never thought it would happen with us since you're not a manticore or shifter. It really never crossed my mind."

Blinking, she blushes a deep red. "Are you telling me that you're impregnating me and that's why we can't separate?"

My heart balls up painfully. "You make it sound as if I'm doing this to you as some kind of punishment. I'm telling you that our lovemaking may have led to our making a child. That's what sometimes happens when people have sex."

She presses her forehead to my chest. "What happens now?"

Every molecule of my body wants to move, to bring us pleasure, and stop her from abandoning me as soon as she's released from the knot. Fighting instinct, I hold perfectly still. "We wait for the bond to loosen."

Rocking her forehead side to side, she says, "No. I mean after this. How do we go forward and if there's a child… You don't have to worry. I can raise my baby. I've always thought I'd be a good mother." Her tears drip onto my skin.

"Do you think I would abandon you or the child?" Can she think that little of me?

"We just met. I don't think anyone expects to make long-term plans after two days. It's nice you want to be part of a child's life. I mean, if I'm pregnant."

My chest is wet with her tears. I grip her ass and pull her tight. Pleasure shoots through me as she comes again.

Her beautiful cries fill the hut and as she arches her neck. I capture her lips, making love to her mouth. She rocks, taking more of me, and we both moan with the next wave of our mating.

As the rapture ebbs, she breaks the kiss. In a sultry voice that sounds contrary, she says, "I don't know if I can take any more."

Rolling to one side, I maneuver so that my back is against the wall and she's in my lap.

"Oh, fuck! Cade! That's…" She rides me while the orgasm crashes around us.

Face to face now, and still intimately locked together, I meet her impassioned gaze. "Listen to me very carefully, Leona. You are mine. You have been since the moment you stepped into my woods. I am your mate and will never abandon you. The only way to rid yourself of me is for you to reject me as your mate. If you did that, it would break my heart, but I will always care for you and our child. Do you understand?"

Tears stream down her cheeks. "I want to believe you."

"Then do. I will never lie to you. If living in your apartment in Brooklyn is what makes you happy, I will come with you. You could stay here, or we can come to another solution. None of those options will include me letting you go." My pulse is so fast, I have to catch my breath. The idea of her leaving, and our baby growing inside her sweet body has made me long for her even more. Nothing short of her rejection will move me on this subject.

Through her tears, she smiles. "Can I ask you something?"

"Anything?"

"Have you knotted with anyone else? Are there little Cades running around the world somewhere?" She combs her fingers through my mane.

"You are my only mate. This is my first knotting." I wouldn't have thought the process would be so emotional or so pleasurable. Older people hardly ever talk about the event beyond saying if you wait, it will pass, and it almost always leads to impregnation. Of course, they were talking about monsters mating. None of them ever mated with a human. Though, it happens. I heard about a family in Western New York state that mated with all human women, and they have had children. None of them are manticores, but I can't help hoping that Leona carries my baby, or soon will.

She pulls her dress over her head and rocks her hips. "Oh, that's so good. If we're going to be linked together like this, my beast, I think we should make the most of it. She rocks again and my cock thickens, pushing us both into another round of ecstasy.

By the time we return to her hotel room, it's only a couple of hours until dawn, and I leave her to sleep. I need rest too, but I have to spend a little time figuring out who tried to keep me in manticore form.

I return to the woods where Leona saved me, and as a full monster, sniff the ground until I find the dart. Shifting back into a man's form, I dress and move the leaves aside until I can pick up the injector.

The side has writing on it, but it's too dark to read it, so I head home.

In the light of my kitchen, I clearly see PremTor in white lettering. So, the dart came from the PremTor Pharmaceutical Company. Did they create it knowing it would keep me a monster? Are they who want me to stay a beast, or did they make it for someone else? There are too many questions without any answers.

I set the alarms for the house and property and head into bed. Maybe it will make more sense after I get some rest.

Not to be, the proximity alarms sound just after the sun comes up. I might have ignored it if it wasn't for the incident of being shot. I head to my office where I can view the surveillance video on my computer.

A powder-blue sports car waits at my gate and behind the wheel is Melony Millar. My gut knots, but I open the gate.

Grinning like the cat that ate the family canary, Melony passes through and up my driveway.

In sweats and a t-shirt, I wait just outside my front door. Whatever this is, it cannot be good.

She pulls to a stop and steps out wearing a skin-tight dress that ends just past her ass. "Cade, I'm so glad to see you."

"This is my house, Mrs. Millar. Who else would you see?" I cross my arms over my chest. Maybe I can intimidate her. "What brings you out so early?"

Unfazed, she climbs the three steps in stiletto heels and faces me. "I thought we might have a little talk."

"What about?" The faint scent of vodka sours her breath.

Pretty to the casual observer, Melony has blue eyes like her sister, but she wears a lot of makeup, and everything about her looks expensive. While her eyes are similar to Leona's, Melony's are tainted with an agenda. She exaggerates the swish of her hips as she walks to the porch swing and nearly exposes herself when she sits. "It has become clear to me that you are dating my sister. Isn't that enough cause for us to get to know each other better?"

"I had planned to come visit with your family today. Why not wait and get to know me then?" I remain standing but close the gap and lean on the front of my house.

She sighs. "My parents, while I love them, can be difficult. I thought if we could talk away from them, it might be cozier."

"And your new husband doesn't mind you going out at the crack of dawn to visit men?" She's up to something, I'm just not sure what it is.

"Derek and I have a very trusting relationship." She looks around the property. "Why don't we go for a walk?"

"What do you want, Mrs. Millar?" My instincts tell me to

get rid of her, but the fact that she's Leona's sister keeps me from tossing her from the porch.

She smiles and lowers her long eyelashes in a way that's meant to be coy and flirtatious, but falls short with me. "Call me Melony. Why not stroll through your beautiful woods and get acquainted? Maybe we could swim in that lake."

I'm not surprised she knows I have a lake. The resort's property and mine share the shoreline. I don't see a bathing suit, so this is an attempt to get me to do something other than talk. "I'm trying to remind you that you're married, madam. I have no idea why you would come here and flirt with me, but my opinion of you was already bad before you came, so say what you have to say and go so I can get some sleep."

She juts out her bottom lip. "I wanted to soften the blow, but if you're going to be mean... I came to warn you about Leona. I know she looks sweet and acts kind, but she'll break your heart like she broke Derek's."

"He doesn't look heartbroken." It takes all my will to keep my temper.

Her smile is wicked. "That's because I cheered him after *she* broke off their engagement. He needed someone to help him through, and we fell in love. Now Leona brings you in to make him jealous, and on our wedding weekend. There's no limit to her betrayal."

"Thanks for the warning. If that's all you want, you should go back to the Greentree now. I have a lot to do today." Nothing this woman says is true. I know it and based on her frown, she realizes she's failing to convince me of anything.

Rising, she skims her hands over her hips and saunters toward me. When she's inches away, she runs her hand along my biceps. "I could make you forget Leona the same way I made Derek forget her. I promise you'll enjoy yourself."

Putting my hands around her waist makes her grin and that glint in her eyes turns victorious for half a second. Then I pick her up and toss her over my shoulder.

"What the hell?" She beats her fists on my back.

I carry her to her car, open the driver's door, and set her on her feet. Stepping back, I wait for her to regain her balance. "Get off my property, Mrs. Millar. Don't come back here. Why you want to hurt your sister, I have no idea, but you're way off base if you think I would have sex with you to help your cause."

Without waiting, I turn and go inside.

She screams, "How dare you? You don't know what you're missing."

Once the car starts and she drives away, I check my computer to make certain she leaves the property.

Calling Leona can wait. Hopefully, she's asleep and will be for a few more hours. Maybe I can even grab an hour or two before I go to see her. I don't know what her sister's motives are, but I hope my mate isn't opposed to only seeing that one at family functions.

CHAPTER NINE

LEONA

I wake up after ten and I'm deliciously sore. Even so, I can't wait to see Cade and find out how much more there is to know about being mated to a manticore. After a long shower, I notice my jeans and a white blouse are missing.

Try as I might, I can't imagine Astra wearing jeans. The idea amuses me. Deciding on a pair of denim shorts and a green Henley-style t-shirt, I put my key card in my pocket, my phone in the other, and head out of my room.

Familiar raised voices from a few doors down make me stop.

Derek says, "Why didn't you get him away from the house?"

"He wouldn't go. I tried. I even let him think I would get naked and go skinny-dipping with him."

I don't know what they're talking about or why they would fight just a few days after their wedding. I shouldn't even be listening. I plan to head directly to the elevator and mind my own business.

"You didn't try hard enough. That stupid sister of yours ruined everything. If I don't get Petroyan, not only will I never get promoted out of the supplements division, I'll lose my job and all those pretty things and vacations you want will go out the window. You need to distract him and get him out of sight. Once he's aroused, he's sure to turn into that monster. Then I just hit him with the CM-234 and we wait."

"You shouldn't provoke a monster into having sex with your wife, but even so, he's not interested in me." Melony's patented whine has made its way into her voice.

"You better make him interested. You are my wife, and you will do this or all your hopes and dreams will be gone. You think I would have had my wedding in the Catskills if this project hadn't needed completion? My boss is counting on me. Now we're a team, Melony. I need him a beast. This time I've got a tranquilizer ready so he doesn't run. No way I'm letting him out of my sight once we've got him."

I've never heard Derek use that tone.

"I'll do my best." From her weepy pitch, I'm sure Melony is crying.

"Do better," he bites out. "Put on something sexy and lure that freak away from the group at lunch, or this marriage and our plans are over."

Fear rushes through me when they stop talking, and I run as fast as I can down the hall and into the stairwell before Derek opens his door.

A minute later I hear the bell on the elevator. Why hadn't I thought of this before? Derek works for PremTor Pharmaceuticals. I mean, he's in supplement sales. At least that's what he told me. It's not relevant how this happened or when. I have to warn Cade to stay away.

I call him. The call doesn't go through. Maybe it's because of all the metal in the stairwell. Trying not to panic, I open the door, intent on going back to my room to make the call.

"Leona? Why are you taking the stairs?" Melony stands just outside her door. She's wearing cut-off jeans shorts that show the bottom of her ass cheeks and a tank top that barely covers anything.

"I needed the exercise." I'm impressed with how normal I sound, considering my sister and my ex are trying to destroy my chance at happiness by sending my mate off to be dissected. Blood is rushing through my ears. I have to push aside those thoughts. "Why are you dressed like a character from a seventies show?"

She swings her loosely curled hair around with a flip. "Isn't it fun? I thought since we have the farewell picnic, I would dress for the country."

"This is New York State, not 1970s Georgia." I head to my room. "Not that it's any of my business."

As I pass her, she slips her arm through mine. "Why are you going to your room? You'll be late for lunch."

"I forgot my purse." I continue to my room, but she holds on. "I'll be right down, Melony. You don't need to come with me."

As I step in, she follows and puffs out that stupid bottom lip of hers. "I could use some girl talk. You are my big sister. Who else am I supposed to ask about things."

My eyes roll of their own accord. There's no stopping them as I grab my clutch from the chair. "You do not need my advice and if you did, you should have married someone else."

"That's not fair," she snaps as if she's the injured party and flops into the chair. "I love Derek, and you didn't really want him or you would have set a date and he'd already be your husband."

"Fine." I sit on the edge of the mattress in hopes that if I let her talk, this will be over in a minute, and I can call Cade. "What do you want to talk about?"

"This guy you forced on us this weekend. Is it serious?" Her eyes are narrowed in the same way Mom's get when she's setting me up to give away something about my life that I don't want to tell her.

That might work for Mom but it will not fly with my sister. "I met him a few days ago, Melony. What do you think?" I hedge, because even to her, I don't want to deny my feelings outright. It would feel too much like a betrayal of what Cade and I have.

"Derek doesn't like him. He told me so. He's going to have him looked into." She tips her chin up like she's said something smart or hurtful.

Standing, I loom over my little sister. "Melony, you need to hear me right now. I don't give a fuck what you or your husband think of me or the men I date. You are not important in my decisions. I'm sure there's nothing for Derek to find out about Cade that he wouldn't be willing to tell me. Now, get out of my room and go to your picnic."

How she manages to tear up at will has always been a mystery to me. She should have been an actress, the way she can cry on command. She dashes a tear from her cheek.

"There's no need to be so cruel, Leona. I've always been a good sister to you."

"Have you, though?" Unable to bear her a moment longer, I leave my room to get away from her.

As expected, by the time I reach the elevator, she's beside me. "Derek and I are married now. There's no going back. You're going to have to live with it and since we're all a part of this family, I suggest you learn to toe the line."

The doors open.

She gets in.

I stare at her. "Toe the line?"

She nods and crosses her arms over her chest. "DeRosas stick together."

As the doors close with me still in the hallway, I say, "I'll take the stairs."

Pulling my phone out again, I call Cade, but the call goes to voicemail. "Don't come here today, Cade. It's Derek. He's the one who…"

The door to the stairs opens and Derek walks into the hall. His eyes widen when he sees me, then he smiles. "The elevator was taking too long. Your mom sent me to check on you and Melony."

Casually, I slip my thumb over the disconnect button on my phone and slide it into my back pocket. "Melony just went down. I decided I didn't need my purse after all. I'm just going to drop it back in my room, and I'll be right out."

He nods but waits in the hall while I toss my clutch on the bed. As soon as I'm back in the hall, he says, "We can go down together, unless you still hate me."

That kind of emotion would take too much energy and he's not worth it. At least he wasn't until I learned that he was the scumbag who tried to hurt Cade. "I'm sure we can manage a ride in an elevator without our emotions overcoming us, Derek."

It must not be the response he expected. He frowns and pushes the down arrow.

On the ride to the ground floor, I pray that Cade gets my message and stays as far away from the resort as possible.

"I never meant to hurt you, Leo." Derek's voice is soft, like he's trying to woo me again.

Unable to stop myself, I laugh. "It's Leona. Of course, you did. But there's no room for regret now. You married my sister."

He closes the distance between us. "But you will always be the DeRosa sister who I love."

"No." I put my hand hard against his chest.

Grabbing my wrist, he presses against me. "I don't like that word, and it doesn't suit you."

Fury rises inside me in a way I've never felt before. I channel it into my right knee and jerk it up directly into his balls.

He gasps and falls to the elevator floor, holding his crotch.

"How about these words? No fucking way, you dirtbag." Leaving him there as the doors close again, I realize that as much as I'd like to believe Derek isn't a terrible human being, it would be a mistake. He is, and Cade is in danger.

I have to find him.

Brian is behind his concierge desk as I enter the main lobby. I have no idea how much he knows about Cade but I need help.

My panic must be evident because Brian is out of his chair, concern etched on his face. "What's wrong? Are you ill?"

"I'm fine. Do you know where Cade is?" I stare out the glass doors hoping to catch sight of him arriving. Maybe I can intercept him and we can drive far away from here. It's Sunday and a lot of people are leaving.

"I thought he was joining you here for your sister's farewell picnic." His red hair flops over his forehead.

Praying this is the right thing to do, I whisper. "He's in danger."

"I doubt that. Cade is a very resourceful, um, man."

Not sure what to say or not say, I straighten. "Of course. He is, and I'm probably overreacting. I'll just wait for him out front."

Brian follows me to the circular drive where bellhops and valets are rushing around helping guests load cars. "Look, if you think he's in danger, I'm here to help. The thing is, do you know him?" he stammers. "I mean really know what he is?"

I nod. "That's why he's in danger. Did he tell you about what happened to him last week?"

Brian's eyes widen. "It was you. You found him. He didn't say who."

"It was Derek or someone from the company he works for. They're planning something this afternoon." My pulse is pounding so hard, that I feel lightheaded.

"Stay here. I'll get my phone and try calling."

Cade drives up to the front door and flips the valet the key fob before smiling at me. "I got your message. I didn't understand. What was Derek? Why did you hang up?"

"We need to get out of here, Cade. It's not safe." I keep my voice low, but the panic inside me shakes my whispers.

Taking my hand, he leads me to the end of the loading

area where no one is milling around. "What's going on?" He cups my cheek, as gentle as he is strong.

Fighting to keep my voice so soft that only he can hear me, I lean close. "Derek works for a pharmaceutical company. He or someone from the company darted you in an attempt to capture you."

The gold eyes of the manticore swirl in Cade's irises. "PremTor. Derek works for PremTor. Is that why your sister came to my house this morning?"

"Melony was at your house?" I fairly scream it.

Pulling me close, he hugs me. "She came and thought she could seduce me or lure me away from the house. I imagine she's pretty angry because I put her in her car and ordered her off the property."

I relax against him. "You did?" I know my sister can be very convincing when she wants something.

"You don't actually think I desire Melony?" He makes a derisive sound. "You are the only woman I will ever want." Holding my face in both of his hands, he tips my face up so that our gazes meet. "Ever. Perhaps I should have said this last night. Things went faster than I intended. I love you, Leona. No one else will ever mean more to me than you."

Emotions bubble out from my eyes. "I love you too." Instinctively, I run my hand over my abdomen. Is our baby growing inside me right now?

He smiles. "Now, let's see if we can't reason with your brother-in-law."

"Why don't we just not show up for the stupid picnic? They only came here for the wedding and family weekend to capture you. I don't owe them attendance." I wave at the valet to stop before he takes Cade's car away.

"I think we should go visit with your family. I just need a quick word with Brian."

We walk inside, and he slaps Brian on the back. Pulling him aside, the two speak in hushed tones.

Brian nods and goes to the front desk.

Grinning like all is well, Cade takes my hand in his, kisses my knuckles, and we walk out the back doors to the garden where my family is gathering for a picnic.

CHAPTER TEN

CADE

My mate's family leaves something to be desired. There's no denying that. Still, I think poisoning me must have some consequence. Now, because that act of violence is what brought Leona to me, I'm willing to make some concessions. If possible, I'll spare Melony.

At the back end of the rose garden is a stone patio with a white canopy.

Patty rushes forward wearing a lemon-yellow dress that flies in the breeze. "I'm so glad you're here, Cade. We've been waiting." She gives Leona a hard look.

"My fault," I say. "I'm afraid my morning went differently than intended, and I had to deal with some issues.

"Oh dear. I hope everything's okay." Patty takes my arm, forcing Leona to walk behind us the last few feet to the table.

A cook from the resort's kitchen mans a grill, and a two-person wait staff bustle around, making up plates as we sit.

The first course is a wedge of cantaloupe wrapped in prosciutto and drizzled with olive oil.

I'm glad to have Leona beside me, but my beast is on full alert, waiting for an attack. Surely, Derek won't do anything in front of his new in-laws and the wait staff. I lean in. "You're not eating, love."

She gives me a side-eye. "You're kidding, right? Who can eat?"

Sympathizing, I don't want to arouse suspicion of the watchful jerk across the table. I carefully cut my appetizer and eat all of it.

"Maybe you can give me some stock tips, Cade." Derek's voice is full of false charm.

"I'd be happy to assist with your portfolio. Though that might be a conflict of interest."

"Why is that?" John asks around a mouth full of food. "I wouldn't mind a few tips myself."

"It can be a bad idea to advise family, and I fully intend to be around for a long time, sir." I shift my attention to Leona and enjoy her rosy blush.

"That's good to hear," Patty says, grinning like a hyena.

John frowns. "I see. I would hope you two would get to know each other for more than a few days before any serious decisions are made."

It's a sensible response from a father. I give him a sober nod. "As a gentleman, I don't disagree with you, sir. Though, as a man smitten, I'm loath to wait any longer than Leona requires."

"Okay. That's enough talk about me and my life. This is still Melony and Derek's weekend."

Right on cue, Melony pouts. "Thank you, Leona. It's about time someone remembered that important fact."

The grilled steak is served with roasted potatoes and asparagus.

Across from me, Melony tugs her shirt so that the thin tank barely contains her boobs. Looking at me through her long eyelashes, she licks her lips.

My stomach turns, and the steak is going to be difficult to eat. I suppose I'm going to have to go along with their scheme for my plan to work.

I never thought small talk would be a relief, but it is and it fills the remaining time at the table while sorbet is served with fresh berries.

As soon as it's appropriate, I excuse myself and head inside, under the guise of needing to use the bathroom.

Inside the main building, Brian gives me a nod, confirming that the appropriate calls have been made.

"Are you alright, Cade?" Melony simpers and gets close enough that her tits graze my arm.

"Fine. I only needed the restroom. Can I help you with something?" A totally loaded question.

Like some kind of femme fetal in an old movie, she runs her hands through her hair and down her face before caressing the tops of her breasts. "I think I may have made the biggest mistake of my life. I mean, I should have been honest when I came to your house. I need help, and I don't know who else to turn to." Now she shifts her hands to my upper arm and chest. "You just seem like the kind of man who would help a girl in trouble."

"What are we talking about, Melony?" I don't even like the way her name feels in my mouth. How did my sweet mate come from the same place as this fake woman who has no scruples?

The whine of her voice sets my teeth on edge. "My

marriage. How could I have married Derek? If I'd only waited a little longer, I'd have known a man like you is available. I know you say you like my sister, but maybe you could spend some time with me. If you knew me better, you'd like me."

Every instinct in me says run, but I have to see this through. "What do you suggest?" As hard as I tried for seductive, the words sound stilted to my ear.

If Melony noticed, it's not evident. She presses her chest against me. "Why don't we take a walk and get to know each other? I know I came on too strong this morning, but I'm a nice girl. We can talk, and you'll see I'm far more attractive than Leona. Everyone always says so."

My jaw aches from clenching. I would give almost anything to never see this horrible woman ever again. The problem is that what I want is a life with her sister and unfortunately, the only road to peace with my mate is through this miserable human. "A walk sounds nice."

She threads her arm through mine and caresses the inside of my elbow.

We go out the front doors and she leads me toward the woods on the north side of the resort. My gut twists like a lamb to slaughter. Let's hope whatever the plan is, I can remain a man until after they fail.

LEONA

This is torture. Knowing that Cade is putting himself in danger to catch Derek or someone from his company in the act or kidnapping is the worst idea ever.

My mother corners me by a fully blooming yellow rose bush. "I'm so happy for you, Leona. I knew this would all work out. You have to admit, Derek is a better match for your sister. Besides, it makes Melony so happy to be first where the two of you are concerned. You've been very nice to let her have her way."

"She didn't exactly ask my approval, Mom. She married my ex and dragged us all up here to spend an entire weekend gloating over it. Then, when I find a man who's interested in me, she flirts with him the day after her wedding." I don't bother keeping my disgust out of my voice.

Mom frowns. "She's just a little jealous of you. It should be flattering for your little sister to want to be like you."

"Well, it's not. It's childish and annoying. I'm here because you and Dad made such a fuss when I said I didn't want to come." I search the garden and there's no sign of either Melony or Derek. My heart speeds up. This is a terrible idea.

Brian walks past the far end of the garden toward the parking lot. He was calling the police to catch Derek in the act. Why is he leaving?

"She's your sister. Be kind." Mom's command no longer has the desired effect.

I keep Brian in my sight and say, "Mom, you should go finish packing. Dad will want to leave for the city in an hour. You know how he is."

Mom checks her watch and her eyes go wide. "Oh lord, you're right." She rushes from the garden.

I jog down the path and out into the parking lot.

Brian is just opening the door of his gray SUV when I reach him. "Where are you going?"

"Um. Home." His skin is pale, and he's sweating.

Searching the area, I don't see a single police car. "Where are the police?"

His lips pull into a tight line. "Look, you should get out of here. It will all be over soon. If you play your cards right, I'm sure we can work out a good deal for you too. Your brother-in-law is very generous."

Oh god. This isn't happening. I back away from him then turn and turn toward the resort. Pulling the phone from my back pocket, I dial 911.

"What's your emergency?" A pleasant voice asks.

"My boyfriend is being attacked by a man with a shotgun." It's the only thing I can think to say.

"Where are you, miss?" Key taps sound in the background.

"We're at the Greentree Resort." I run faster.

Brian's SUV screeches to a stop in front of me.

"Hang up that phone, Leona." Gone is the pleasant concierge and in his place is a sweating, lying villain.

"Come quick."

"Officers are en route. Tell him you're hanging up." The dispatcher is just as calm as she was when she answered.

"Okay." I pretend to push the button and lower the phone so it faces my thigh. "I can't believe you would jeopardize your job here by helping Derek with his plan. It's a crazy plan."

There's no humor in Brian's laugh. "This job sucks and Millar pays well for information. He needed someone like Cade, and I gave him the location. I've done nothing wrong."

"Except betray your friend," I bite back.

"You know what he is. Why protect that."

Police sirens blare and grow closer.

Brian's eyes widen, and he looks at me as if he might kill me before he jumps in his SUV and burns rubber out of the parking lot.

I run as fast as I can to the front of the resort. My side

hurts from overexertion, but I push on. Not sure where to go, I head for the woods where I first found Cade. The small clearing is empty. Closing my eyes, I try to feel him. If we're mates, true mates, shouldn't I be able to find him?

A spark flashes to life inside me, like a match strike in the darkness. Turning right, I run down the hiking path.

Cade's voice stops me. "We're getting pretty far from the resort. We should head back."

"Oh, just a bit farther. I saw a pretty view up ahead." Melony's voice is sweet and full of that helpless damsel act that men always seem to love.

The sound of sirens is loud now.

The shot firing cracks the air almost at the same time as those sirens go silent.

"Got him." Derek's voice is triumphant.

Instinct tells me to run to my mate, but I need the police to find us. Drawing in as much air as possible, I start screaming. The sound cuts the silence like a knife. "Here! They shot him! Hurry!"

As soon as the police breach the woods and their radios and heavy stomping reach me, I run toward where I heard Cade.

"Hurry. Follow me." I keep up my loud yelling, knowing the dense woods might make it difficult for the police to find us.

Derek grabs my arm. "Shut up, Leona!"

I scream as loud as I can.

He slaps me across the face, and I fall to the leafy ground. "Shut up, or you'll get far worse.

A strong female voice says, "Step away from the woman, sir."

Once I give the officer's gun a good hard look, I turn and

scramble to my feet, running through the trees. I find Cade lying on the ground with Melony standing over him in just a bra and lace panties.

Her face is twisted in anger. "Why don't you turn?" She kicks him in the side. "Change into the monster."

Pushing Melony out of the way hard enough that she stumbles and grabs a tree for support, I kneel next to Cade.

A dart with red feathers at the end sticks out of his arm.

Two police officers barrel through the woods.

I pull the dart out and toss it to the ground. Cupping Cade's face, I pray he'll wake up. "Don't you dare leave me."

"He was supposed to change. He's a monster. Why didn't he want me?" Melony grabs her breasts as if in offering to the unconscious Cade.

An officer holds her arm. "You might want to put your clothes on, ma'am."

Someone touches my shoulder. "Let me have a look at him."

I back away a few feet to give two EMTs and an officer room to examine Cade. The officer sniffs the needle. "I think this is a sedative." He shakes the vile. "Still a few ccs left. Must not have fully injected."

Derek yells. "He's mine. I'm not getting left out of this."

The female officer grabs him by his cuffed hands and pushes him to the ground. "If you run away from me like that again, sir, I'll be forced to manacle your legs as well."

"What? Why is he like that? Where's the manticore?"

With a groan, Cade blinks his eyes.

A young officer with dark hair and eyes, says, "Mr. Petroyan? Can you hear me? Do you know what day it is?"

"Jose? It's Sunday. What the heck happened?" Holding his head, he sits up.

"Easy," the EMT warns. "You've been given a potent tranquilizer, Mr. Petroyan. We're going to go slow, take your blood pressure, and then we'll decide if we should move you on a stretcher."

"Leona?" Panic laces Cade's voice.

Filled with relief, worry, and anger, my voice is tight. "I'm here. I'm fine."

Lying back down, his eyes unfocused, Cade relaxes. "Okay. Take my blood pressure. I could use a rest."

CHAPTER ELEVEN

CADE

Because the dart malfunctioned, only a fraction of the contents made their way into my blood.

Leona and I are in the police station giving our accounts of the events.

This time, Derek opted for a tranquilizer. I guess he thought to kidnap me and get me to change either with his wife's help or by some other means. Who knows what he planned? Whatever it was, it was foiled by my brilliant mate.

Brian's betrayal hits hard, but I'm going to try to let the authorities handle the punishment. Most of the local police know me as a man who gives to their charities and participates in local events. So, when Brian and Derek go on about me being a manticore, they get put in a mental ward until they can be evaluated for sentencing.

Keeping my attention on Leona while she finishes her report to the police, my heart swells with pride. When she finishes, we leave the station, and she drives since I've recently been drugged.

"How did you keep from shifting?" she asks when we're alone on the road back to the resort.

"Do you think your sister could tempt my beast?" Reaching across the console, I tuck her hair behind her ear. The bruise on her cheek fuels the anger of both man and beast, but I'm fully in control of myself.

She smiles. "No. I didn't think Melony could change you or that you would shift because of a sexual stimulus unless you wanted to. But I think anger and protective instincts might make you shift. How did you keep from changing to protect yourself?"

The memory of her screams forces me to close my eyes and push my beast down. "I can control the beast, but when I heard you in distress, it wasn't easy."

"I had to alert the police to where we were before Derek heard me. It was all I could think of." She shrugs.

"You saved me again, little lioness. If not for you, Derek might have hauled me away before the police arrived."

Frowning, she turns down the road to the resort. "Derek is a terrible person. I don't know why it took me so long to realize that. My sister isn't much better..."

There's more to her thought. I can see the wheels turning in that gorgeous head of hers, but she doesn't say it.

"What else troubles you?"

She huffs out a long breath and stops before we reach the valet parking area. "Brian was your friend. You've known him for years. Why would he betray you?"

"Money makes some people do things even they might not expect." I wish that were not the truth, but it is.

Continuing to the front door, she sighs. "I suppose, but I don't know why you're not more upset about it."

"I'm disappointed in him, but I have you and nothing else really matters to me right now."

That brings a small grin to her pretty face. "I just need to pack and check out. It won't take long."

Patty and John are sitting in the lobby, surrounded by luggage. Getting up, Patty has tears in her eyes when she wraps her arms around Leona. "I don't understand what's happened, but I'm so relieved the two of you are safe."

John shakes my hand. "Why would Derek want to harm you?"

"He thinks his company can use me to make money." It's true but leaves out a few details.

Hugging me tight, Patty says, "He said that you're some kind of monster. He called you a beast and said you don't have the same rights as we do."

"I'm sure that's what he thinks." I pat her back.

Holding me at arm's length, she gives me a long look with narrowed eyes. "Do you promise to always put Leona's happiness above your own?"

"Of course."

"Then I don't care what you are, Cade. I've never seen my daughter happier than she's been these last couple of days. Make her happy and we'll stand behind you no matter what comes." Patty kisses my cheek. She gives Leona another hug. "We packed your bags." She points to a small suitcase and Leona's purse.

John asks, "Are you coming home with us, Leona?"

"No. I'm going to stay here a while." She gives me a questioning look. Once I nod, she smiles, and my heart soars.

John hugs her. "Probably for the best. We've got to go and

collect Melony, and I can't imagine the two of you in the same car right now would be a good mix. It was nice of you not to charge her for her part in whatever happened today." He shakes his head. "I'm sure Derek will make bail in a day or two. What happens after that, I can't imagine."

We see them out and load Leona's bag in my car. Once they leave, I turn to my mate. "How long will you stay?"

Without responding, she gets in the car and starts the engine.

Once I'm in, with my seatbelt buckled, she pulls away and heads to my house. "How's your head?"

"Clear now. I can drive if you want." I guess she's not going to answer. Maybe she doesn't want to hurt my feelings. I'm happy to have her for now anyway.

Shaking her head, she pulls to a stop at the end of the road, then turns right toward my house. "You can drive tomorrow if you want. Maybe we'll just stay inside for the day. Actually, it might be a few days before I'm willing to let you out of my sight."

I like the sound of a few days. "You're welcome for a lifetime, love." My throat tightens when she remains silent. After a few miles, I say, "I may have to leave here. If Derek told his company about me, they'll start looking. I don't want to have to worry about being shot every day for the rest of my life."

Still quiet, she pulls into my driveway and parks the car. Once we're in the house, she rolls her suitcase into my bedroom. "I'm going to have to go to the city."

"I understand." My chest hurts as if she'd driven a knife through my ribs.

"My landlady is nice. I'll bet she'll give me my deposit and not hold me to the last three months of my lease. My boss may be a little harder to convince about living outside the five boroughs." She shrugs. "There are other jobs."

Staring at her as she pulls open drawers in my dresser, I don't know what all of that means, and I'm afraid to hope.

Reaching the last drawer, she puts her clothes in. "I have some laundry. Do you think you can make room in one or two of these for me?"

"Yes." It's all I can manage to get out.

"Where would we move?"

Maybe she was going to say more, but I stopped any other questions by scooping her up in my arms. "We?"

Her sweet lips tip up, and she runs her fingers through my hair. "Of course. There's a very good chance I'm carrying our baby. Not to mention that I'm madly in love with you. Where you go, I go. Unless you had other plans?"

I capture her mouth with mine and kiss her until neither of us can catch our breath. The idea of our baby growing in her sweet body makes me feel reverence, but everything about my mate drives my desire. "Are you sore?" I skim my fingers along her bruised cheek. At some point, Derek will have to pay for touching my mate, but that can wait until he serves the human sentence.

"A little." Gripping my neck, she wraps her legs around my waist. "Not too sore though."

"Maybe you have a bit of nymph blood running through you, Leona." I lay her on the mattress. I never made the bed after my abbreviated sleep this morning.

She unbuttons her shorts and strips them down her smooth legs, along with the strip of lace panties. Her shirt goes next and then the bra. She pushes to the middle of the rumpled sheets and stares up at me with dilated eyes. Her sweet pink tongue slips between her mesmerizing lips and wets them.

I strip out of my clothes. To keep from going mad, I wrap my fist around my cock and stroke it. "I need to taste you more than I need air right now, little lioness."

Locking her gaze on my shaft, she makes the most beautiful little whimper. She bends her knees then lets them fall open, revealing her glistening folds.

My mouth waters at the sight, and I use my shoulders to spread her farther before licking her from bottom to top.

Her screaming my name fills my bedroom and fuels my need to give her pleasure.

I swirl my tongue around her clit before sucking the bud into my mouth and sliding my finger inside her.

She bucks her hips, riding my face and fucking my finger.

When I add a second finger, she comes with a long keen. Her pussy pulses around my digits.

"You're perfect, mate." The manticore is close to the surface. The tingle of hair growing to form a mane around my face, and the waving off of the last of the sedative is the signal that he won't be denied some part of our connection.

As soon as she relaxes, I move to all fours and hover over her.

Gripping my mane, she purrs, and it's the most beautiful sound. With a sexy grin, she rolls to her stomach, then lifts her ass in the air. She backs up until my cock touches her slick folds.

My manticore roars as we drive inside her with one long, slow thrust. I hold still, giving her time to adjust.

Calling my name, she tips her hips higher, taking more of me, then pulls forward and crashes back.

I won't last long like this. Gripping her hips, I pound into her sweet body, every move bringing us both closer to heaven.

Her pussy grips my cock and she calls my name. Her orgasm stretches out while I pump three more times and fill her with my seed. She collapses onto the mattress, and I slip free. Still half hard, I lie beside her and pull her into my arms. "I'm thinking farther west. Maybe still in New York."

"Where is that family you told me about?" Her voice is scratchy, and her breath uneven.

"The monsters? Havendoor. It's a small town in the southwest part of the state." Man and beast like the way she thinks. There's safety in numbers. It would be nice to have a community.

"It has a nice sound to it." She wraps her delicate hand around my cock. "I'm insatiable when it comes to you." She follows her hand with her mouth.

Turning her ass around so she's lying on top of me, I have a perfect view of her pretty pussy. While she sucks me, I lick and tease until she's writhing on the tip of me and comes all over my face. "I could live on this pussy alone."

As if I'd issued a challenge, she sucks me deep and hard, taking most of me into her mouth and throat. When I hit the back, she eases me out, grips the base, then gives me the best blow job of my life.

So close to coming, I lift her away, turn her, and let her impale herself on my shaft. She rides me like the goddess she is and comes again as I come inside her.

Collapsed on my chest, she kisses my chin. "I can't get enough of you."

"Good. I'm all yours, so you needn't try to get it all tonight."

She giggles. "Will you come with me to the city? It will take me a few days to pack up."

"Lioness, I'll follow you anywhere." I kiss her long and slow, letting our tongues tease and tempt each other before she tucks herself against my side and sighs.

I don't know how I got this lucky, but I'd brave a hailstorm of darts to have this woman by my side.

EPILOGUE

One year later

LEONA

The baby is crying and we're already half an hour late for a picnic at Scrim Hall, the home of our new friends here in Havendoor. Dashing across our house, I nearly trip over a stuffed dinosaur.

My phone rings in the kitchen.

"I'm coming, Aithan."

He stops crying.

Stalling in the hallway in case he's gone back to sleep, I listen.

Cade's strong voice coos from the nursery. "That was a lot of fussing when you know your mommy will be here soon enough."

The phone goes silent and since I've missed whoever it was, I continue to the bedroom.

Cade has Aithan cuddled against his chest. The baby is big for his three months, but he looks tiny in the arms of his father. A healthy, happy baby is all I could ask for and more. "Does he need a change?"

The phone ringing starts again.

Smiling warmly, Cade bounces Aithan and kisses his head. "I've got him. Go get the phone."

Our house isn't as big as the place in the Catskills, and it needs work. We bought it from people who had been on the property for generations. It's a good-sized piece of land and it's adjacent to the Pettigrew land, so when Cade needs to run, he's safe. Who would have believed there is an entire family of monsters living in a small town a couple of hours from Syracuse? I never dreamed there were vampires, wolf and dragon shifters, and more in existence. Now they feel like family.

I grab the phone and answer because it's my mom. We're late, but I don't like to put her off. She's been surprisingly supportive of my choices since the fiasco with Melony and Derek. "Hi, Mom."

"You didn't answer the first time. I was worried," she says quickly not bothering with hello.

"Aithan was crying." I stare down the hallway toward where Cade continues to speak to our son in low tones.

"Is he sick?" Mom must have forgotten that babies cry.

"No. He woke up from his nap. Cade's taking care of him. We're going to a barbecue at our friend's house. They have a big family and a lot of the local people will be there too." I grab the diaper bag and start filling it with the bottles I prepared earlier and other things I'll need while we're out. It's amazing to me how much stuff one small person needs to get through a few hours outside the house.

"That sounds nice." She drags out the last word as if she wants to say more.

"How are you and Dad?"

"We're fine. You know... um..." Her fingernails are tapping on something, probably the kitchen counter.

"What is it?" I add a couple of pacifiers to the front pocket.

"Today is your sister's wedding anniversary. You might call her and try to make things right between you two."

It's almost laughable that my mother thinks Melony and I can mend our relationship. However, it's obvious from her tone that she's serious. "You know, Mom, I'm not that concerned about it. Melony is married to a man in prison for trying to kidnap my husband. I don't wish her ill, but I don't need that kind of selfish greed in my life or my baby's life. I know you want to make everything okay again, but really, it never was that great."

Mom sighs. "You might never have met Cade if not for Melony."

"True, but it doesn't change my mind."

"I understand. Have a good time with your friends today." She sighs again.

"Why don't you and Dad come out here for a week and spend some time with your grandson? He's growing so fast you might not recognize him if you wait much longer." I'm filled with joy as Cade carries Aithan into the great room, dressed in the cutest jeans and a lumberjack-plaid shirt. In Cade's other hand is the stack of extra clothes I left on the changing table.

I have no idea how I got so lucky.

"We would love that," Mom says. "How about at the end of the month? We can stay in town at that little inn. We don't want to inconvenience you." Mom's nail-tapping gets louder and faster.

It's hard to not laugh since Cade can hear her and he's raised one eyebrow in a comical look of disbelief. I wave him off and put the extra clothes in the bag. "That's not necessary. We finished the renovations on the guest bedroom and bathroom last week. You'll be very comfortable here."

"If you're sure—I'm putting it in my calendar for the twenty-seventh."

"We've got to go. I'll call you tomorrow." I tell her I love her and end the call.

Cade puts the carrier on the counter and buckles Aithan in before kissing my cheek. "She wanted you to wish your sister a happy anniversary?"

"How did you know that?" I'm shocked he would ever think of my ridiculous sister and her horrible husband.

Wrapping his arms around me, he captures my lips in a long kiss that leaves me breathless. "You don't think I could forget the day I met you, do you, little lioness? It was the greatest moment of my life when you stepped into that clearing and saved me from certain doom."

We stare at our perfect son. Cade keeps a possessive arm around me with his hand resting on my hip. It's perfect. I have exactly the life I want, even if it's nothing like the one I imagined. "I'm pretty sure you saved me too, my love."

Kissing the top of my head, he hugs me tight. "If we weren't already late, I'd take you to bed to see if we can make another one just like this." He runs a gentle finger along our son's cheek.

Aithan makes bubbles and smiles. We have no idea if he'll ever be a manticore like his father, and we won't know until he reaches five or six, but I have a feeling there will be at least one more monster in this house. My womb longs to be filled with another baby. "I'm all yours, and I would love to fill this house with a passel of manticore babies, but later, after the party."

The beast inside him swirls in his eyes.

Rising on my tiptoes, I press my lips to his. "Later." And I meet the monster's sexy gaze.

He growls low and it eases into a purr.

Aithan yawns and his eyes drift closed.

Ever so gently, Cade places the carrier on the floor in the living room. He pulls me close and runs his hands over my ass, hauling me in so I can feel his cock straining against his jeans. "We can't wake the baby. No one will notice if we're a bit later than late."

Wrapping my legs around his hips and my arms around his neck, I wish we were already naked. "How did I ever get so lucky to find you in a world full of humans?"

Just a few strides later, he carries me into our bedroom. The beast growls. "You are my mate. If you didn't find me, I would have hunted the earth for you."

As he lays me on the mattress and stares into my eyes, I know that it's true. Nothing could have kept us apart. Not even Derek and Melony had that kind of power. We are meant to be. This is our destiny.

Thank you for reading Cade and Leona's story.
I hope you love them as much as I do. I have thoroughly
enjoyed writing all my monsters and the ladies they love.

Turn the page to find out what happens with Astra,
the nymph in the woods, in **Promised to the Satyr**.

PROMISED TO THE SATYR

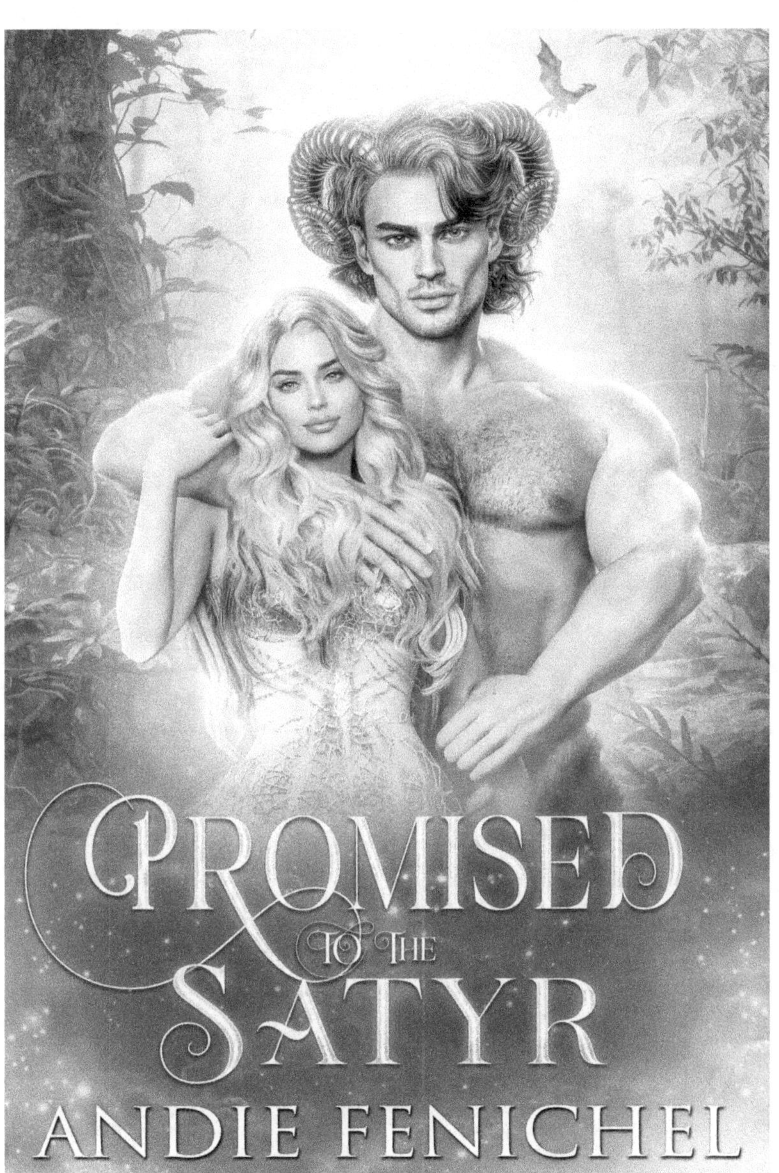

PROMISED
TO THE
SATYR
ANDIE FENICHEL

PROMISED TO THE SATYR

CATSKILL MONSTERS

ASTRA

Being a nymph, people generally think of me as a mythological character, but I'm a real woman with things that I want out of life. Having spent my entire existence in the woods of Upstate New York, I long for more. Now my father has promised me to a satyr named Niko whom I've never met. This is my last chance to get away, so I charm a local wyvern who's had his eye on me for many years into flying me far away from this place, my father, and that satyr.

Only Niko finds me before I reach the meeting place. And damn him, but he's charming. He's not at all the careless beast I expect. Still, I'm not giving in to an arranged marriage. Of course, that means I'll never see my father or my woods again. It's an impossible choice.

NIKO

I was reluctant to agree to an arranged marriage, but once I see Astra's picture, I know she's my destiny. When word reaches me that she's running to avoid the match, I go after her. Even after finding her fleeing from me through the woods, I'm smitten. If she feels the bond between us, she hides it well. Unwilling to give up too soon and never have a life with her, I make a deal. If Astra will give me one week at the house I bought for us, I will abide by whatever she decides and make things right with her father.

CHAPTER ONE

ASTRA

I'm wearing clothes! Real clothes. It's a first for me. Nymphs never wear anything that will shed when stepping inside a tree. I have a closet filled with sheer magical gowns and not one pair of jeans. However, the manticore Cade's new mate told me I could take what I wanted from her room at the resort to make my getaway. I can't exactly go into the human world with the wyvern shifter naked. I suppose that was one of the ways Father kept me in these woods and out of sight.

In jeans and a white shirt tied at the waist, I look like every other human roaming the earth. All I have to do is get to the meeting place by the lake and Drayce will fly us out of these woods forever.

My father thought he could give me to a satyr without even bothering to let me meet the fiend. Old-fashioned and high-handed, he set a date and kept it from me until the day before my wedding day.

Well, I hope Father will be very happy when there is a groom and no bride for the ceremony. A stupid tear tries to escape at the thought of leaving my forest, and I suppose Father too, but I force my anger aside.

These little white sneakers are not as comfortable as running barefoot, but I'm starting to get the hang of it.

The clouds gather and I begin to worry that a bad storm might keep the wyvern from flying. He thinks he's in love with me, which is unfortunate. Most creatures fall in love with me. It's part of being a nymph. We are alluring to men, women, and monsters alike.

However, it doesn't work both ways. While Drayce is nice, I don't love him and probably never will. I don't think I've ever loved anyone. He's my ticket out of this place, so I'll use him to escape, and then I'll find him someone he's really in love with. His love for me is only because of my magic.

That tear makes its way to my cheek and I dash it away.

The underbrush rustles to my left.

I stop and crouch in case Father has come after me. Inching closer to a big oak, I slip inside the trunk to wait for him to pass. The human's clothes fall away in a heap at the base of the tree.

The bushes move and the deer trail I was using fills with a man. He's tall and broad. His dark hair catches the breeze. His eyes are intense and his full mouth tips up as if he knows a joke and won't tell. Horns curl back from the top of his head. Though he wears a kilt, there is no denying the hair-covered bend of goat's legs.

The satyr.

He's far more beautiful than I imagined, but that doesn't make him more appealing. I'll not be forced to wed anyone, no matter what they look like.

My body says differently as I can't help wondering what he hides beneath that kilt. I close my eyes and my arousal shakes the leaves of the tree I'm hiding within.

"I know you are in there, little nymph. Come out so we can talk." His voice is deep and seductive.

Damn him.

I'm staying right where I am. I'm not going to be bullied by him, either.

He picks up my borrowed jeans and they look tiny in his hand. "What would I have to say to make you come out, Astra?" He holds the denim close to his nose and breathes deep. Closing his eyes, his lips tighten and the crease between his eyes deepens as if in pain.

I swear his kilt flares, but it's probably just my overactive imagination. Though, he is a satyr after all.

He sits and folds the jeans and shirt and makes a little pile next to the tree's trunk before smiling at the sneakers and placing them next to the clothes. Leaning back against the rough trunk, his shoulders are nearly as wide as the old oak.

If I crouched, I could touch him, but that would give myself away. I shouldn't want to touch him, but heavens help me, I do.

"Shall I tell you about myself? Will that make you more inclined to come out of hiding?" He lets out a long breath. "Maybe your father told you that my name is Niko Barbaros. I was born in woods similar to these in Canada. It's colder there, but I was happy. I had hoped to find a bride there when your father sent a letter. He asked if I would marry his daughter as she was becoming restless and needed a husband."

Rage at my father rushes into my chest and if I'm not careful, I'll solidify and have to jump free of my place within the wooden rings that hold me.

He touches my clothes. "I didn't think nymphs wore clothes." After a long pause, he says, "I initially told your father no, but then he sent me a photograph of your face and I said yes. I think you are the most beautiful woman I've ever seen."

Beauty, ha. Of course, that's why he wants me. When he tires of my looks, he'll move on to the next. I suppose I could wait for him to tire and appease my father. Why doesn't anyone care what I want?

Picking up one of the sneakers, he studies it from different directions. "It might have been better if I had come sooner and introduced myself, but I had a life to sort out up north. When I arrived, I learned you were apprehensive about our arrangement. I asked your father why you hadn't responded to any of my letters. He said he'd kept them from you and that it was better for you to know me after our marriage. An old-fashioned idea."

His back stretches as he takes a deep breath. "Astra, you don't have to marry me."

My heart is beating so fast, I may pass out and become part of this tree forever. I gather my wits. "How can I know you're not lying?"

The tree's leaves shiver with the vibration of my voice.

"I suppose you can't." He stands and faces the tree and me. "I swear on the old gods, I will not force you to do anything you do not wish for. I promise to go away if that's what you want. All I ask is that you spend a week with me without distraction. If you don't like me and never could, I'll return to Canada and your father will blame me for the failure."

"One week?" I like the idea of having a choice, and he is beautiful to look at.

"I heard you were planning to run off with a dragon. Do you love him?" There's a tight warning in his otherwise caressing voice.

I step from the tree.

Niko scans my body from head to toe. "Lovely." He focuses on my face. "Do you love the dragon?"

I pull on the jeans and shirt, which I button and tie at the waist before slipping my feet into the sneakers. "Drayce is a wyvern who is very fond of me. He thinks he loves me, but he is only lured in by my nature. I had hoped for him to take me far away from here and then find his true mate for him." I have no idea why I told him all of that. It shouldn't matter what he thinks of me, but I don't like the idea of being some femme fetal who uses men.

A hint of a smile pulls at his lips, and it's totally distracting. He stares at me, his hands on his hips and his head cocked. "Do we have a deal, Astra?"

"Where would we go that there wouldn't be distractions and what would you demand of me once we arrived?" Half of me wants one thing, the other, another. Honestly, more than half can't get the idea of being pressed up against him out of my head. What's wrong with me?

"There is a cabin several kilometers from here. I bought it when I agreed to your father's offer. We can go there unless you have another place you'd prefer. I will make no demands other than you spend at least one hour talking to me each day and we take our meals together." He crosses his thick arms over his chest.

How can any man be this perfectly formed? He makes my mouth water.

I don't want to lose my father, and this plan makes Niko the villain. Father is controlling and misguided in the ways of the modern world, but he is my only family. "I agree to your terms. After a week, you can leave and Father will blame you. I can go back to the way my life has always been."

He bows. "If that is your wish, Astra, that's how it will be." He reaches a hand out.

Hesitant but not wanting to look cowardly, I take it and shake. Heat rushes through me at his touch. I pull back. "I have a message to send." Closing my eyes, I call the owl roosting high in the trees.

It soars down to me, landing delicately on my arm. Its long talons are gentle on my skin, and it hoots.

I whisper along his feathers. "Tell the wyvern I cannot come. Tell him I'm sorry."

With a flap of his wide wings, the owl lifts into the air and flies toward the lake.

"Ready?" Niko smiles at me as if he's won something.

I'm not a prize. "Keep your grinning to yourself, satyr. I only agreed to one week. After that, you and I will never see each other again."

It's almost sad when his smile falters.

We walk through the forest, moving west, then north.

After twenty minutes, something nags at me. "What did you write in your letters?"

Shrugging, there's a hint of a blush on his smooth cheeks. "I wrote the things a young man writes when he wants to impress a woman."

Not much of an answer. "Why didn't Father give them to me?"

"Perhaps he worried you would use the letters as an excuse for disobeying him." Niko probably isn't far off.

Father likes to be obeyed without question and when I was a little girl, that was fine, but I'm grown and have a mind of my own. Perhaps my father never expected to have a child. Mother died when I was small. She was human. That's all I know since that's another subject forbidden in his house.

A sigh escapes.

Niko stops. "If you are tired, I will carry you."

Dammit, does he have to be so sweet and charming? "No. I'm thoughtful, not tired."

"Would you like to share your thoughts?"

"Not really," I say. "I wonder if Father read the letters?"

"He did not." Niko turns down a driveway that ascends a mountain.

My thighs and calves begin to ache. Maybe I shouldn't have said no to being carried. "How can you be so sure?"

"He gave them to me and they are all still sealed." As if sensing my distress, he lowers to his knees with his back to me. "My legs are much stronger. Please, let me carry you?"

Against my better judgment, I wrap my legs around his waist and grip his shoulders. "Only because climbing mountains is not in my daily routine."

Holding my calves in his hands, he runs up the mountain.

I hold tighter, afraid that if he hits a rock, I'll go flying off and roll to my death. "Why are we running?"

His voice is tight. "Because having your body pressed to mine is more than my cock can take. Galloping is a distraction and if I don't, it will be difficult to walk."

I stifle my amusement. "Then why did you offer me a ride?"

"I am a gentleman and didn't bring you proper transportation. Thus, carrying you is the least I can do." He grunts and a hint of what's under his kilt nudges at my foot.

My body tingles with lust. I think it's going to be a long week.

CHAPTER TWO

NIKO

With her arms wrapped around my chest and the rest of her flush to my back, it's hard to concentrate on putting one foot in front of the other. She's more beautiful than her pictures led me to believe. When she stepped out of that tree, my heart skidded to a stop. She's clever and smells of wildflowers. The few nymphs I've known have had no interest in defiance. Astra is different.

We crest the last rise and my new cabin comes into view. I bought the place through photographs only and hired a team of people who spent the last three months fixing it up.

Astra gaps. "This is your cabin?"

"Yes. Do you like it?" I hold my breath.

It's a two-story log cabin with porches and a stone chimney. From this distance, it's part of the mountainous landscape with a view of several lakes and the top of the Appalachian range.

"I've never seen anything like it." She unwraps herself from my back and stands next to me, gaping. "When did you buy this?"

"In the spring. I—"

"The spring!" She spins to face me. "When did you agree to this arrangement with my father?"

It feels as if whatever I say next will be wrong and important. Lying is not an option. "It was in March that he first sent me your photograph and I knew then that I would agree to whatever terms he offered."

"March." She storms toward the cabin. "March."

I follow. "What's wrong, Astra?"

She throws her hands up in the air. "March was five months ago."

"I don't understand." My gut is twisted and my heart pounding. I have no idea why March is significant or what is going to come next from her. Even so, the sway of her hips and the high color of her cheeks have me enthralled.

"You've written letters to me since March. Didn't you think it odd that I never responded?" She puts her fists on her hips and faces me.

Back in Canada, I longed to hear some word from her. I wanted to know her and begin our relationship. Her image, though beautiful, was not enough. "I was disappointed that you didn't wish to let me know you. Of course, now I understand your father didn't share my correspondence."

Shaking her head, she turns and continues down the drive. "Father never gave me those letters. Do you know what else he never did? He never told me anything about you or the arrangement the two of you had made. I found out yesterday that I was to be married today."

I lope to catch up. Her legs may be much smaller than

mine, but she walks fast. Feeling like I'm losing her, I take her arm. "Yesterday. That's not possible. Who made all the wedding arrangements?"

There's rage in her bright eyes and her delicate jaw ticks. "I would imagine someone who works for my father. I know nothing about it. He informed me yesterday—" She pulls her arm from my hand. "That I would be married at three o'clock today."

I sit back on my haunches. "No wonder you ran."

Her gaze gentles for a moment and then she frowns. "One week, Niko Barbaros. That's all I'm giving you and that is only so that I can remain in my forest. I've lived here all my life and despite my father's heavy hand, this is my home, these are my trees, my rivers, lakes, and creeks."

Offering her my hand, I force a smile. If all I have is one week, then I have a lot of convincing to do in a very short time. "One week and then you decide our future."

With a toss of her silken hair over her shoulder, she takes my hand. "The future is that I will go back to my life and you will return to Canada. Actually, I don't care where you go. All I know is I'm not in your future beyond this week."

"You promised an open mind." It breaks my heart to think of her walking away from me. I've wanted her from the moment I saw her, maybe even from the second I knew of her existence.

"I promised one week. Show me your house." She presses her full lips tightly together and looks at the cabin. "It's very well situated."

"It is." Getting to my feet, I lead her the last few hundred yards to the wooden stairs to the lower porch that wraps around the house.

Dropping my hand, she looks back up the well-worn

drive and the woods that roll across a seemingly endless mountain range. "I've never been up here. Who owned this house before you?"

"A half giant named Bard." There are double doors with glass panels leading into the house; I open the one on the right. "Would you like to see inside?"

"Bard played the lute at festivals. I had no idea he owned such a fine property. He kept to himself." She pauses a moment before crossing the threshold. "I'm not your prisoner."

"You are my honored guest, Astra. I'm very sorry your father has made this uncomfortable for you." When I see Nocturn again, I plan to give him a piece of my mind.

"Father loves drama almost as much as he loves obedience." She crosses the great room without giving the kitchen, living room, or dining room a second glance. The large windows that span the back wall offer a spectacular view of her home forest. "This is beautiful."

Her blond hair cascades down her back in waves like the ocean and stops at the swell of her shapely ass.

Silently, I thank the tree for not allowing her within wearing the human clothes. Seeing every inch of her body was a gift. I hope to know more once she allows my touch. Actually, nymphs are usually naked or nearly so. "Where did you get those clothes?"

Running her hand along the denim, she grins. "A friend gave them to me. Well, she's only an acquaintance so far, but she's mated to my good friend, so I imagine, one day, we'll be friends too."

"You charmed her into giving you her clothes." It is her nature to seduce.

"No." She shrugs. "Maybe, but she offered. I can't help

what I am, Niko. Humans and monsters alike are drawn to me. It's not my fault."

I find it odd that she's defending herself and to me, of all people. "I wasn't admonishing you, Astra."

Her cheeks flush. "No?" Turning away, she shrugs. "Well, we don't know each other." She runs her hand along the back of the long brown leather couch. "All new furniture?"

"I wanted to make the place fresh and clean. Bard's furnishings were dated and worn." I'm fascinated by every move she makes. I love the way she touches each item: the club chair, a lamp, the live edge of the coffee table. "I hired a human named Marissa to decorate. Do you know her?"

Astra nods. "Marissa Monet has a shop in the valley. Of course, I've never been there because I was never allowed clothes. I run around my woods and pop in and out of trees without purpose or profession." Bitterness rings in her voice.

"What would you like to do?" My hooves clomp on the wood floors as I cross to sit on the couch. If I'm not careful, she'll be aware too soon about just how attracted I am to her. My cock has been between hard and half-mast since I first saw her. The kilt can only hide so much. Sitting makes it easier to disguise my condition.

Propping herself at the edge of the club chair, she plucks the red pillow from the back and hugs it, eyes wide. "You're the first person to ever ask me that. No one expects a nymph to do anything useful."

It's true, but again, it's clear she's different. "Most of your kind are happy to pop in and out of trees or water and seduce humans for fun. I sense you wish for more or you wouldn't have attempted to escape my horrible clutches in favor of a wyvern with whom you are not in love."

With a long release of breath, she slumps. Still hugging

the pillow, she meets my gaze. "I would like to paint or write. I don't know if I can do either, but there are images and stories in my head..." Blushing, she stops talking. "Never mind."

Damn. She was so close to opening up. I suppose it was too much to ask for her to bare her entire soul after knowing me for an hour. "Shall I fix us something to eat or are you tired?"

"I'm not sleeping in the same room with you." She tightens her grip on the pillow and straightens. The flash of fire in her sky-blue eyes is mesmerizing.

It's going to take every ounce of my patience to keep my hands off Astra. I may not be susceptible to her magical allure, but I'm already lost to her charm. "I have a very nice guest room or you can have my room and I will take the guest room. It's up to you where you sleep."

She stands. "I would like to rest for a while. Alone."

I show her upstairs to the two guest rooms and the main suite. "Would you like me to go and get your things from your father's house while you rest?"

"Do you have a phone?" Taking the smartphone from me, she walks out of my bedroom and chooses the guest room with the best view of the forest.

I follow like a lamb.

Sitting on the edge of the queen bed, she dials a number. "Hi Paula, it's me. No. I'm fine. I understand. Can you pack a bag for me? A satyr will come and pick it up. A week. Thank you." She hangs up and hands me my phone.

"I'll be back before you wake up," I promise. "You don't have a phone?"

Pushing herself to the center of the bed, she rolls to her

side and curls into a ball. "I've never had pockets before." The sorrow in her voice breaks my heart.

Kneeling at the side of the bed, I brush her hair from her face. "Astra, you can do anything you want. Sleep here, paint a masterpiece, run off with a dragon, and write a novel. You have free will."

A large tear runs down the bridge of her nose. "Free will is an illusion for humans. That's what Father would say." She closes her eyes and another tear joins the first.

As silently as my hooves will allow, I step from her room. Winning her trust means undoing a lifetime of repression, but I'm up for the challenge. At the tree earlier, I thought I could dominate my nymph into submission, but once I met her, I knew that wasn't the way, not for her and not for me.

The wyvern may have been satisfied with her joining him out of desperation, but I need more. When Astra comes to me, it has to be a decision she makes from her heart.

CHAPTER THREE

ASTRA

I hate to admit it, but I slept better in the satyr's house than I have in my life. Despite being promised to him, I don't feel like a captive. He believes I will keep my promise to stay for the week, and I will. After that, I'll figure out a new living arrangement. I'm never going back to my father's house.

I stretch in the bed and gaze out at the pinks and purples lighting the sky with the setting sun. From here, I can see my entire forest, and it's lovely. Sitting up, I note my luggage near the door and a large bag from a department store. Curious, I gather the bag and dump it out on the bed.

Jeans in several colors, shorts, dresses, blouses, shoes, and underthings the likes of which I've never worn tumble out.

There's a knock on my door.

"Yes?" I look up from the human clothes.

Niko steps in, leaving the door open. He looks from me

to the bed. "I hope you don't mind. I asked Marissa to do me a favor and buy you a few things to wear. I assume what's in your valise is…nymphlike…and thought you might prefer human clothes."

My borrowed clothes are wrinkled and got a bit dirty when they fell off as I entered the tree. I rub a grass stain on the shirtsleeve. "That was thoughtful." I want to dislike him, but he makes it very difficult. "Thank you."

His kilt twitches. Turning slightly away, he nods. "I've made a salad and some fish. Paula said you rarely eat meat, but that you like fish."

Damn Paula for giving him any information. Though, I'm sure she only worries that I'll starve. I'd refuse to come to dinner, except my stomach is empty as I've not eaten since yesterday before Father told me about my impending marriage. Besides, I did say I would take my meals with him. Still, I feel foggy and grimy. "If you don't mind, I think I'll bathe and change before I come down."

He opens the door to his right. "Take your time. This bathroom is shared between the two guest rooms. It is yours for the week." He turns as if to leave, but then stops. "If you need a larger tub, my bathroom might be preferable."

I'm about to make a scathing remark when he holds up a hand. "I promise to give you your privacy."

Without another word, he walks out and clomps down the stairs.

I wonder how he managed to get to my door without me hearing him coming. His hooves are loud. Satyrs are known for large, ready cocks, not stealthiness. My body reacts to the idea of his shaft twitching at my words of thanks. Is he always aroused or is it me?

It makes no difference. I open my suitcase and pull out a

brush and other toiletries, then walk into the shared bathroom. The tub is slightly deeper than a standard bath and the other fixtures are very nice. The tile is made to look like coppery stone and the double sinks are slightly raised from the long vanity.

Curiosity gets the better of me. Niko is the kind of man who will always keep his word. I'm safe upstairs. I stride down the hall, intent on looking at his tub. It can do no harm to look.

I step through his bedroom, which has a large king bed and two picture windows. The walls are painted a dark grayish blue, and the tray ceiling has hidden lights that cast a warm, sensual glow. Double doors open up to a bathroom with marble floors and a huge shower. The dark wooden cabinetry has marble tops and smooth copper-colored glass basins. Sitting under the window that faces my forest is a deep cream-colored tub with a rolled top, big enough for two, even if one is a very large satyr.

My body aches to sink into that and lifting my chin, I plunk my toiletries on the vanity, then start the water. In the cabinet under one sink, I find shaving supplies and other manly items. Under the other is rose-scented milk bath and a stack of fluffy white towels.

Once the bath is filled and scented, I strip out of my borrowed clothes and sink into the warm water. Staring out at the mountains and trees, I sigh with contentment. If only the satyr wasn't here, this would be perfect.

Even as I think it, it I'm not sure I mean it. He's been a perfect gentleman other than not turning away when I was naked. However, I have no shame since I've been naked all my life. People gape and stare and fall in love with me. It happens every day. Only Niko didn't gape or gush over me.

He looked, then kept his attention on my face. He talked to me as if what I said was important to him.

Only creatures like Cade the manticore ever showed interest in me as a person. He wasn't lured in by my essence because he can only want his true mate. Some creatures are not affected by nymphs. Why am I disappointed that Niko didn't instantly fall in love with me? No. It's better this way. I can leave at the end of the week without any guilt.

Sinking lower, I let my head fall back, soaking my hair. I wash and relax until my stomach's grumblings overwhelm my enjoyment of the bath.

When I return to my room, I find an envelope on the nightstand. It's addressed to me and postmarked from March.

Not ready to read the letter and curious to know how Niko got up those steps without being heard, I pull on a pair of white shorts and a pink shirt that says Pretty in Pink on the front. I don't bother with the underwear as I can't imagine such items being comfortable.

I like the way the clothes feel on my skin. Somehow putting them on feels naughty and rebellious.

I step into the great room and the scents of food fill the air. Niko's back is to me and he does something at the stove. He's broad, and the way his waist narrows and the curve of his ass is far sexier than I'll ever admit. I clear my throat. "Have you always cooked for yourself?"

His smile as he turns melts me from the inside out. My body abandons my demand to not be attracted to him, and my clit pulses with need.

"I like to cook." He nods to a cookbook on the counter.

On the cover is a photo of him without horns. His name is written in shiny black lettering across the top. I blink and shake my head, expecting that to be some kind of illusion that will disappear. "You write cookbooks?"

He shrugs. "I'm a chef and cooked in my own restaurants for a long time. When my nature became known, I retreated to the mountains. I hired chefs and on-site managers, and started writing books. Eventually, people forgot about the half-goat man who cooked them risotto, and I have led a peaceful life ever since. That was a long time ago."

I wish I didn't find him so fascinating. "Thank you for getting me clothes."

Nodding, he brings me a plate with toasted baguette slices covered in bruschetta.

Too hungry to refuse, I eat two before I think about the price of his kindness. "I'm not going to marry you just because you fed me or let me use your bathtub."

"I know," he says without looking at me.

"I don't need you." I wish the fish didn't smell so good roasting in some kind of tomato-based sauce.

"Of course you don't." He turns off the oven and faces me. "You're a grown woman who can do anything she wants. You are not even required to stay here for the week."

"I promised." Why does it hurt to think he might prefer me to leave? Is he having second thoughts about the deal we made?

Rather than continue the discussion, he smiles and offers me a seat at the dining table.

*H*ours later, I'm filled with food and wine and curled up on his couch, looking into the darkness of the mountains.

Niko sits, sipping bourbon, and has been quiet ever since he joined me half an hour ago.

"Why did you move here, Niko?" If I am to keep my promise, I may as well get to know him. Who knows, perhaps we can become friends. A nymph can never have too many friends who aren't lured in by the magical appeal.

He puts the crystal glass on the coffee table. "I have known a few wood nymphs and water nymphs and they all loved their places in the world. Your father told me you are special and have ties to both woods and water. Still, I thought you'd prefer to stay in your forest."

"I wish Father hadn't made this arrangement." I meant for the comment to be light, but it comes out whiny.

"I know you do." Sorrow laces his tone.

Hating that I've hurt his feelings, I sit up and move beside him. Resting my hand on his arm, I say, "It's not your fault. I'm sure you're a nice man. I don't like being manipulated. This was unfair to both of us."

His kilt rises, but he keeps his gaze on mine. He covers my hand with his. "It was not fair. I still can't wish this away."

Jerking my hand back, I sit back a foot. "Because you want to have sex with me. You're a satyr and I'm a nymph. It's expected that we are sexual beings. Father likely thinks he won as I won't be able to resist you. You are both wrong." I cross my arms over my aching breasts, wishing my body would listen to my words.

Danger flashes in his dark eyes. His full mouth pulls into a tight line. Leaning toward me, his large hand flattens on the cushion. "We are what we are, Astra. You lure in men and women with the essence of the nymph. You care for your woods and rivers as if you own them. I play and compose music just like my ancestors before me. Make no mistake, I want you. My cock has been thick and ready since the moment I first saw your photograph. It is our nature, and neither of us can fight nature. The only things standing in the way of sex are that you have not agreed, and I want more from you."

It's hard to breathe. The depth of his tone and intensity in his stare has my pussy screaming to give him what he wants, whatever that might be. "More?"

"Yes. I need my wife to be a partner in all things. You don't want me, though I think you're attracted to me." Pulling back, he shifts so his kilt covers the effects of being close to me. "Either way, your father is not the one who will win or lose, Astra. This is about us, not him."

Even knowing he's right, I can't stand the idea of my father winning this battle. "My father will not see it that way." I get up and, pushing aside the hurt look on Niko's face, I head to the guest room, where I lock the door against an invasion I know will never come.

CHAPTER FOUR

ASTRA

*W*hen the sun comes up, a mist hangs over the mountains outside the bedroom's window. I want to ignore the letter still perched on my nightstand, but it calls to me.

Picking it up, I note the way his handwriting is neat, curved, and masculine. He has strong hands, but he said he's a musician. He cooks like it's all he'll ever do. The dinner last night was one of the best meals of my life.

Niko is interesting, and I can't escape thinking about him. I slip my finger under the corner of the envelope and tear the paper.

Dear Astra

First, I would like to thank you for agreeing to this marriage. At first, I was hesitant, but your father insisted that a match between us would be favorable. Generally, I'm not led by the will of gods or demigods like Nocturn, but he convinced me to think about it.

I apologize for not coming to New York directly. While I long to meet you in person, I have a life in Canada that I need to sort out. I own three restaurants for which I have to hire a general manager. Each has its own, but with me out of the country, I'll need someone to oversee the entire operation.

As you can imagine, this will take me some time. I will come as soon as possible. I said at the start of this letter that I was initially uncertain about this arrangement. However, from the first moment I saw your photograph, I knew this was my only path.

I hope you feel the same and look forward to getting to know you before I arrive.

Sincerely,

Niko Barbaros

The soft sounds of a guitar filter through the house as I hold the letter against my chest. What did he see in the picture? What photo had Father sent? It would be just like Father to send a photo to this stranger while leaving me in the dark about everything. Father didn't want me to have time to make plans and run away.

If I had known Niko was kind before I came out of the tree, I would have told him I was tricked and wanted to leave.

A tear spills from my eye at the thought of never touching my forest again.

Dashing it away, I tuck the letter back into its envelope and get out of bed.

This deal with Niko ensures that I'll never have to leave my home.

Once I'm wearing a light-blue sundress, I follow the

sound downstairs, where I find a sticky note on the counter next to a smartphone.

The phone is for you. Pancakes are in the warming drawer. N

Grinning like a child at Yule, I tuck the phone into the pocket of my dress and round the counter to find the scent of vanilla and a blue light, which lead me to a stainless-steel drawer and a plate full of palm-sized pancakes.

There's syrup on the counter, but I eat the delectable morsels plain.

He's trying to win me over with the best food of my life and so far, it's working. However, I'm still leaving in six days. I'm just doing so with a full belly.

On the porch overlooking the lake and valley, Niko sits strumming an acoustic guitar. He smiles as I open the French door. "Did you eat?"

"Yes. Thank you. They were delicious." I walk to the railing and breathe in my trees. "This is a good view."

"I'm glad you like it." He stops playing.

"Thank you for the phone. You didn't have to do that. I've managed a great many years without one." I touch the glass object in my pocket.

"But now you have pockets and I can call you." Chest bare, he puts the guitar aside and steps beside me.

"Buying me clothes and objects will not make me stay past our deal." There's no point in giving him false hope. I've already hurt the Wyvern this week, I don't want to hurt Niko too.

"I know that, Astra. I thought you might like to go into town or to the lake, and I would like the ability to come to your aid, should you need me." He grips the railing with white knuckles, but his expression is soft. Only the whitening of his knuckles indicates he's less than under control.

"Have I upset you?" I slide my hand over his, hoping to ease whatever I've done.

"No." He pulls his hand away. "I'm unable to control my arousal and I feel foolish. That's all."

Mind your own business and go in the house. You can go for that walk and that will get you away from him and ease his situation. I'm practically yelling inside my head to go, but I face him and study the set of his jaw and the kindness in his dark eyes. "I've heard that some satyrs are always erect. That must be inconvenient." My nipples tighten and rub against my new dress.

One side of his mouth tips up. "I imagine that's true, but until a few weeks ago I had been in full control of my cock since my teen years."

"Oh. Then I'm the problem. I'll go for that walk." I never want to harm anyone and his condition must be very uncomfortable.

Before I can get away, he wraps his hand around my upper arm. His breath tickles the shell of my ear. "You are not a problem, Astra. Wanting you is not an inconvenience."

The soft, strong tone of his voice reminds me that his hands have the same quality. It's likely he's a very good lover with both tenderness and intensity. My clit pulses and my breath catches. "That's a nice thing to say. I'll visit my trees and you can…do what you need to do to…" My cheeks heat. I can't remember ever being embarrassed before, but I'm sure I'm blushing.

"Does the notion of me masturbating bother you?" His

grip eases and he skims his fingers along the inside of my elbow.

Bother is an interesting choice of words. "I'm going for a swim." I step out of his reach and without looking back, rush through the house and out the front door.

Even as I run my fingers over the trunks of trees and hear their deep voices echoing their health, my mind will not give me peace. I envision Niko's big hand wrapped around his thick, hard cock. I know he's running that hand from base to tip and thinking of me, or maybe about some woman he left in Canada. Why should I feel jealous? He's not mine. It's normal to be sexually aroused by a man with a large cock. It's normal to want to have sex.

I run through the woods, kicking off the uncomfortable shoes so I can feel the earth beneath my feet. Moving faster and faster down the side of the mountain, I only slow when I hear a strange beep and my pocket vibrates.

It can only be one person. It can only be a beautiful satyr. I lift the phone from and see Niko's name on the screen. I click and a text opens.

NIKO:

I'm not chasing you. Why are you running?

I look back at the house. Can he see me this far away? Do satyrs have exceptional senses? I should have studied harder when I was young.

ASTRA:

I would know if someone was chasing me. The trees would tell me.

NIKO:

Good to know.

ASTRA:

Are you angry that I left?

Three dots blink for a moment then disappear.

NIKO:

No. Come back when you're ready. I have things to occupy my time until you return.

I slip the phone back into my pocket and continue to wonder if he's masturbating. Why can't I get him out of my head? I never fantasize about sex. I'm the seducer, not the one who is seduced. Men want me because I'm a nymph and my magic is to lure people away. I've never been much for keeping any of the lovers I've seduced. After a while, it's a bore to manipulate humans and monsters. Besides, it reminds me too much of my father's passion for getting people to do his bidding.

At the edge of the lake, I strip out of my dress, careful to make sure my new phone is safe. I wade in to my thighs, then deeper. The cold water helps alleviate some of my pent-up longing for Niko and his big cock. The way I'm thinking about it, it's as if I've seen him naked. Perhaps it's worse to have an idea about something than the truth. However, there's little doubt from the way it moves his kilt that a lot is hiding under there.

I swim to the center and float on my back while the sun rises higher in a clear blue sky. Still warm, the day should be perfect. As I become one with the water, it occurs to me that I like Niko. Damn. That's the problem. Father ruins everything. If he hadn't forced a satyr on me, it might be different. There's no way I'm letting Father win. "Never!"

Damp from swimming but no less aroused than hours before, I walk up the path from the lake to the house. I touch as many trees as I can. At the bottom of the stairs that lead up to the porch, I take a deep breath.

Niko is wearing a chambray shirt with the buttons open to mid-chest. He has a glass of iced tea halfway to his lips when he stops to watch me climb the last few steps. He puts the glass down. "Are you alright?"

"I need sex. Can you help?" It's the only thing that makes sense. Once the deed is done, the aching for it will disappear as it always does. This is just my nature.

His kilt jerks violently. Closing his eyes, he groans. "Astra, is that really what you want?"

Sitting next to him, I'm careful not to touch him.

"I could seduce a human. There's a campground ten miles—"

"No." He swallows hard, his Adam's apple bobbing alluringly. "I mean, please don't."

"I tried to take care of it myself, but that was not satisfying and I think it's because you are here. I could run far away, but I promised you a week and this is only the second day. All I'm asking is for some mutual satisfaction and then we'll both be more comfortable." It's hardly a difficult matter.

His face tightens as if I've caused him pain. He runs his hands over his hair and grips one of his horns.

Suddenly, my need to touch his horns grows. I wonder if they're smooth or rough, warm or cool. I've never been much for longing. In fact, I'll admit to being a bit spoiled. Freedom is really the only thing I've ever lacked and even that is a matter of opinion. My father didn't lock me in a tower; he demanded I follow the old ways, which includes my marrying at his whim.

I stifle my thoughts about both men and focus on what I want. I need relief from sexual tension. "Will you help me?"

"This is not how I imagined you wanting me." His voice is tight and deeper than usual.

His phone vibrates from the middle of the tray holding a pitcher of iced tea and two glasses.

Father's name flashes at the center of the screen.

My need is replaced with anger. "What does he want now?"

Picking up the phone, Niko sighs. "He delayed the nuptials and now our wedding hour approaches."

Looking at the clock on my phone, I realize he's probably right. It's afternoon. I get up and narrow my gaze at Niko. "Neither you nor my father will bully me."

CHAPTER FIVE

NIKO

I watch her storm into the house. She's nearly as beautiful angry as she is when full of lust. I slide the screen to accept the call.

Nocturn's angry voice forces me to hold the phone away from my ear. "Where are you? Where is my daughter? Why are you not here?"

"Why didn't you ask Astra if she wished to marry? Why didn't you tell her you had arranged a marriage? Why didn't you give her my letters?"

He can try, but I'm hard to push around.

There's a long pause. "She told you that? You saw Astra?"

Tired of questions and no answers, I calm my burst of annoyance and keep my voice even. "Astra has agreed to spend a few days in my house as my guest. She has not agreed to the marriage."

"Bring her here. I'll expect you in one hour." He grumbles

something about disobedience. "Tell her that if she doesn't show herself, I will drag her home and keep her from her precious trees."

Even though I have no intention of allowing Nocturn to punish Astra, I say nothing about it. "I will convey your request, but I expect you to honor the agreement she and I have made. There will be no wedding today unless it is what Astra wishes."

"Be careful of your tone, boy. I'm not any ordinary monster." Darkness thrums in his warning.

I could throw a similar warning back at him. While my parents were not gods, my grandfather was a demigod. "I shall not take a wife who doesn't want me."

Softer in tone, he says, "I only wish to talk to her. She'll listen to me."

I have my doubts. "I'll see if she's available to pay a call in one hour."

Before Nocturn can protest, I disconnect the call.

I carry things inside and put the tray on the kitchen counter. The house is so quiet, I wonder if Astra has run away, but she promised the week and I believe she will honor her word. Making sure my hooves are heard on the stairs, I go to her door and knock. "May I come in?"

"I suppose so." She sounds petulant even though her father called me. She acts as if I'm in cahoots with him.

I step in and feel torn between being saved by the bell and wanting her amorous gaze back. She stares out the window with her arms crossed over her chest. Her phone is on the nightstand with the opened letter from yesterday and the one from today still sealed in its envelope.

Part of me hoped she'd read it right away, but I knew she

probably wouldn't. "Your father has requested that we pay him a visit."

"You mean he demanded I come." She meets my gaze. "Did he make threats?"

"I won't lie to you. He said that if we don't come, he'll drag you home and lock you away from your trees." My gut tightens.

"Then, I suppose, I have no choice." She picks up her phone and puts it in her pocket. "I can go by myself, Niko."

Pushing down my urge to strip her naked and give her what she asked for on the porch, I close the distance between us. "Astra, I would never allow you to come to harm, not even at the hands of your father. He will not take you away from your trees or anything else that brings you joy. I will accompany you, unless you forbid it."

She worries her bottom lip between her teeth. "I'm not getting married today."

"No. I have informed your father that there will be no wedding this afternoon." Unable to stop myself, I run my fingers along her upper arm. Her skin is soft and warm. She prickles with gooseflesh at my touch and I don't know if that's good or bad.

Swaying slightly toward me, she blinks and catches herself. "Unless you want a fight with my father on your front door, we should go. It's a long walk."

"We don't have to walk. I have a vehicle." I can't help grinning when her mouth opens and now words come out.

"You are too big to fit in a human car." She cocks her head, but amusement lights her eyes and I like that I've put it there.

Once I've escorted her downstairs, I pull my specially made Jeep to the front driveway.

Astra gapes from the steps and then laughs. "That's the biggest, blackest, baddest Jeep I've ever seen." She skips to the passenger's door and leaps in and buckles her seat belt. "I love it."

Happy that I've done something to make her smile, I shift into gear and head toward her father's house. Even with the alterations, my head reaches the top of the roof and I'm happier when I can take the top off. I suspect it will rain. I wasn't willing to risk drenching us both and the interior for my comfort.

"Can we ride in this one day when the weather will be better?" She's grinning and my heart soars at the sight.

"I think tomorrow it will be sunny all day. We can ride with the top off." It's such a small thing, but her asking me for this seems bigger. No strings. No rules. Just going out and having fun together.

"I know a place that will be perfect to ride and after the rain this afternoon, it should be a lot of fun." She grips the grab bar on the dashboard with both hands as if it's the safety bar on an amusement ride.

"What other activities amuse you?" I pray she doesn't say anything alluring. The effects of her request have not fully vanished, nor do I expect they will any time soon.

"I like to swim and run with the whitetail deer that live in the woods. I climb my trees from the outside and oversee the forest. I have a few friends who are not under the spell of my sexual appeal and I visit with them. I study the stars and enjoy astronomy as well as astrology." She sighs. "I like books, though rarely make the time to read much these days."

"It sounds like a lot of fun." I wanted to go and watch her

swim today, but it would have defeated the point of her wishing to be away from me.

"Do you have hobbies?" She blushes as if this is the first time she's inquired about someone.

"I read a great deal. I can't climb a tree, but I do enjoy taking a book and reading under them. I can swim, though I'm not very graceful in water." At least I won't drown. "I told you I enjoy cooking even though it is technically my profession, and I play several instruments better than most."

"Why are you so big?" She stares at my legs, then scans up to my face, with an adorable crease between her eyes.

"What do you mean?" It takes all my will not to get fully hard again.

She lets out a breath. "Goat legs shouldn't be so large. You could be part horse, but that wouldn't explain the horns."

"I am man and goat and perhaps because of my ancestors, bigger than most of either species. My father was the same." I shrug and make the turn that leads the last few miles to Nocturn's house.

"Who is your mother? Is she a monster?"

Thinking of my parents always makes me smile. "Mother is a Lycan. Very beautiful and very fierce. She can shift to human form but prefers to stay a beast. I think Father prefers it too."

"They live in Canada?" Her tone has grown sadder the closer we get to her home.

"Yes. In the mountains near Alaska. It's very remote and suits them." I touch her hand and she offers it for me to hold. My pulse speeds and my chest tightens. This small gesture of tenderness means so much more than her earlier offer. "Your mother was human?"

"She was a lovely person with little understanding of what I would become or what Father truly was. Then an illness took her away when I was small. Father took her to the human doctors, but they said there was nothing to be done." Her tone is even, as if she's told this a hundred times, or maybe the story was told to her and she's merely repeating it.

"Did he love her?" It's hard to imagine the overbearing demigod having an emotional attachment to anyone, let alone a human.

Astra cocks her head. "I don't know."

The house comes into view. It's as close to a palace as I've ever seen in North America. Three tall stories of white and blue with spires reaching to the sky. A golden gate is centered on a ten-foot, black, steel gate. As we approach, the gate opens.

To the left, a wide lawn is covered with white flowers and chairs streaming with tulle. Servants are bustling around, and I can't tell if they're tearing it down or putting things in place. "Do you think he still believes we'll be married in two hours?"

"Yes. Father doesn't like to be wrong." She releases my hand and draws a deep breath as we pull to a stop near the grand stairs leading up to an enormous arched entrance.

Standing in the open doorway is Nocturn. His appearance is that of a large man with pale hair that flows around his shoulders as it catches the breeze. His bright blue eyes burn with fury and his thick arms are crossed over the white dress shirt.

No one can doubt that Nocturn is formidable, even if he is misguided.

I get out and rush around to open the door for Astra.

Offering my hand, I hope my support is obvious since we both know she doesn't need my help.

"What are you wearing?" her father bellows from above.

Unfazed, Astra steps toward him with her hand still in mine. "Clothes, Father. I plan to wear clothes and do as I please from now on." She drops my hand and steps around her father, into the house.

Smiling after her, I look Nocturn in the eyes. "She's strong-willed. I like her very much."

"You're more foolish than I expected. Nymphs need to be controlled or they will seduce everyone in their view." He rolls his eyes as if this is common knowledge that I'm too stupid to know.

"I hope those employees of yours are removing that wedding setup. It's going to rain and no one is getting married today." I cock my head. "Unless you're taking a bride, sir."

Jaw tight and muscles testing the threads of his dress shirt, Nocturn growls. "What is the arrangement the two of you have made?"

Facing him, I take the same stance. "Astra will tell you if she wishes you to know."

Frustration etched in the creases around his mouth and eyes, he spins and walks into the house.

I follow, trying to hide my amusement.

Astra lounges on a royal-blue chaise. It has rolled arms and Queen Anne feet. It looks as if it was plucked right out of the eighteenth century and dropped in the ornate sitting room. The large room is separated into three conversational areas and a fourth corner with a white grand piano that Liberace would envy.

My fingers itch to play the magnificent instrument.

Instead, I sit in a chair far too delicate and small for me. Its only appeal is that it's next to Astra.

Nocturn glares at her.

Paula calls Astra's name. "Astra, my dear." She is the woman who runs the house, as far as I could tell from my earlier visits. She's a human with salt-and-pepper bobbed hair and large dark-rimmed glasses and no fear at all. Rushing in from a door at the other end of the room, she's grinning. "I'm so happy to see you. Shall I call for tea? I love this sundress. You look lovely."

Astra stands and hugs Paula. "Thank you."

"No tea," Nocturn commands.

Neither lady reacts to his loud voice. They continue to chat to each other.

After a few minutes, Paula says, "No tea, so we're going to have a chat and then what?"

"A wedding." Nocturn scowls at Astra, then me.

I stand. "It's nice to see you again, Ms. Paula."

"And you, Mr. Barbaros."

Letting my hooves clomp more than is polite, I say, "There will be no wedding today."

Nocturn sits in a very large chair that resembles a throne with a wide, fanned back that extends above his head. "What is the arrangement between the two of you?"

I offer my hand to Astra so that she will sit beside me on the love seat and I can abandon the smaller chair.

She looks confident and sure, but her hand shakes and her inhalation has a hitch.

Smiling, I give her a nod. I hope she knows I will stand beside her no matter what she says.

CHAPTER SIX

ASTRA

As much as I love to make my father angry, I don't like to disappoint him. I know that is exactly what I'm doing now. Having Niko beside me somehow makes it easier. "Father, I will not get married today. Niko is a good man and very kind, but I don't know him and he doesn't know me."

"You will know each other after the marriage," Father growls.

The help can be heard arranging the ballroom across the foyer. My anger returns. "If you had told me about this plan months ago and not intercepted the letters Niko sent, you might not be sending your guests away today."

Paula gasps. "Nocturn, you didn't."

"She would have run away in March if I had told her." Father is less sure of himself.

I shrug. "We shall never know as I wasn't given the

179

chance and now, I have an agreement with Niko to spend enough time together to decide if we wish to spend more time together."

"How much time?" Father demands.

"That is none of your business. You will stay out of our way. You have already made a mess of this. If you so much as step foot on Niko's property, I will leave this forest, which I love, and never return." My chest aches with the idea, but I mean what I say. At least, I think I do.

Father opens his mouth and sorrow darkens his eyes.

Drawing a deep breath, I say, "It is to Niko's credit that I agreed to give us both an opportunity to walk away or stay."

"You agreed to this?" Father's question to Niko is full of accusations.

"It was my idea. Astra is a grown woman with a mind of her own. She's different from other nymphs who are satisfied to frolic in the trees. We will get to know each other, then each decide if we suit." Niko looks at me gently, then at my father with a glaring disapproval.

The longer he defends me, the more I like him. If my father wasn't here, I would take Niko's hand, but I won't give Father the satisfaction. He doesn't deserve to know that there might be affection between us. Honestly, I'm not sure there is. I like him more than I planned to, that much is certain.

"Fine." It's a monumental agreement for my father.

Paula claps. "Excellent. Will you two stay for dinner?"

"Not tonight, but thank you." I hug Paula and tell my father goodbye before practically running from the house. The clomp of Niko's hooves is my only comfort. Knowing that he's behind me is the most security I've ever enjoyed.

When we've returned to Niko's cabin, I go directly to my room and lock the door. Disappointing my father, his showing no care for me, and even Niko being so kind and supportive, all make me feel less somehow.

I strip out of my sundress and lie on the bed. I do like the option of human clothes, but it's good to be in my natural state.

Rolling to my side, I pluck the unopened letter from the nightstand and open it.

Dear Astra,

I am disappointed not to have received a response from you. It occurs to me that the reason for your silence is because of me. I am to blame as my first letter was disjointed and uninformative. My only excuse is that the notion of marriage was still new to me. I imagine it is the same for you. Please forgive me.

Hopefully, it will please you to know that I have purchased a home and large property in New York. I thought you would prefer to remain in your home forest as it has been my experience that nymphs are deeply attached to their trees.

The house requires updates. Would you like to be involved in the renovations? Of course, this is entirely up to you.

Though I have not cooked in my restaurants for many years, I still design the menus and enjoy cooking very much. I would happily cook for you. What type of food do you enjoy?

I look forward to hearing from you.

Yours,

Niko

I hug the letter to my chest and close my eyes. Why does he have to be so nice? I imagined a brutish and bullying goat more like my father. Niko is modern-minded and kind. It's possible he was going to refuse my offer of sex earlier today had Father not interrupted.

There's a soft knock on my door. Niko says, "I have a tray with food for you, Astra. I know today was difficult."

I sit up, staring at the closed door. My heart has lodged in my throat. I want to open the door but if I do, what will it cost me to trust him?

"I will be downstairs if you need to talk." He clomps away.

When I'm certain he's made it to the bottom of the steps, I go to the door and pull the tray inside before locking myself inside again. It's silly really. First, it's unlikely Niko would barge in without an invitation. Second, the door's lock is not likely an obstacle to a very large satyr. Still, I like the idea that I can lock the door. This space feels as safe as being inside one of the trees.

There's a little desk in the corner and I place the tray there before removing the cloche. The scent of Greek oregano, tomatoes, and cheese fills my senses. A perfect slice of pastitsio with mushrooms rather than the traditional beef. The lasagna-like dish is comfort food. I suspect that's why Niko prepared it for me.

How he can know I need comfort is a mystery. I have no

idea what he needs. I've spent no time trying to understand him in the last two days.

Recovering the dish, I pull on jeans and a blue shirt adorned with small pink roses. Carefully, I carry the tray downstairs, and when I find Niko eating at the long dining table, I join him, sitting to his right. "Thank you. This is one of my favorites, though I usually have to eat around most of the meat."

A hint of a smile plays on his beautiful lips. "The mushrooms make a good substitute."

I eat and relish the rich flavors of an old country that I've never seen, but know is part of my ancestry. "This is delicious."

"I'm glad you like it and I'm happy you decided to come down for dinner. I would have understood if you wished to stay in your room." His soft voice sends a thrill through me.

After eating half of the large portion, I put my fork down. "I find my father's machinations exhausting and they make me sad."

Niko rises and takes a bottle of wine from a small refrigerator in the island. Gathering two glasses, he returns, opens the bottle, and pours. "I imagine you would prefer him to show some affection. May I suggest that securing your future is his way of doing that?

"Are you taking his side?" I put the wine down. "He would marry me to a stranger without a second thought. What if you were abusive? What if you dragged me back to Canada without my permission? He couldn't have known your character before he chose you."

"How do you know that?" His smile hasn't wavered in the face of my rage. He's calm and his voice is soothing.

"Father wouldn't have chosen someone so agreeable to

me. He thought you would dominate me the same way he has always tried to control my life." Yet, Niko has done neither of those things.

"Would you prefer that I drag you to the altar and force a life on you?" He sips the wine.

It's a stupid question, so I reclaim my glass and let the fruity Italian blend come to life on my palate. I close my eyes as the wine slides down my throat. When I open them, I look into Niko's almost black irises and the caring there boosts my courage. "I would have liked to have met you at a party without any intervention from Father. Maybe we would have shared a drink and talked about the weather at first. You would have told me that you make a far better brochette than what was being served. I would have laughed and said that you would need to prove that. Maybe at the end of the night, we would have agreed to a date."

Sorrow pulls the smile from those lips I have not stopped admiring since first seeing them. "That is not our story thus far, Astra. Does it follow that we must have a tragic or unsatisfying end?"

I put the wine down. "I don't know."

"I hope not." The way he looks at me sets my heart throbbing in my chest and other parts also take note. "I like your letters." It's dim in the dining room with only a small lamp on the buffet at one end, but I think he's blushing.

"I'm glad. Shall I give you the last two?"

I nod. "I would like to read them."

"I think I would have written more than four had you been allowed the opportunity to respond. Your father did us both a disservice. If he believed me the right man for you, he should have trusted you to see it." He reaches across the corner of the table and takes my hand. He massages my palm, then the knuckles of each finger. "I am happy you agreed to stay here for the week."

That couldn't have been easy to admit with all I have said and done, trying to escape him, and telling father I wouldn't do as he told me. "I'm glad I did too." Tears clog my throat and I have no idea why I'm filled with emotions.

He grins. "I have an idea."

Hoping it includes mindless sex that we can take with us as a memory when this all falls apart, I say, "Okay."

"I can run very fast and the rain has not yet started. Will you allow me to take you for a run in the woods?"

It's hard to breathe. "You want me to ride on your back while you run through my forest?"

His grin is full of mischief. "If you think you would enjoy that."

Pulse racing and skin tingling, I can't contain my excitement. "I think I would."

We clear the table while the sun sets. Each time his arm brushes mine or his hand grazes my back, I want all of him touching me. I want to feel his body move as he runs. I'm more excited than I've ever been, and while this is not about seducing him, I begin to wonder if perhaps the tables have been turned on me.

When Niko takes my hand, I shiver with anticipation. He threads our fingers together. "Would you like to go now?"

I nod, liking the way our hands fit together despite his being twice the size of mine.

He leads me out on the porch. "I'm ready." His voice is deep and tinged with warning. He strips out of his shirt, but leaves his kilt in place.

Together, we take the stairs. When he reaches the bottom, he stops me three steps up so that I can mount him. As the words enter my mind, I groan. Touching his smooth back, I trace a line to where his hip is covered with fur. "Why does this feel so erotic?"

Looking over his shoulder, he meets my gaze. "Because that lovely mind of yours is a dirty mind, Astra."

I pull my hand back, though my mouth is watering with desire to kiss him. "And you don't like that."

He spins to face me. His chest an inch from mine, he leans in and whispers in my ear. "I never said that. There's nothing about you that I don't like."

Moisture pools between my legs. "Turn around, Niko." I like the way his name feels on my tongue. Before climbing on, I strip out of my jeans and shirt. I burn as my breasts press against his broad back. "*Mmm...*" inadvertently rumbles in my throat as I wrap my legs around his waist.

His hands cup my calves. "You feel heavenly."

I'm about to agree, when he leaps into a full run down the mountain. Wind whips through my hair and my pussy rubs along his spine. My juices drip with each undulation of his muscles.

He turns and takes a deer path through my forest.

Gripping him tighter, I don't know if I can hold off coming. I bite my lip to try to stifle a moan. It comes out as a squeak. "Niko."

His hands wrapped around my calves, he races through the underbrush like he's been here a hundred times. Reaching back, he grips my ass and pushes me higher before letting his fingers press the flesh. "Do you like riding me?"

"I'm... Oh gods. I don't know if I can hold off, Niko," I whisper against his neck.

He groans and slows as we approach an old oak with a wide canopy that has pushed aside all the other forest growth. Gripping my ass, he pulls me around his hips so that my legs wrap around his back and my dripping pussy is spread along his abdomen. The head of his cock is hard and bobbing against my ass. "Come then." He presses my back against the rough bark of the oak and captures my mouth with his.

His tongue collides with mine and it's as if I've waited my entire life for this kiss, his kiss.

Every sense engaged, I explode as my pussy pulses and longs to be filled. I break the kiss and scream nonsense while the pleasure contracts and releases again and again.

I could slip into the tree and leave him alone in the woods. My pleasures should be sated, but I also long for his pleasure. I want it in a way I've never wanted anything.

CHAPTER SEVEN

NIKO

I knew that running with Astra would be erotic but her juices dripping down my back was almost too much to bear. The more I ran and felt her excitement building, the harder it became to run with my cock bouncing against my abdomen.

As her screams of pleasure fill the woods, I kiss her neck. "You are the most amazing creature I've ever known."

She reaches between us and grips my straining cock. "I need for you to come, Niko. I've never cared about another's pleasure as I do now." She caresses up and down the length of me, her small hand unable to encompass my girth. "So big."

Holding on by a thread, I press my forehead to the tree. Maybe I can lighten the moment and keep myself under control. "I'm a satyr. Why do you think I wear a kilt?"

Her lilting laugh plays in the air. "I had a feeling, and

knew you were attracted to me." Unwrapping her legs, she slips to the ground and grips me tighter with both hands. She strokes harder, then lowers her mouth and sucks the bulbous head between her sweet lips.

Threading her hair through my fingers, I watch the tip of my shaft disappear inside the warm wetness. Her teeth scratching on each release is maddening.

I've never wanted to have a moment last forever, but this one is perfect. I could die and be nearly satisfied, knowing her need is as great as mine.

Naked and perfect, she lets me pop from her lips and stares up the length of my body. "I want you inside me. Will you give this to me, Niko?" Gently, she caresses my cock from base to tip and runs her soft fingers around the head.

Her touch is the sweetest torture.

Lifting her, I grip her ass in both hands. "I would have made this better with a large bed and all the comforts."

She shakes her head. "No. Against this ancient tree is more than perfect." She wiggles until my head slides along her wet slit.

Gravity is all that is needed for her to take me in. I go slow, stretching her tight pussy and giving her one inch at a time.

Arching her back, she presses her back against the trunk and grips tighter with her legs. She's stronger than she looks and takes more of me. "Good. More. That's so good."

One hand on her ass and the other braced against the tree, I press in with one steady thrust, expecting to reach the limit of her much smaller body, but the more I give, the more she takes. I moan as I fill her and our hips meet.

Our cries mingle in the breeze.

Clutching my hair, she makes the most sensual cry. "Niko. Oh, gods, you're magnificent."

I'd like to give her time to adjust to my size, but I'm driven by forces beyond my control. I kiss her hard and press my tongue into her mouth as I pull out to my head, then thrust inside her again. Pleasure rockets through me each time I move. Every cell in my body is alive and tingling with the electricity of our connection.

She's so wet and tight, this is heaven. I find a pace that makes her scream and moan with each entry. Again and again, I fill her, suck on her tongue, caress her curves, and pinch her nipples.

She calls my name as she comes again around my cock. Her juices drip down my legs as her sheath tightens, pulsing around me.

I thrust harder, faster, as my own release sends a tingle down my spine. My legs shake and I shoot my seed inside her. I barely recognize the roar that falls from my lips as she comes again and draws every drop of cum from me.

Holding her tight as my softening cock still fills her, I never want to let her go. "Are you alright?"

"So good." She rubs along my flesh like a satisfied cat.

I slip free of her and miss her body's embrace. Shifting her in my arms, I carry her toward the house.

With a sigh, she rests her cheek on my chest and wraps her arms around my neck. "We could just sleep here a while."

"It's not far. I'll get us home." I kiss her forehead and revel in the way her eyes close with trust. "You are the first woman who could take all of me inside."

Those bright blue eyes open to meet my gaze. "You are the first man who has really filled me." She looks away as if the admission was an accident.

Even if it's not true, I like that she said it. Though, I'd hazard to guess, I'm her first satyr. My goal will be to be her last lover of any species. "It was wonderful, Astra. Why do you look away from me?"

She cups my cheek. "Did I trick you or was that what you wanted?"

"Trick me?" Holding her tighter, I jog to the back of the house, and up the steps. At the back door, I suck her bottom lip between mine. "You didn't trick me. I've wanted you since seeing your picture."

A tear slips over her lid. "I'm a nymph. Everyone wants me. I seduce even when I don't want to. It's my nature." Pushing on my chest, she forces me to put her on her feet in the living room.

As she heads to the stairs, I catch her hand and turn her toward me. "I'm not affected by the magic that nymphs possess, Astra. I'm not attracted to you because you're a nymph."

"How do you know? The seduced never know they're under my spell." She combs her fingers through my hair, grazing my horn and sending a thrill through me.

Tugging on my kilt, I let it fall on the floor. My cock is fully erect again. "Canada has a good many nymphs because they love the vast woods. I've met many and none lured me in or enraptured me." I grip my cock. "This is for you. The house is for you. If you want me, I am also for you."

She grips her breast with one hand and bites her bottom lip. "Maybe you have me under *your* thrall." She slips her fingers between her thighs. "I want you so much, I ache with need."

"I don't have that kind of magic." The scent of her arousal

fills my nostrils and a goatish sound escapes me. Lifting her, I carry her up the steps to my bedroom.

As soon as I release her, she crawls to the center of my mattress with her ass high and her legs spread. Her pussy glistens with readiness.

It's tempting to slam inside her fast and hard, but she looks too tasty and I lie on my back and slide along my blanket until my head is between her knees. Gripping her ass cheeks, I pull her to my mouth and slip my tongue inside her sweetness. I lick and suck her clit until she's crying out and undulating against my face.

"Niko…"

I'll never get enough of hearing her cry my name in passion.

She stands before I can draw out her orgasm. Straddling me, she lowers to her knees and takes my cock deep in one motion.

Pushing myself the rest of the way onto the bed, I grip her hips to keep her from going too fast. "Slow, Astra."

Sweat beads across her forehead and her chest rises and falls hard and fast. "I can't. I need…"

It's impossible to deny her anything. I ease my grip. "Take what you need."

Thunder crashes outside and rain patters on the roof and windows.

She rises and falls like the goddess she is.

Every move is pure ecstasy. Fully seated inside her smooth, soft wetness is something I've never experienced before tonight. Knowing that this woman should be mine for all time heightens my pleasure. My heart pounds, my body tingles. The hair on the back of my neck prickles as if warning me.

Astra presses her palms to my chest and raises and lowers her ass hard and fast. Her screams fill the room and mingle with my groans and moans.

The storm grows and lightning flashes illuminate her and the room. Thunder is close behind with sheets of rain pounding down. It's the perfect music for our lovemaking.

She digs her nails into my skin.

The tiny pain adds to the tension building in my balls.

Her pussy tightens. She slams onto me and calls my name, then bites my pectoral.

Pleasure and pain collide as her body squeezes my cock and I explode inside her. Gripping her hips, I hold her in place while a low grunting sound escapes me.

Still joined, she stares at my chest with a look of horror. "I marked you."

Rising to my elbows, I glance at my chest and the two rows of red dashes where her teeth nearly drew blood. An unnatural swell of pride fills me. "I'm not hurt."

She scrambles off of me. "I'm not some animal marking their mate."

Before she can run from the room, I scramble after her and wrap an arm around her waist. Drawing her back to my front, I whisper, "I know who and what you are. You have nothing to be embarrassed about, sweetheart."

"I lost control. This entire night has been—"

"Please do not say it was a mistake." My gut tightens.

Relaxing against me, she sighs. "No. It was too good to be wrong. Still, I would like to go to my own room."

Pushing aside my disappointment, I breathe in her earthy scent and kiss her shoulder. "Of course. Will you wait one moment? I have something for you." I let her go.

"I don't need gifts, Niko." There's tightness and insecurity in her voice and she won't look at me.

I take the last two letters out of my nightstand drawer and walk to her. "You said you wanted these."

She tips her head to look, then meets my gaze. Tears pool in her crystal eyes. "Why are you so kind when I am awful?"

Pressing my fingers lovingly over the space above my heart where she marked me, I say, "You are wonderful." I inch the hand with the letters forward.

After a moment's hesitation, she takes them. Clutching the envelopes to her chest, she rushes from the room.

While I want to go to her and convince her she's beating herself up for no reason, I suspect there's more to her reaction than a little bite mark that will be gone in a day or two.

Grabbing a kilt and shirt from a drawer, I do what I always do when I have a problem. I go to the kitchen and cook.

CHAPTER EIGHT

ASTRA

I know it was cowardly to leave him last night, but I felt as if my heart was going to explode. It wasn't the sex. It was the feelings. The onslaught of emotions bombarding me from the way Niko looks at me, touches me, and talks to me are something I've never experienced before.

Exhaustion allowed me to sleep, but now I'm taking my time in the shower. The more I think about seeing him, the more my heart pounds. I long to see him and at the same time, I'm terrified of all of these new impulses.

I wrap myself in a towel and comb my hair, thankful for the steam covering the mirror and keeping me from seeing the fainthearted woman in the mirror.

Unable to stall any longer, I dress in shorts and a red shirt with puffy little sleeves.

Relief floods me to find the kitchen empty. I scan the

great room. Niko sits drinking coffee on the deck. In his other hand, he grips a flute.

Lowering his cup to the table, he brings the flute to his pursed lips. The faintest hum of his music gets through the windows. It's soft but there's life to the lilt of it.

Drawn to both the man and the sound he produces, only the need for caffeine keeps me in the kitchen.

The coffee smells divine. There's a brown shipping box on the counter. I head around the island to pour myself a cup. As I sip, I see my name on the box's label. I've never received a package at home, I can't imagine having something come for me here. Maybe someone sent a wedding gift. I sigh. I suppose I'll be sending whatever it is back.

On the vertical side of the box is a yellow sticky note. *I thought these things could get you started on discovering your dreams.*

Putting the mug down, I open the box. Inside is a laptop computer, three notebooks each with a different pretty cover, a sketchbook, and art pencils. I pull everything out and line it all up on the counter. My chest aches with joy at the idea of creating something. I don't even know if I'm capable of such things, but the fact that someone wants me to find out is overwhelming.

"If you want to paint, we can order watercolors or oils."

Not having heard him enter, I spin toward his voice. I brush a tear away. "You ordered all of this before last night."

He cocks his head and his horns catch the sunlight. It makes him look almost angelic. "I ordered them after you told me about your desire. You should be able to pursue anything that makes you happy, Astra."

Last night he called me sweetheart. I long for the endearment. "I'm sorry I didn't stay with you last night."

A hint of a smile lights his face as he approaches and kisses my cheek. "It's alright. I had time to come up with some new recipes."

I'm not surprised since my dreams were all food-related. I'm sure he was angry even though he didn't show it. "If you want me to leave, I can stay with my friend Cade and his woman."

Standing at the counter, Niko is only inches from me. "I don't want you to go. I understand you were overcome and needed some space. I'm not upset with you."

I run my hand over the laptop box. "I don't know how to use such things."

"I will show you." He takes my hand and kisses it. "First, the rain has made our other plans quite appealing, if you'd still like to show me the area for riding in the Jeep."

Rather than being angry with me, he's understanding of something he can't possibly fathom. He offers me friendship and I have nothing to give him in return. Rather than say anything more about my failures, I will give him what I've already promised, the rest of the week.

We bounce around a muddy field, getting stuck twice. But with a satyr, it's not an issue. He lets me get behind the wheel and pushes us out of the mud with ease.

"No one has ever taught me to drive," I say as I return to the passenger seat.

His eyes narrow for a moment before his smile returns and he steps on the gas, driving us through another mud puddle. This time we make it through and drive up the embankment before spinning in a circle and driving down into the field again.

I can't remember when I've laughed as much. It's as if all the troubles of being my father's daughter have disappeared for the moment.

Two hours later, we are both covered in mud and I can't stop grinning. "This was more fun than I've had in a long time."

"Why don't I show you how to drive and you can begin to check some of your life's restrictions off the list." He wipes a clump of dirt from his cheek and another drips from his horn.

I force my mouth closed. My pulse pounds and more feelings rush in. "You want to show me how to drive this Jeep?"

He nods as he finds a clean inch of shirt to wipe his eyes with. Stepping out, he offers his hand for me to climb into the driver's seat. Once he's seat-belted in, he tells me how to shift gears.

Before I know it, I'm driving around the field's outer edge. I slow and downshift. Coming to a grinding halt, I hold the steering wheel with both hands and press my forehead to the top. "My father is not a bad man, but his capacity for the show of emotion is limited. He expects things of me, but I don't think he has ever loved me. You asked if my parents were in love. Mother may have loved him, but I'm sure he only wanted her. He never mourned. I think I am like him."

Niko's silence is heavy in the air.

Unable to bear it any longer, I turn my head and look at him.

His eyes are filled with sympathy and maybe pity, which grinds in my gut.

I'm about to tell him that I neither need or want whatever he's about to offer.

He says, "Thank you for sharing that. I know it was difficult for you. Let's get you back home and cleaned up."

On cue, a dried clump of mud flakes off of my arm. I laugh. "We should hose off before we set foot in your beautiful house."

Something I said dims the joy in his eyes, but he reaches across and squeezes my hand.

On the fifth day, I push aside my fears and decide to open Niko's third letter.

After two wonderful days of learning to drive, attempting to draw, and toying with writing, I can't help but feel happy. Niko patiently showed me how to use the computer. Granted, I prefer notebooks and pens for the moment, but I like the way he teaches with patience and kindness. I like the way he does everything.

For the past two nights, I have gone to my own bed early, claiming exhaustion. It wasn't a lie, but I'm afraid that sex opens me up too much. It's terrifying losing total control.

I run my fingers over his scrolling handwriting.

Butterflies awaken in my belly and I have no explanation for why.

Dear Astra,

Your silence is concerning but your father ensures me that you are not much of a writer and that you are thrilled (his word) with our upcoming marriage.

I shall tell you more about myself.

From time to time, I enjoy drawing. I'm enclosing a rough sketch I made of you. It is copied from my only photo of you, so forgive its simplicity. One day, if you permit me, I will do a better rendering. When I know the silk of your skin and the texture of your hair as it falls through my fingers, I will create something more fitting.

I hope you're not offended by the personal nature of this letter. I find the closer the time of our meeting draws, the more aroused I am. Will you write or call and assure me that your feelings match mine?

Yours,

Niko

I turn the envelope over and another paper falls out. It's folded in thirds and then in half. I open it and find myself staring back. It's a softer version of me. A me with love in her eyes. An emotion that the real me is incapable of expressing or feeling. Niko deserves the kind of love in this picture. He deserves someone who will feel all the things I cannot.

I dash away my tears and hold the letter and picture close.

The clomping of hooves on the stairs alerts me that Niko is approaching. His soft knock has those butterflies bumping around inside me.

I swallow my strange feelings. "Yes."

Opening the door, he pops his head in. "What would you like to do today?"

Part of me knows I should say that I'm content to sit in the house and write, and I would be, but the more vital side of me wants to try new things. "I'm not sure you can give me what I want to do."

It's so adorable when he cocks his head that way. "Try me."

Gathering my wits, I stand and put my beautiful picture and letter on the nightstand.

His eyes shift to the pages, then back to me. Longing practically pours from his gaze, but he keeps any thoughts or feelings to himself.

"I'd like to go to a bookstore and perhaps out for lunch like humans do." Unable to stop myself, I glance at his horns, then legs, and know this isn't possible.

With a light laugh, he says, "It's an easy thing to give you. It only requires a bit of a disguise and a little magic, sweetheart."

That endearment raises the hairs on my arms and I step close to him. Reaching up, I run my fingers along his warm slightly rigged horns. "How will you hide?"

A low growl starts in his chest and rises. His eyes darken and the front of his kilt tents. He wraps one arm around my waist and places the other flat on my abdomen. His fingers rest just under my breasts, making them ache to be touched. Searching my eyes, he presses a gentle kiss to my lips. "My horns are sensitive, Astra."

I don't remove my hand. Instead, I caress the arching protrusion to the tip then down to the base. In spite of my resolve to not have sex with him again, my pussy aches with need and my nipples bead. The cotton dress I'm wearing rubs them. I need his hands. I need his mouth. I glance at his growing erection and know I need that too. "How intriguing."

Lowering his head, he kisses me deeply. His tongue sweeps into my mouth, sliding along mine. He makes love to my lower lip, tastes my mouth, sucks my top lip, then goes back to deepening the kiss.

It's hard to catch my breath as my body has completely overridden my brain.

Niko walks me backward until the backs of my legs touch the mattress. He drops to his knees and looks up at me, wrapping his hands around each of my calves. "Astra?"

I take hold of both of his horns and caress them as if they were his cock.

He groans, slides his hands up my legs, and nudges my mid-thigh dress up. With a growl, he licks my slit and slides his tongue against my clit.

Unable to hold my own weight, I sit and spread my legs wide. With every suck he delivers, I caress his horns and press my pussy against his mouth. Within seconds, I scream his name and shake with pleasure. "Niko." I collapse back and curl into a ball while the pleasure rushes through me.

Niko lies beside me and pulls me close. He kisses my hair and the exposed flesh where my neck and shoulder meet. "I love to watch you come."

"I lose myself with you." The admission wasn't meant to be spoken. I wish it back as soon as I say it.

Tightening his hold, he whispers, "Are you sure losing is what you're doing, sweetheart? Maybe we're both discovering new aspects of ourselves."

It's hard to think with his cock so hard and thick resting against my ass and back. Pulling to all fours, I flip my dress up over my hips to expose myself. "I don't think you're right, but I can't deny my desire for you." I wiggle my ass.

The sound he makes is half man and half goat and my pussy pulses to be filled. Kneeling behind me, he grips my hip with one hand.

I look over my shoulder.

He's discarded his kilt and shirt. Beautifully naked, he holds his cock and slides it through my wetness, teasing me.

Pushing back is futile while he holds me in place and continues his sweet torture. His fingers replace his cock and he spreads my juices up to my tight asshole, teasing that sensitive place.

I cry, "Yes. Gods, yes."

He presses the tip of his thick finger inside.

Breaking free of his grip, I push back to take a little more. "Niko. I need all of you inside me."

The head of his cock notches at my pussy. "I will always give you what you want." He thrusts deep and hard, again and again.

I take all of him, both cock and finger, until my body is pulled so tight I'm sure I'll explode.

He grunts and moans. His fucking gains momentum. Over and over, he slams inside me.

My body loving every inch of him. As he pulls back, I long for him. As he fills me, I relish the stretching. It's perfection to have Niko inside me, fucking me, giving himself to me.

On a long guttural cry, he fills me with hot seed.

I scream as the orgasm takes me. My pussy pulls and grips at his shaft, drawing every last drop of cum from his magnificence.

Niko wraps his arm around my waist and eases his finger, then his cock free.

Jerking with the sudden emptiness, a small cry escapes as I collapse on the bed. How have I resisted this for the past two days? More importantly, how will I do so for another two before I leave him?

CHAPTER NINE

NIKO

There are no words to describe how good this
woman feels or how attached to her I've become
in such a short time. She thinks she can't love, but I'm certain
she's mistaken. Having lived a long time, I'm wise enough to
know that telling her how to feel is of no use. My biggest
obstacle right now is the damned ticking clock that I set in
motion. Time is running out.

She stares at me from the now clean and covered Jeep's
passenger seat. "How did you remove your horns?"

"It's a glamor. A witch taught it to me long ago and it has
served me well. Since it's only for show, it doesn't work for
hiding my legs. The loose trousers and a cane to indicate
some infirmary is enough to keep humans from asking
questions." I turn into the parking lot of the large bookstore
in a neighboring town.

She tugs her black tee shirt down over the top of the jeans

she changed into. "I've never been out in the human world. I stay in my woods and when they pass through…"

"You seduce them." I'm not in the dark about the nature of my nymph.

Shrugging, she blushes. "I have. Though, not in some time. I decided a few years ago that I wanted to find a way to defy my father." Her laugh holds no humor. "I couldn't even manage to get myself clothes."

Reaching across the console, I take her hand. "Looking in the rearview is of no use. Look at all that is before you, Astra." I point to the large green letters above the store's double doors.

She laughs and nods.

Once we enter, she stares at the aisle and tables filled with books. "I had no idea it would be so much."

I stay close without crowding her as she flits from one table to the next, each with a different genre of books. When she looks at one longer than another and seems conflicted, I put it in the basket I'm holding.

A man with gray hair and a white golf cap pulled down low on his forehead stops next to me. "Were you injured in the war, son?"

"No, sir. I was in a car accident. It's been a while. I'll likely always have a limp." I shrug as if it's of no concern.

He slaps me on the back. "You still managed to catch the prettiest girl I've ever seen."

Not even men in their seventies or eighties are immune to Astra. I look up to find her and she's not at the shelf where last I saw her. "Speaking of which, I'd better find my lady."

The man chortles and walks toward the history section of the store.

Panic rises in my chest as I search each row. Wishing I'd

taken her to a small indie store, I curse. Reminding myself that Astra is not fragile and if she left it was of her own accord, I still continue the search. In the back of the store, I find her sitting on the floor surrounded by half a dozen books with astrological signs on their black covers.

She looks up with bright, excited eyes. "These books are fictional romances based on *our stories*." She whispers the last two words. She holds one up to me. "I'd like to read this one."

Crouching down, I gather up all six and put them in the basket.

Blushing, she stands and gapes at the overflowing books. "You shouldn't buy me all of those. You'll spoil me."

Pressing my lips to her temple, I inhale her floral scent. "That is my devious plan, sweetheart."

"To lure me in with books and other gifts?" She smiles, but there's hesitation in her tone.

Leading her toward the checkout, I say, "To see to your happiness despite knowing only you are in control of such things."

"Am I?" It's only the faintest whisper, but I hear her.

I pay for her books, then take her hand while balancing the cane and heavy bag in the other. "What would you like for lunch?"

"I always see the tourists eating sandwiches served on long baguettes. Can we try those?" She looks all around the area where shops line the street and a mall backs up to the bookstore's parking lot.

"I offer you the world, and you want a sub." This woman brings me pure joy in all things. She only knows of her magical allure, but even without magic, she is spectacular.

After dinner we lie on the couch and I borrow one of the books she chose while she reads another. Tucked in the crook of my arm, she pores over the pages. "They got so much wrong, but it's very entertaining."

"One should never let the truth get in the way of a good story." I wink when she stares at me. "Mark Twain said it first, but I think he had it right."

With a laugh that sets my pulse thrumming, she nods.

If this were to be my life, I would be perfectly happy. Astra in my arms and all the things we'll discover about her as she finds her own dreams, I would be sated.

She shifts and pulls something from her pocket. "I've been waiting to read the last one."

"Do you want me to leave the room?" It's personal to write a letter and unconventional for a letter to be read in the writer's presence. A shiver of unease shoots up my spine.

"Only if you want to. I've liked each letter very much." She opens the envelope and unfolds my letter.

Dear Astra,

This will be my final letter as the day draws near for me to journey south to you. It will be a longer trip as I have to use certain magic to cross the border between our countries. It's not as if the border patrol has seen a satyr before. However, I know a witch who has conjured the required "passport" for me to get to you.

My longing has not waned, though my worry over your feelings has increased exponentially throughout the last five months.

I wish you would have written. It seems strange to feel as if I know you, yet I've had no words from you. Perhaps you worry I won't care for the voice of your writing. None of it would have mattered. I was smitten from the moment I first saw your picture. Not in the way nymphs can seduce people. My connection to you is far deeper and is magic of another kind. The oldest kind.

I am yours. Nothing will change that.
Niko

The air seems to leave the room in a whoosh, then silence follows.

Astra carefully folds the page before asking, "What kind of magic were you referring to?"

It's too soon. She's not ready to hear this, but lying is unacceptable. "I believe you are my true mate, sweetheart."

"Do such things exist for nymphs?" She shakes her head. "I don't believe they do. Certain creatures like the manticore are doomed to only have one love that binds to them for life."

"Doomed? Do you think finding your one true mate is fatal?" I put my book on the table and lean away to look her in the eyes.

She clutches the letter to her chest. "I don't know what I believe anymore. I can tell you what I know, Niko. I'm not capable of returning your affection. I'm cold as the stones that built these mountains. There is nothing in my heart and you can only be hurt by wanting more than temporary sex and companionship from me."

The pain in my chest feels as if someone has split my rib cage open with an ax. "I don't believe that's true, any of it..." I have a dozen more things to say to show her how wrong she is.

Someone or something pounds on the front door hard enough to shake the hinges and rattle the windows.

We both jump to our feet. My instincts take over and I push Astra behind me, blocking her from whatever danger is at the door.

"Father." Panic vibrates in her voice. "He never leaves his compound."

"How do you know it's him?" I have my hand on her hip, keeping her behind me.

"I know."

Nocturn's bellowing voice vibrates the windows almost as thoroughly as his pounding. "Open this door before I tear it off its hinges."

"Stay behind me." I go to the door and open it. "There is no need to approach as if this is a battleground, Nocturn." I remain blocking the threshold with Astra at my back.

"I want a wedding and I want it tomorrow." His eyes are bloodshot and his skin red with rage. He's a few inches taller than me, but not as broad.

I have no doubt he has magic that could be dangerous.

Astra yells in a voice full of anger and panic. "I'm not getting married just because you want something. It's my life."

"What is this obsession with a quick marriage about?" I force myself to use a civil tone in hopes the other parties will follow suit.

"My reasons are my own! Marry her or leave these woods and I'll marry her off to someone else." His neck bulges, and he raises his fist in the air. "The troll in the cave north of here is looking for a wife. He'll know how to keep you in line."

It's not lost on me that he's implying I cannot do the job.

It never occurred to the demigod that I have no wish to control his daughter.

"I'm not some toy for you to maneuver on a chessboard." Astra sounds as if she's close to tears.

"That is exactly what you are, daughter. Mine to do with as I please." He raises his hand and blue lightning crackles in the palm.

I grab his wrist and hold him at bay. "Don't."

"How dare you?" Nocturn pulls his hand free. "Are you going to marry her tomorrow?"

There's no opportunity to look into Astra's eyes and see how she feels. All I can do is rely on what she has said. "She doesn't wish it, and I will not force her hand."

Nocturn spits on the front porch in front of me. "You shame the gods' lineage inside you, boy. If you want her, you should take her."

"That is an old-fashioned idea and not how I wish to gain the love of a woman."

Astra's sharp intake of breath makes my heart contract. Why did her father have to show up now?

"Love," Nocturn scoffs. "That's for humans."

Telling him that I disagree would do no good. "Why don't you come in and we can discuss this calmly? I'll open some wine."

"Very well." He steps through and narrows his eyes on Astra. "You have made a mess of this."

"You shouldn't have kept the arrangement from me. Maybe if you had given me Niko's letters when they arrived, we wouldn't be at odds. Secrets and plots are all you know. Why do you want me to marry so urgently?" While her voice is strong and sharp, she backs away, keeping her distance from her father.

It warms my heart that the letters mean something to her.

"If you like him now, just marry him, but it must be tomorrow." He mumbles something that I can't quite make out.

"Pardon me, Nocturn, what was that?" I would swear I heard the word "wager"

in his mutterings.

"Nothing." He stares at me. "Marry her tomorrow or face my wrath." He lifts that hand again.

"I don't answer to you." I narrow my gaze on the magic pooling in his palm. "You would be unwise to attack me in my home, Nocturn. I will not like it."

He looks at his daughter. "I'm not losing to Prede. Marry him!"

"No," she cries. Her eyes widen and she braces for the impact of his strike.

I step in front of her just as the bolt of blue light shoots from Nocturn's fingers. The magic burns through my chest and my knees hit the floor.

With another scream of denial, Astra runs out the front door.

I grab Nocturn's wrist to keep him from chasing after her. Fury rushes through me as I absorb his spell. I don't know what effect the magic might have had on Astra, but I feel pain, and push back with my grandfather's power. "I warned you."

Eyes wide, Nocturn backs up a step while surrounded by a red bubble of my weakening spell. He drops to his knees then falls to his back. "What is this?"

Rising, I stand over him. "It's a bit of your own medicine, sir. You cannot bully me or Astra for the sake of some bet you made with another demigod. What a foolish and childish man you are."

The bubble grows smaller until it pushes inside Nocturn. His powers diminish and he's just a man, at least for now. I can't help the small amount of pleasure I experience from taking him down a peg.

"You don't understand. Prede said I had no power, not even over my own child." He gets up slowly and winces at his ordinary aches and pains.

"You once called Astra spoiled, but it's you who is the brat. Now she's run off in the middle of the night. I will promise you this, Nocturn. Should any harm come to her, I will make it my life's work to destroy you. Go home." I storm out of the house and start searching.

CHAPTER TEN

ASTRA

I've been running for an hour. I'm exhausted and dirty by the time I reach Cade's house.

His mate Leona opens the door. The red and blond highlights in her hair catch the moon's light. She cocks her head when she sees me. "Astra, are you alright?"

"I need help." I've never said those words in my life. Tears pour down my face and I can't catch my breath. "I don't know what to do. I'm sorry."

"Cade!"

"What the hell?" Cade's voice is stern, but he lifts me off my feet and carries me inside his house.

"Put her on the couch. I'll put water on for tea." Leona is a blur through my tears.

I sob. "I didn't know where else to go."

Cade hands me a box of tissues and sits in the chair adjacent to me. "Of course, you should come here. We've been friends a long time."

"But Leona." I can only imagine what the pretty human thinks of me and my friendship with Cade. "I don't want to cause trouble for you."

Leona plops down on the couch next to me. "No trouble. I know you are old friends. Would you like to tell us what happened? If I make you uncomfortable, I can leave the two of you alone to talk."

I take her hand. "You are very kind." I knew she was the moment I saw her in the woods. I heard her sweet nature in my head. "Stay."

Squeezing my hand she says, "How did you get here? I didn't see a car."

"I ran." I take two tissues and wipe my face.

"How far?" Cade asks.

"From who?" Leona asks.

I sigh and shrug. "Quite a ways. My father struck Niko and it's all my fault. He's a good man and I can't marry him." More tears come. Never have I cried so hard or so long. I ache from the effort.

The teapot whistles in the kitchen and Leona gets up to make the tea.

"Astra, what's going on?" Cade's golden eyes are filled with concern.

"Who is Niko?" Leona calls from the kitchen.

"Niko is the satyr that your father arranged a marriage with?" He extrapolates from what I've told him in the past.

"Yes."

Leona brings a tray with three mugs steaming with tea and a bottle of bourbon. "I thought we might need something a little stronger."

I reach for the bourbon and pour a healthy dollop into

my tea. "Thank you. I knew you were good the moment I met you."

"Because you read my mind." She sits on Cade's lap and puts a little bourbon in her own mug.

I sip and let the warm tea and burn of whiskey distract me for a moment. "I can't help it with humans. Your thoughts are very loud."

Cade pours his bourbon into a Glencairn glass that Leona provided. The delicate glass looks precarious in his big hand and knowing that he can shift into a terrifying manticore makes it even odder. "Is the satyr trying to force you into marriage?"

It almost makes me angry for anyone to think badly of Niko. "No. He has been very understanding and patient."

"But he wants to marry you?" Leona asks. "Of course, he does. Who wouldn't? I'd marry you." She blushes.

"Niko is not subject to my magic the way you are, Leona. Yes, he wants to marry me. At least, he did." My chest hurts and my eyes fill again.

"Don't cry anymore, Astra. What happened?" Cade's command is gentle but effective.

I wipe my eyes and tell them about the deal I made with Niko and about my father showing up at his house.

They both stare with mouths agape. Cade speaks first. "Niko took the full blow of Nocturn's magic to save you."

I nod.

"Would that kill him?" Leona grips her mug with white knuckles.

"I don't know what Father's intentions were for me. I saw Niko fall and I ran. If he survives, he'll hate me for running like a coward. I thought Father would chase me." I down the remainder of my spiked tea. "I'm no good for him. Just like my father, I have no ability to love."

Cade wraps an arm around Leona's waist. "Why are you crying if you don't care about Niko?"

How dare he. "Of course, I *care*. Not wishing death or magical enslavement on someone is not the same as being able to love them."

"That's true." Leona puts her mug down and leans forward. "Why did you run?"

"I thought my father would be distracted, run out of Niko's house, and leave him alone. If I could have lured Father away, then Niko might have been strong enough to withstand one blow. Besides it's unlikely Father wanted to kill me. He probably would have bespelled me and forced me to marry tomorrow."

"Can he do that?" Leona's eyes are wide.

I nod. "He's a demigod. He could have done so before, but he thought to trick me instead. Maybe it was part of the terms of his wager with Prede."

Gape-mouthed, Leona blinks several times. "There was a wager about your marriage?"

Cade holds up a hand to pause whatever else his woman was about to say. "Let's come back to your father's behavior later. We already know the nature of demigods is to toy with the lives of others for amusement. When you ran out of the house, you wanted to protect Niko. Did you enjoy your time with him?"

"Yes. He is kind and we had fun." I don't say that his music soothes me, his hands calm me, his cooking nourishes me, or that his body fits mine perfectly.

"Maybe you just wanted to have a good time and then go on your way to find the wyvern you were rushing to when we saw you last. Niko was a fling." Leona leans against Cade's chest and wraps her arms around his neck.

A rush of longing sweeps over me. I want what these two have found, a sense of belonging and being a part of something special. "No. It wasn't meaningless."

"Do you miss him?" Cade nuzzles Leona's hair.

"I've only been away from him an hour." A knot tightens in my gut and my chest feels hollow.

"Then you know he's not dead?" Cade stares at me.

Leona smiles. "Do you sense him the way Cade senses me?"

Closing my eyes, I search the world and instantly, Niko is there. "He's alive. I feel him." I sit up straight. "I feel him. Why can I feel him from this distance?"

"Maybe he's your true mate." Leona sighs.

I shake my head. "Nymphs don't mate for life."

"Satyrs do." Cade runs his finger along Leona's upper arm.

I stand and walk to the window. A shiver runs up my back and gooseflesh pops out on my arms. "I know nothing of love or mates. I have lived my entire life under the thumb of my father, and he does not love me."

"You love your trees and the lakes here." Cade leans back and Leona snuggles against his chest.

"That's different. They are a part of me and care for me but cannot love, nor can I." These damned tears keep coming and I brush them away. I pace back toward my friend. "Explain love."

Both of them stare back at me as if I have three heads.

Leona recovers first. She stands and takes a deep breath. "It's hard to put into words."

"Try." Frustration wells up inside me. I want to do what's

best for Niko. It would be wrong to tie him to a woman who will never share his feelings.

A hint of a smile tugs at her lips. "When I'm with Cade, I'm happy. When I see him smile or laugh, it brings me joy. When I'm away from him, my heart yearns to find him again. If something good happens, I want to share the news with him first. If a tragedy came to me, it would be his shoulder I'd want to lean on for support. That's love. At least, that's the way it feels for me."

Cade stands and wraps his arm around her shoulders. He opens his mouth as if he has something to add, but then shakes his head and blinks away some moisture in his eyes.

"I do miss Niko. I want to protect him. He listens to me when no one else in my life ever has. He not only wants me, but he's excited about who I might become when I find my passions. I wrote a short story the other day and wanted to share it with him more than anything, but I was afraid." The ache in my empty chest deepens.

"What were you afraid of?" Leona asks.

"That I could need him and he could leave." It hits me like a bucket of cold water. "I'm in love with Niko."

Nodding, Cade smiles. "It would seem so, old friend."

"What if Father kills him? I've got to go." I run to the door.

"Wait. I'll drive you." Cade grabs keys from a small table near the door.

We step onto the wraparound porch as the security at the gate beeps.

Stepping back inside, Cade looks at the screen. "I think your satyr found you."

The Jeep is on the screen, and in the window, Niko's teeth are bared. "Is Astra here?"

Without answering, Cade presses a button. "He'll be here in a minute." He nudges me toward the steps. "We'll be right inside if you need us."

Leona takes his hand. "But I doubt you will."

Once the door is shut with me on the outside, I stare down the driveway as the headlights get closer. My legs shake, so I sit on the wooden steps. The bottom of my dress is covered in dirt and a leaf falls from my hair.

The Jeep stops and my satyr climbs out. "Are you alright, Astra?"

I look at him as if seeing him for the first time. His dark hair is wavy, the perfect frame to his handsome face, and the sensual curve of his horns. His shoulders are broad and his torso tapers to a narrow waist. I can practically feel the ripple of his six-pack abs. He's looking at me with worry and caring.

My bottom lip quivers.

"Sweetheart?"

I run into his arms. "I shouldn't have left you with him. I'm sorry. I never should have run, but I thought he would follow me and leave you alone."

"Shh…" He combs his fingers through my hair. "I'm fine. He would have chased you, but I will never allow anyone to cause you harm, not even your father. I held him in the house and resolved his magic."

"How did you do that?" My father is very powerful. I've never seen anyone stronger.

"My grandfather was a demigod. Nocturn's magic will not work on me. Besides, I will always protect you, even if you don't want to marry me, Astra. No one will force their will on you, I swear it."

I press my hands to his chest and look at his strong jaw and beautiful mouth. "Why?"

A soft smile tugs at his lips. "Because I love you, Astra. I have loved you since first seeing your picture. Our bond is not breakable, no matter what decisions you make. I will respect your choices, but I'll never abandon you."

There seems to be no end to the number of tears I can produce. My heart pounds and my soul yearns to be one with this magnificent satyr. "I was wrong, Niko. I'm not like Father. I can love. I love you. It's only that I had nothing to compare all these feelings with."

Cupping my jaw, he kisses me softly. "I would have waited a lifetime to hear you say those words."

"Can you forgive me?" My throat tightens, knowing I don't deserve his forgiveness.

"What for?"

I don't even know where to start the list. "For making you wait and being the cause of whatever Father tried to do."

"Your father is back at his own home, licking his wounded pride. He'll have no magic for several days and hopefully will have lost his bet and learned a lesson."

"Now I'm really sorry I ran. I would have loved to have seen you squelch his magic."

As Niko lifts me into his arms, I wrap my legs around his waist. "Can I take you home now, Astra, or should we visit with your friends first?" His cock is thick and trapped between us.

I grind against him. "We can visit with them tomorrow."

With a growl, he leaves his Jeep behind and runs with me into the woods.

The thrill of it sends a shiver of excitement through me.

My forest, my satyr, my love.

EPILOGUE

NIKO

*R*unning through the woods behind our house, I cannot catch Astra. Spring has brought her to life in a way I couldn't have dreamed. She's lively and fast, not to mention filled with lust.

She jumps from the trees and lands beautifully naked in the path. Her grin is intoxicating. "You can catch me now if you want."

"I would run myself ragged trying. Are you always so quick and elusive in the spring?" I slow my pace and close the gap.

Caressing my chest, she wraps her arms around me. "This is when my forest comes back to life. Don't you feel the vibration of it?" Swinging around, she mounts my back.

A goaty sound bays out of me and my cock comes to full attention. I grip her legs and run through our woods. "I wish I could feel the earth as you do, my love."

The oak where we first made love is on my right and I stop under its canopy of burgeoning leaves.

Touching her feet to the ground, she takes my hand and leads me to the trunk. "Would you really like to?"

My heart speeds up. "If it were possible, I would revel in hearing the trees as you hear them."

She blushes. "The night my father came, and I ran, I knew you had not been killed. I knew it because I felt you as I feel my forest."

"You never told me."

"No. I didn't want you to think you were like the trees or the blades of grass. You were and are so much more. Still, I feel you, and I think that if I opened my senses to you, you could become part of everything. At least you might hear this tree." She runs her fingers along my horn, down my cheek, and rests her hand on my shoulder. "If you want?"

When she touches me, it's magic that has nothing to do with her being a nymph. Wrapping my arms around her, I stare into her crystal eyes. Every nerve is awake and ready for more Astra. Still, we've lived together through eight months, and never has she made such an offer. "Why now?"

Tears spill over her lids. "All these months you have loved me without asking for anything in return. You make no demands. You never again asked for the marriage you came to New York for. I want to share this with you. It is something I have never shared with anyone else."

Emotions swamp me. "Show me."

She stands between me and the tree with her back to my front. Taking my hand, she presses the palm to the rough bark of the oak's trunk. Her small hand covers only half of the back of mine.

A soft hum vibrates inside me as our hands sink into the

tree. A rush of calm falls over me despite my instinct to pull away; I trust Astra and remain in the grip of the unknown. "Should I be afraid, sweetheart?"

"Never. Close your eyes and feel."

Opening myself to whatever is to come, I do as I'm told. Rather than the darkness of the backs of my eyelids, I see light and shadows. The rings of the trees are in shades of brown, the beat of life within shines white, and the acceptance of the new connection reflects a calm green. The hum is all the life of the forest mingling like a crowded room buzzing with conversation.

Love for Astra flows through me to her in waves that band around my heart.

Inside my mind, Astra's voice says, *"Legends say my beauty is my greatest gift, but this is more."*

"To me, this is a reflection of your beauty, Astra. You are lovely inside and out." I draw an unsteady breath as she releases me from the essence of the tree.

Facing me, she stares with emotion glistening in her eyes. "Can you see why I run through these woods each day?"

"I feel blessed that you ever leave those voices to come home to me." I trace the curve of her cheek with my fingers, seeing more of her light than I've ever noticed before.

Her cheeks pinken. "You are even more tempting than the forest. When the weather is warmer, I will share the water's voice with you." She hesitates. "If you wish."

"I do wish it, Astra. I want to know everything about you. Thank you for sharing this." I wrap her in my arms and hold her close. Her floral and earthy scent fills my nostrils. She's like an addiction. The more I'm with her, the more I need her.

"I will never leave you," she whispers against my heart.

The words seep into my soul. "You are the only woman I can ever love, my beautiful nymph. If you ever left, I would wait for you to come back."

"And you're certain I would return to you?" She kisses my throat.

"We have long lives, my love, and I can wait a very long time." Kissing the top of her head, I lift her off the ground.

She wraps her legs around my waist. "You shall never have to wait on me, Niko." Cupping my cheek, she kisses me. Her tongue slides across mine and she moans against my mouth.

Leaning her against the tree, my cock thickens between us.

On a needy sound, she breaks the kiss. "I want to marry you."

Frozen, I stare at her as if she might evaporate in my arms. It's too much to ask that I heard her correctly. This must be a dream, the dream I've had a hundred times, but always woken up from. "You didn't wish to marry."

She shakes her head. "I didn't want to be bullied by my father or a satyr whom I'd never met. I let too much time pass. I was happy and thought changing our status might change how we felt."

"I love you, Astra. Nothing will ever change that." I brush her hair out of her face and study her eyes. They're clear and determined, without a hint of doubt.

"Will you marry me? I can understand if you no longer wish it."

Part of me could laugh at the thought that anything could change my desire for this woman. "I no longer require a formal pledge from you because we are more than that now." I touch her chin to keep her from looking away. "I still very much want to marry you."

She squeezes my neck and laughs. "I would like a small wedding here under this tree. My father will be invited, but not until the day before."

Joy bubbles up from deep in my soul. "Fitting. When would you like to marry?"

Running her hand along the trunk, she studies the limbs of the trees. "When the leaves have lost their sap and are in full face to the sun."

Not sure what that means, I ask, "Is there a calendar date for that?"

Her giggle is pure joy and music. She shrugs. "Next month."

I touch the sticky pale-green leaf that's just trying to open above our heads. "I would wait a monster's lifetime for you, my nymph; a few more weeks won't hurt. Besides, you saying you'll never leave me would have been enough."

She takes my hand and kisses my fingers. "I am yours until the end of time, Niko."

Pressing my lips to hers, my heart is lodged in my throat. Once I catch my breath, I complete the vows, "And I am yours, Astra."

The trees sway in the breeze, reveling in the joy of the moment.

Thank you for reading Astra and Niko's story.
I hope you enjoyed them as much as I do. Turn the page to
read **Wild for the Wyvern** to find out how Drayce
gets his happily ever after.

WILD FOR THE WYVERN

WILD
FOR THE
WYVERN
ANDIE FENICHEL

WILD FOR THE WYVERN

CATSKILL MONSTERS

DRAYCE

For half my life I longed for the nymph who frequents the woods of Upstate New York. Finally, she told me she would be mine if I took her away from here. Then she stood me up and mated with the satyr. Having sworn never to be bothered with romance again, I spend my days plotting revenge. I've set my trap to humiliate them. When the alarms indicate the trap is sprung, I rush to meet my prey. What I find is the most beautiful human I've ever seen. I don't even like humans, but I can't take my eyes off this one. She struggles against my net in a vain attempt to escape me. The longer I look at her, the more certain I am that this woman is mine.

KORI

I lost my friends on a hike in the woods. If that wasn't bad enough, I walked into some kind of animal trap and now I'm dangling twenty feet off the ground in a giant net. I scream, but the odds of someone hearing me seem less than zero. It's more likely that I'm about to be eaten by a bear or mountain lion. The last thing I expect is a dragon to fly through the forest and stare at me with giant golden eyes. My screaming turns to whimpers. Terrified, I start babbling, the way I always do when I'm afraid. Instead of devouring me, the monster's eyes soften, he releases me from the trap and cradles me in his arms. I pass out and end up in the house of a stunning man. If I'm not dead, then this fairy tale is my dream come true.

DRAYCE

$\mathcal{I}$t seems as if I've waited a lifetime for the nymph to be mine. It has been many years of pining. She says she doesn't love me, but she does need me. I will carry her away to a new home with new trees for her to cherish. I can give her everything she wants.

Standing in our meeting spot by the lake, I think of all the arrangements I've made to make my treasure happy in our new home. I've been making these plans for weeks. I want her to be comfortable and happy. I want to cherish my jewel for an eternity.

It's a clear day, which will make our flight more pleasant. I fashioned a sling to carry her away in. As a wyvern, I have no arms, and as a man, I can only take her so far.

The sling will keep her comfortable and safe while I hold the thick rope handles with my talons. It's a long flight to our new home in the Smokey Mountains. I must keep my nymph safe.

The lake glistens as a light breeze blows through the Catskills.

An owl hoots, then circles overhead.

Narrowing my eyes and shading out the sun with my hand, I get a better look at the bird.

It circles lower before landing on a branch several feet above my head. It's a great horned owl with tall tufts above its eyes and a regal look about it. Staring at me, it turns its head this way and that for a long moment.

Silly bird.

I cast my gaze back toward the woods, where Astra will soon appear, ready for our journey. She's begun to wear human clothes, which is slightly disappointing and quite strange for a nymph. Nymphs generally go naked or wear magical sheer gowns, which allow them to pass through nature. For instance, she can become part of a tree or the water in the lake.

Still, if she wishes to wear clothes, I have no objection. She will be mine and that's all that matters. Soon my obsession will be a reality.

The owl warbles out a few notes.

It almost sounds like speech, and I cock my head to hear the animal better.

There are words hidden in the owl's sounds. *"I'm not coming, Drayce. I'm sorry."*

Rage rushes through me. Not coming. Not coming? How can she do this to me? She asked me to take her away and save her from her father's tyranny. I made arrangements to make her happy and keep her safe.

My bones crack and grow as I shift into my wyvern.

The owl screeches and flies in the opposite direction. Smart beast. I'm angry enough that no one is safe. A roar erupts from deep in my chest and pushes from my long snout, filling the sky as I take wing.

Staying just above the top leaves of the trees, I scan the forest for my nymph. She will face me.

Moving east, I hit a magical blockade that nearly bumps me out of the air. Regaining my balance, I sniff the magic. It's foreign, not from a monster I know. Carefully, I circle the barrier. It surrounds a large house on a ridge twenty miles from mine.

There!

With her hand in that of a satyr, my nymph walks up the steps to the house.

Fury rises in me and I batter myself against the magic, trying to push through, but to no avail. I don't even get the satisfaction of either of them looking up at me.

They will pay for making a fool of me. She sent a bird when I waited half my life for her to realize I was the only man for her. Then that spoiled nymph agreed to marry a satyr she barely knows. I've been devoted to Astra for years. How could she do this to me?

Unable to contain my rage, I've laid my trap. When they're captured, they'll see what it's like to be humiliated in front of the community. Every monster on the mountain is laughing at me, but I will get the last laugh.

Just because my nature is a wyvern and I'm fierce when in that form doesn't mean I don't have feelings.

Covering the net with last year's leaf fall, I survey the spring on the trap. When the nymph or her satyr step inside the net, the trap will grab them and no magic will free them.

Then I'll leave them to hang there until I get my proper apology.

She thinks sending an owl is enough to make up for all the plans I arranged and all the trouble I went through trying to make her happy, then leaving me for a stranger to the woods. I will have revenge.

CHAPTER ONE

KORI

"Why me?" Why is it always me who gets lost? I mean, I set out on this silly hiking trail with my three best friends. I can guarantee they are still walking through the wooded property surrounding the Greentree Resort in the Catskill Mountains. Meanwhile, I'm lost in the middle of nowhere with no path and no clue which way the hotel is.

I'm not outdoorsy. I'm a put me up in a nice hotel with a good book. I'm a stay home with a cozy blanket and a book. Just give me a book and leave me alone. I love my friends and I know they mean well when they bully me into venturing out of my comfort zone, but it's called a comfort zone for a reason. What's wrong with wanting to be content and not adventurous?

Every tree looks the same. The sun is mostly shaded by

the late-spring leaves of the canopy far above my head. That stump seems familiar. Oh lord, I'm going in circles.

Stopping, I try to figure out which way is east. We set out from the hotel, walking away from the sun, and it was early. My stomach is growling, which probably means it's afternoon. The sun is pretty high, but maybe that way is east.

I turn right at the stump and hope it takes me out of these woods and onto a road where I can find someone to take me back to the resort. It would be my luck to be picked up by a serial killer and no one will ever hear from me again.

Trudging farther, I sniff the air. Maybe I smell wood burning. That could be the big fireplace in the lobby. I break into a jog and follow my nose.

Something under the old leaves catches my toe. I hit the ground hard and let out a yelp. Keeping still, I assess whether or not I'm injured while the damp seeps into my clothes at the knees and elbows. I push my hands against the ground and a stick pokes my palm. "Ouch."

There's a loud crack and snap. The world turns upside down. Something grabs me from every direction. I'm screaming, but I don't even know what's happening. Everything is moving. I'm whipping away from the ground at lightning speed. My stomach lurches.

I'm bouncing in the air. After a second, everything slows. The rope net that I'm trapped in is like something for a bear and the stiff material cuts into my arms and legs. Fresh leaves fall from the trees.

Slowly, my bouncing stops and now all I see is the ground, and the creaking of the branches makes my panic button go into full alert. I'm going to fall thirty feet to my death in this godforsaken woods and no one will ever see me again. Maybe I'll just hang here and die of dehydration or starvation. I would have been better off with my fictional serial killer.

"Help!" *Don't look down, Kori. Hold yourself together and don't look down.* "Help!" I feel as if someone is watching me. "Is anyone out there!"

There's movement below me and a loud rustling.

"Help me!" My scream echoes through the woods.

A shadow passes over the sun.

Turning forces the ropes into my ribs. I stifle a grunt and stretch my neck to look toward whatever is blocking out the daylight. Shades of turquoise and green, mixed with gold beautifully shining iridescent. I scan the scaly surface, my gaze rising until I find a large gold-and-garnet eye staring back at me. "What?"

The eye narrows and its owner's huge nostrils flare.

My scream is trapped in my throat. I'm going to be eaten by a dragon in Upstate New York and that is why no one will ever hear from me again.

Its elongated nose shifts to view me with its other eye as its spiked tail wraps around the bottom of the rope trap. It opens its mouth revealing razor-sharp teeth.

My scream finally finds a voice as the creature snaps its jaw shut on the thick snare above my head.

Cradled in its cool wings, it jumps with me to the ground.

"Dragons don't exiiiist!" I scream as I fall through the tree's limbs. I land so softly that it takes me a moment to realize I'm on land. I'm on my back and the trap falls away. I can't catch my breath as I scramble backward and try to get away.

It cocks its head and bares its teeth.

Had it understood me? I stand on wobbly legs. "I'll just go and you can go back to not being real."

A low rumble echoes from its throat and it blinks at me.

Taking a step away, I stumble and a beautiful wing whips out to keep me from falling. Palms flat on the scaled surface, I sense the blood rushing through the appendage. "This is the most realistic dream I've ever had. I'm sure that any moment now I'm going to wake up safe and sound in my bed at the resort. None of this is real. Either that or I've had a psychotic break and I'm going to die in these woods."

I'm back to the fact that no one will ever find my body or hear from me again.

The dragon lowers its nose and inhales long before letting out a low rumble. It steps closer. The claws dragging through the forest's underbrush are at least four inches long and razor sharp.

"Time to go." Even as I say it, my feet won't move. I'm mesmerized by the beast's magnificence. "I'm sure there's a logical explanation for why you're here. It probably makes perfectly good sense. You probably don't get out much and that's why no one has ever reported seeing a dragon—ever—anywhere." Finally, my legs listen to my brain's command and I step away. When I look back, the dragon is watching me.

The problem is that I still need to figure out how to get back to the Greentree. There's no path and I have not gained a sense of direction in the last hour. I keep walking away, but it's like the world is going faster and I'm going slower. My brain won't process what I've seen and touched. The feel of its scales against my fingers and his warm scent. Yes, I'm sure the dragon is male. I don't know how I know, but I do.

Just keep walking, Kori. Don't look back. Don't think about anything but getting away.

Thirty minutes later, I'm standing in front of a giant rock

formation jutting out of the side of the mountain. "Now what?" I'm tired and dirty. There's no doubt I've lost my mind. And I'm no closer to the resort. I'm sure I'm farther away.

The wind whips up and the leaves crash down like rain as the dragon lands on top of the boulder.

I stumble backward and fall hard on my ass. A screech escapes and I moan when the pain of whatever is under the leaves and forest floor bruises my ass. Closing my eyes, I try to decide if I'm injured or just hurt.

The heat of his huge body forces my eyes open. As beautiful as when I first saw all the colors of his iridescent scales, he stands in front of me. His golden eyes are soulful and locked on me with the red irises narrowed to slits.

One clawed foot wraps around my middle.

I scream, but it's stifled as he lifts me from the ground and maneuvers through the tall trees into the air. Certain he's going to drop me, I keep my eyes closed.

His other talon wraps around my bottom half, and he cradles me more gently than any hammock or the softest bed. Somehow, before I'm about to be dropped to my death on the forest floor, I feel safer than I have in my entire life.

Then I look down. It's a long way and my panic increases until I'm screaming and can't catch my breath. My vision narrows and then... nothing.

DRAYCE

The woman's scent is intoxicating. She's scared of me, and I don't like that. I should take her to the resort and leave her close enough that she'll find her way back. Though, I'm skeptical that would work since she walked in the wrong direction. Now she's lying limp in my claws and I'm starting to panic.

I speed through the air, just above the treetops, and make my way home. Any higher and the locals might see me. There's safety in keeping low. Rarely do any tourists come this far up the mountain, but you never know.

Landing in my yard, I gently place her on the ground and let the change take me. My vision shifts from the sharpness and colors of a dragon's eyes to the central focus of a man. Bones pop and rearrange, and my size shifts, as does my shape, until I'm human.

It might be a good thing she's unconscious because I'm naked as I lift her from the ground and carry her to the house. Still, her scent is almost too much as I place her carefully on my couch. I brush her warm brown hair from her face.

Kneeling beside the couch, I study the line of her pert little nose and the way her jaw curves. Not only did my beast get lured in by her scent, but the man in me finds her stunning. Her hair is streaked with gold and bronze and cut to just below that jaw I so admire. Even covered in dirt with a leaf sticking out of from behind her ear, she's beautiful. Her black tank top hides nothing and every inch of her fullness makes my mouth water.

The rise and fall of her chest assures me that she's only passed out and not injured. Part of me wants to stay and watch her, but I have work to do. I can be back in ten minutes.

Stepping outside, I return to my beast form and fly back to reset my trap. Once that task is done, I return home at a dangerous speed. The pull toward this human woman is strange and overpowering.

Kneeling beside the couch where she rests, I try to pull myself together.

Her lips part on a short gasp, and she opens her bright blue eyes. They lock on mine. "Who are you?"

There's no fear in her voice, only curiosity. She studies my face, scans my neck and bare chest. Her eyes widen. "Are you naked?"

The fact that I should be serious doesn't seem to matter. She's adorable. A short laugh escapes. "I'm afraid so."

She blinks and her cheeks turn the most charming shade of pink. "And my other question?"

"I'm Drayce Webb. You were lost and then you passed out. I brought you to my house. I can get dressed and return you to your resort…" I trail off. If I could think of a way to keep this strange human here, I would.

She tugs the leaf out of her hair, then looks around for somewhere to dispose of it before keeping it in her hand. "Was there more to the offer?"

Even in my human form, the scent of her is intoxicating. I want her. My dragon wants her. How is that possible? I don't know this person, and she's human. Humans are weak and terrified of monsters like me. Taking the leaf, I put it on the coffee table. If I stand, she might run away since my cock is already thick and aching just from the sight and scent of her. "I could run you a bath and wash your clothes if you want. I would be happy to cook you dinner."

"Is it dinner time?" She touches the ends of my hair. "Who are you?"

"It's four o'clock. I told you. I'm Drayce Webb." I swallow, my heart feeling as if it's lodged in my throat.

"Your eyes look almost like the dragon. Of course, there's no such thing as dragons and you probably think I'm insane."

She studies my face and lifts her hand. She pulls back before actually touching my cheek.

Wanting her touch is totally irrational. I want Astra. Even if she doesn't return my feelings. I waited years for her.

"I wouldn't mind a bath and some food. You don't have to do my wash though." Something in her tone makes me think she's nervous I'd turn her away even after making the offer. She's tentative and her eyes won't meet mine.

Perfect joy fills me. It's been so long since something truly made me happy, I press my hand to my chest. Maybe to keep from bursting with the feeling. Not sure what to say to put her at ease, I stumble and mutter, "I'll go run the water for you."

CHAPTER TWO

KORI

The beautiful man stands up and every perfect inch of him is hard and muscled. And, I mean every inch. His thick cock stands out perpendicular to his chiseled abs and thighs that I couldn't wrap both hands around and have my fingers touch. He's enormous.

My cheeks are on fire but I meet his stare. "I'm sorry."

His smile is criminally gorgeous.

My entire body clenches and a little swirl happens in my stomach.

"What could you have to be sorry for?" he asks, completely unbothered by his nudity.

I, on the other hand, am bothered in the most base way possible. "For looking, I guess."

His laugh is round and full and makes his cock bounce and my mouth water. "I'd be sorry if you didn't." He turns and walks away a few steps before stopping and looking back at me. "What is your name?"

The sight of his round tan ass has me speechless for several beats. I take a deep breath. "Kori. Kori Devers."

"Kori." He repeats it softly, as if to himself. "Relax. You've had a fright. I'll let you know when your bath is ready."

I manage a nod before he turns and strides across the room and down a hall.

Immediately, I sit up. The house is rustic, with tall ceilings, rough-hewn beams, and exposed rafters. Skylights let in the afternoon sun. A stone fireplace sits in the center and faces the living room and seems to open to the outside as well. Behind a wall of windows is a flagstone patio that overlooks the Catskill Mountains. It's a stunning vista with every shade of brown and green on display.

Taking it slow, I rise to my feet. Once certain that I'm stable and not at all dizzy, I walk to those windows and stare out before giving a full turn to look at the great room belonging to the strangely familiar Drayce Webb.

Maybe it was Drayce who found me in the woods and I had some weird fantasy dream about a dragon. His eyes are the same, though not slitted at the center or red. There's something strange about the man, but I like his voice. I wanted to touch him. Not once in all my twenty-seven years have I met someone and longed to feel their skin the way I did when he was in front of me.

On the other side of the room, spanning right from the front door, is a kitchen with black cabinets and a huge island. The countertops look like white marble with black veining. It's stunning. The fixtures are brushed gold. It's a touch of modern in the rustic house and it works better than I would have thought.

I make my way to the place where I feel most comfortable and admire his forty-eight-inch cooktop and double oven with its red knobs. I would kill to have one of these of my own. It would never fit in my apartment. I have plenty of burners at the restaurant where I work. This is a luxury I can't afford and would rarely have time to enjoy. I might never leave the house if I had this stove.

"Do you like to cook?"

His sudden question startles me, and I spin around. He's clothed in cargo shorts and a white tee shirt.

I'm at once relieved and sorry. I almost giggle at my stupidity. "I'm a chef. You have a beautiful home."

"Thank you. A chef. That's wonderful. Where do you work?" He rounds the island.

One step at a time, I back away from his approach. He's so big and male, and my body longs for him in a way that isn't normal for someone I just met. I don't even have time to date a man who lives in the city, let alone one nearly three hours upstate. "At No Reservations downtown. This is my first vacation in two years." I keep backing up as he steadily closes the gap. "So, of course, I get lost in the woods and have a mental breakdown."

He stops, and I do too. Scanning me from head to toe, he takes a deep breath.

I probably smell like a warthog. My cheeks are on fire. As I back up, my hip hits the corner of the island, and I stumble. Before I can brace for the impact of hitting the floor, Drayce's arms wrap around me and steady me.

Breathless, I look into his golden eyes. "Sorry."

"You have nothing to apologize for. I'm happy to keep rescuing you all day and night if you'll let me." He takes a deep breath and groans. His voice is rough. "Your bath is ready."

"Thank you."

He takes my hand and leads me down a hallway to a bedroom.

I stop at the door and my heart pounds. I'm an idiot. Now I'm going to be raped and killed by the most stunning man on the face of the earth and no one will ever hear from me again.

He releases me. "The bath is in my en suite. I won't touch you. I promise." He crosses to the wooden barn door and pushes it aside to reveal the steaming tub. "There's a latch inside if that makes you feel better. But I promise not to enter unless invited."

Drawn to the scent of roses and the giant claw foot tub, I step inside the room and turn to close the door.

Watching me, he shifts from foot to foot. "Put your clothes outside the door. I'll take care of them. I left a robe inside for you."

I nod.

Before I get the door closed, he stops it with one hand. His eyes shine with intensity like nothing I've ever seen. "You're not crazy, Kori. You did see something. But dragons have four legs. You saw a wyvern." He closes the barn door.

I back up and stare at the spot where he was. Nothing makes any sense. A wyvern? I pull my phone out of my pocket. It had no service in the woods but I have three bars here. I type in wyvern and a two-legged dragon pops up.

"Idiot." I swipe away the internet and dial Dean's number. The phone goes dead. I try again, but the battery is dead.

With a sigh, I strip out of my clothes and put them

outside the door with my useless phone on top of the pile. Once I latch the door, which I'm certain Drayce could push open without much effort if he wanted to, I get in the rose-scented water and sink all the way down. This is heaven. My aching muscles all seem to sigh at once.

Before he told me I wasn't crazy, he said he wouldn't come in unless invited. Does that mean he's as attracted to me as I am to him? No. He's so far out of my league, he's in a different stratosphere. Men who look like him don't date struggling chefs. Men who live in houses like this on the tops of mountains don't rescue lost city girls either. This may all still be a dream. I'll wake up and none of it will have happened.

Closing my eyes, I wish the dream would never end.

Before I get too pruney, I wash and get out of the tub. There is a stack of fluffy white towels on a chair and I wrap myself in one before securing a second around my head. On the vanity, which is made of the same white-and-black marble as in the kitchen, is a brush, toothbrush, toothpaste, and a hair dryer.

This guy might be the best host in the world, besides being the best-looking human ever. Rather than dry my hair, I give it a good brushing. I put on the robe and hang the towels on the brushed-gold hooks that match all the lovely fixtures.

Mustering my courage, I step out of the bathroom. I'm on

the fence as to whether I'm relieved or disappointed that the bedroom is empty. I pad down the hall and find Drayce in the kitchen, stirring a pot of sauce. "That smells great."

He turns and smiles. There's no surprise in his reaction. He knew I was here. "I'm no chef, but I can make sauce, which I can myself, and I thought I'd wait for you to tell me if you like meat or only basil in your sauce with penne."

"I'm in favor of both. Can I help you?"

He shakes his head and his long brown hair shifts from side to side.

I can still feel the texture of those strands.

"You should let someone cook for you once in a while."

I sit on one of four stools and watch the muscles of his broad back flexing under his shirt. "Should I?"

"Yes."

"Why did you say there are dragons?"

"Wyvern, but there are dragons too. There are many monsters in these woods. This is our home." He stiffens his back.

"Our?" I know what I heard, but my brain is not processing the information. "What do you mean? Are you a monster?" I don't even believe in monsters, so it's a stupid question.

With a heavy sigh, he turns to face me. He switches off the fire under his pot, then crosses so only the island separates us. His eyes are full of need and passion. "Maybe we should eat dinner first. I think if I tell you everything now, you'll grab your phone and call someone to get you out of here. I'd really like for you to stay for dinner."

"My phone?"

He points to it sitting on a small table near the front door. It's plugged into a charger.

"Thank you for charging it." If I was smart, I would grab that phone and call for a ride immediately. No one has ever accused me of being smart. "I will stay for dinner, Drayce, but I don't believe in monsters."

His smile is panty-melting. "You say that now, but you know what you saw in the woods, Kori Devers."

What did I see? I saw a dragon or a wyvern. "What's the difference?"

Cocking his head, his beautiful full lips purse. I can't take my eyes off them when he finally asks, "Difference?"

"Between a dragon and a wyvern?"

Then he smiles. Oh god, that smile has my pussy aching with molten desire. I have got to get a grip on myself. However, I continue to stare at his mouth as he answers.

"To the naked eye, a dragon has four legs and a wyvern has two. However, each has its own attributes and they're different species."

The thing I saw in the woods had the most beautiful iridescent wings, but no front legs. It was terrifying and magnificent. I shake myself. I probably hit my head and imagined the entire thing. "I see." Time to get real. "I'm going to call my friends at the resort so they don't worry and send out a search party."

"Of course."

I feel his gaze on me with every step I make to my phone. Picking it up off the small entry table, I call Dean. "Hi."

"Oh my god, are you hurt?" Always dramatic, his voice rises in both volume and tone.

"No. I'm fine. I made a new friend and we're having dinner."

"Is that a code for, you've been kidnapped and I should send help?" Oh, the drama.

I laugh nervously, since not long ago I was thinking the same thing. "No. I'm glad you didn't already call out a search party."

"We figured you got a little turned around and would find your way back. Now it's getting dark and we were worried." In the background, Meg and Lori are asking rapid-fire questions.

"I did get lost, but I met Drayce Webb and he's cooking me dinner. He'll bring me back to the resort later." I figure if I don't turn up at least Dean knows whose house I was last at. I scan over to the kitchen and Drayce is browning beef in a pan.

He smiles and nods to confirm he'll do as I told my friends. There's something about him that makes it hard to look away. My heart speeds up and my stomach tightens every time I glance at his broad back, long legs, and perfectly shaped ass. I will never forget how he looked naked. It was like looking at the flesh and blood version of a Michelangelo statue with every muscle perfectly defined. The image is burned into my brain.

I might be ruined for life.

"Drayce," Dean says with a teasing lilt. "I never get rescued by good-looking men."

I want to ask him how he knows Drayce is good-looking, but since the subject is still keeping me in his sight, I hold back. "I'll talk to you tomorrow or later tonight if you're still awake."

"We'll be waiting up for this story." All three of them laugh as I hang up.

I leave my phone plugged in on the little table and return to the island. "My friends are silly but fun. I hope you couldn't hear all of that."

"Every word, but they just sound nice to me." He adds the drained beef to the sauce. "Do you drink wine?" He sets the burner on a low simmer and puts the lid on.

The sauce may be at a slow bubble, but I'm about to boil over just from looking at him.

CHAPTER THREE

DRAYCE

I lean on the island and watch her blush the most delicious peach. Keeping the large slab of granite between us feels necessary. The space allows me to act as if every moment with this human woman isn't significant, despite my monster's voice in my head telling me to claim her as my own.

She looks down at the countertop, then meets my gaze through the waves of her chin-length hair. "I thought I was being kidnapped, and maybe I am, but I've never felt safer in my life."

There is nothing sexy about what she said, but my cock thickens just the same. "You are safe, Kori. I will never let anything harm you."

With her arms crossed and leaning on the granite, her breasts push up between the folds of my robe. I've never been more jealous of a piece of material. She licks her bottom lip, then pulls it through her teeth. "What was that trap supposed to catch? Was it for the thing I saw?"

It's strange that though she knows she saw my wyvern, she won't acknowledge him. "No. It was to embarrass someone who wronged me."

"Who?" She shakes her head. "Sorry, it's none of my business."

"I think I'd rather save that story for another time. If I told you now, you'd form an opinion of me that I don't think I would like." Thinking about it, I don't like it either. The fact that I went back while she was sleeping and reset the trap makes me feel even worse.

"You make it sound as if we'll be seeing each other after today." She grips the edges of the robe and pulls it tight around her neck before walking to the wall of windows that look out over the valley and the mountains beyond. "How long have you lived here?"

"I built this house fifteen years ago but I've lived in the Catskills all my life." The wyvern prompts me to get closer to her despite knowing it's a bad idea. She's human and has no knowledge of monsters. She passed out just from the sight of me when I carried her here. This isn't where she belongs.

"Do you go to town much? I noticed a nice little bistro when we drove through the other day." She wraps her arms around herself but doesn't look at me.

A foot from her, I stop and force myself not to reach out and touch her, not to pull her back against my chest, and not to slide my hands inside the robe covering her from neck to her shapely calves. It's pure torture. "Rialto. It's a very nice Italian restaurant. I go to town from time to time. I'm not a shut-in, but I do prefer these woods and my home to crowds."

"What do you do for a living?" She peeks over her shoulder.

"I trade in precious metals for exclusive clients." Unable to resist, I run my hand from her shoulder to her elbow. There's an inch of terry cloth between my fingers and her flesh, yet it still feels intimate.

The little hitch in her breathing increases my longing. "It sounds interesting or illegal."

Fuck but she's adorable. "I like it so it's interesting to me. I assure you, it's perfectly legal."

When she turns, it brings her even closer. Arching her neck to look me in the eye, her lips part on the hint of a gasp. "None of this is any of my business. You saved me from myself in the woods. You're not obligated to tell me anything. It's only…"

My hands ache to feel all of her and my wyvern growls inside me, practically screaming for me to take her, mark her, and make her ours. I skim my thumb along her soft jaw. "I would tell you anything. Everything."

"Is that all you want? To talk?" She leans her head against my hand and presses her lips to my palm.

The monster's growl makes its way through me and escapes as an audible moan. "Kori, what exactly are you offering?"

Inching closer, she rises to her toes and kisses my neck. "I'm not like this. I don't get rescued by handsome men. However, I do often need rescuing. I never go home with men I don't know. It's only, there's something about you. My brain says one thing and my body says another."

Lowering my face to her wild, wavy hair, I breathe in her scent as if it's my last gulp of air. "Which one are we listening to?" I let my hand rest on the small of her back and ease her close enough that my painfully hard cock presses against her. "Because I think my desire is apparent."

"Because you're into damsels in distress? I know men like women who can't take care of themselves. You didn't really see me at my best today." She stiffens but doesn't move away.

I thread my fingers through her hair. "No. Not because I think you're helpless. It's deeper and very difficult to explain. Everything about you summons me." Without explaining the entire nature of monsters, that's the best I can do.

"Maybe you could kiss me now?" She meets my gaze with utter faith that I won't hurt her.

Cupping her cheek, a bubble of joy wells up within me. I've never felt anything like it. I press my lips to hers and the rest of the world falls away. It's only Kori and me in the entire universe.

She grips my shoulder and lifts up onto her toes again.

While I band my arm around her back, I nibble her bottom lip and run my tongue along the seam.

Her warm tongue touches mine, and she makes the most guttural deep moan. She wraps one leg around mine, pulling her center tight to my shaft and grinding forward.

The beast growls and I press my tongue inside, exploring every centimeter of her lips, tongue, and teeth. "Kori," I mutter against her lips.

She answers with a longing cry.

Giving the tie on the robe a tug, I free it and slip my hand along her hip to her soft thigh. "I don't want you to do anything you'll regret. I want to be a gentleman."

Looking up at me, she stills and brushes my hair out of my eyes. "You think I'm being hasty?"

Kissing the palm of her hand, I brush my knuckles along her pelvic bone, then along her abdomen, to just under her perfect tits. "What I think doesn't matter. I want you. I long to bury my cock deep inside you and make you come a dozen times. I want to taste every inch of you then start at the top and taste you again. But only if that's what you want and need, sweetheart."

The haunting sound of yearning that breaks in her throat is nearly my undoing. "I feel safe with you. Even now. I haven't had that many places or people who make me feel that way. I know I should play coy and tell you to take me back to the resort. Still, I can't make myself do it. I want you to make me come a dozen times. I want to give you pleasure and maybe for you not to forget my name the moment I'm back in the city and you're here."

I wrap one hand around her ass and then the other before lifting her off the floor.

She grips me with her legs and arms, watching me with questions in those steel-blue eyes.

Passing through the kitchen, I shift her weight to turn off the stove before carrying her down the hall to my bedroom. Carefully placing her on the bed, I follow her down. "I will not forget your name, Kori Devers, or any other part of you."

"Do you promise?" She slips her arms out of the robe.

Easing back, I strip out of my clothes and take in every inch of her perfect body, from her rounded tits that my hands ache to mold, to the swell of her hips. She's petite and luscious. Breathing in the scent of her longing, the wyvern keens deep inside me.

I kneel on the floor and pull her toward me until her thighs hang over my shoulders and the heady perfume of her sex intoxicates me. "I promise."

She gasps and lifts her hips. "Drayce. Please."

I slip my fingers between her folds and find her so wet,

my cock throbs to be inside her. I lap up those sweet juices and circle her clit before sucking and pressing my finger deep.

On a low keen, she grinds against my digit and mouth. "That's. I'm so close. I…"

I suck hard and her body pulses with her release.

I lick my finger, then lap up those intoxicating juices. Looking up the length of her sweet body, her cheeks and chest are pink. "That was beautiful, Kori."

"I couldn't hold off." She covers her face with her arm.

Kissing a path up her stomach to her perfect tits, I suck one nipple into my mouth while gently adjusting her to the center of the mattress.

She arches her back and says my name. I want to hear my name again and again from her.

"I never want you to hold back. Your pleasure is everything." I suck her other nipple while worrying the first between my fingers. "I want to show you how much rapture is possible. Promise me you won't hold anything back." I use my teeth on the sensitive bud, then lick.

"I… I promise. God, that feels so good." She turns her head from side to side and bends her leg, opening for me.

Slipping my fingers into her wetness, I tease her clit and she gasps and jerks. I gentle my touch but don't pull away completely. Slowly circling and teasing, as light as a feather. "Does that feel good?"

Lifting her hips and lowering in the same slow cadence as my fingers, she says, "Oh, god, yes. I'm. I can't. Oh, fuck." Her orgasm crashes a second time.

Before I go for a third round of her pleasure, she wraps her hand around my cock. "Kori."

She runs her hand from tip to base gently, then bolder.

"I've never come twice in such a short time before. You're magic."

Closing my eyes, I let her pleasure me with those soft fingers, teasing, then stroking, then brushing soft as a feather again. I want to tell her that she's the magic one. I long to tell her about my real magic and see if she still desires me when she knows my nature, but I can't speak with her hands on me.

Before she takes me too far, I grip her hand and groan. "If you continue, I'll come, and I'm hoping for the privilege of being inside you."

Her hand around my cock and my hand around hers, she stares into my eyes. The sunlight streaks through the bedroom window, making the reds and golds in her hair shine. She's a goddess. "I want you inside me more than I want to draw another breath." Bending both knees, she lets them fall open.

The beast inside me pushes forward, wanting to claim her, mark her. I breathe and fight to control him. Scaring her away is the last thing we want. *She's not ready for that.* He roars within but pulls back.

Covering her body, I notch at her sweet, wet pussy. I brush her hair off her cheek. "You can tell me no. There is no point of no return."

With a smile, she lifts her hips. "I don't want to tell you anything but yes and more."

"Kori." I press in an inch, stretching her.

She moans and her breath quickens.

I kiss her cheek, and her jaw, then take her lips possessively. Every molecule wants to fill her, but I'm big, and she's tiny. I push another inch and let her adjust before continuing to fill her, one excruciating stretch at a time.

Her eyes close, and she winces.

I pull back and let her juices ease me in over and over until she's pressing up to meet me, and I'm buried to my balls. Nothing has ever felt this good. She's perfection. Her pussy was made to be filled with my cock.

Kori tilts her pelvis and wraps her legs around me, bringing me in deeper. "Oh. My. God. You're. I'm." Her body pulses, and she screams through the orgasm.

Holding perfectly still, I let her pleasure ebb before I ease back and fill her again. "You're the magic one, sweetheart. I could die here."

Her nails bite into the flesh on my shoulders. "More. I need more." She rocks her hips.

I start slow before quickening my pace. Thrusting hard and fast, my orgasm builds as a tingle at the base of my spine. I hold back, sliding my hand under her ass. That lets my shaft rub her sweet clit and her pussy milks my cock, sending me over the edge.

The tingle of a knotting hold begins at the base of my cock. Panicked, I pull free and spill my seed between us before the knot can set. Wrapping her in my arms, I roll so she's sprawled on top of me. I kiss her temple, her hair, as emotions swell inside me.

Mate. My beast growls.

CHAPTER FOUR

KORI

’m not innocent, but that was by far the greatest sex of my life. I’d be willing to bet it was the best sex of anyone’s life. I probably should feel some shame for urging a stranger to take me to bed, but all I feel is sated and, well, great.

"Are you alright?" He combs his fingers through my hair and holds me as if I’m precious to him.

I sigh, wishing this moment would never end. "I’m fine."

"I didn’t hurt you?" There’s a hint of panic in his deep voice.

Pressing on his broad chest, I look him in the eye. "No. It was wonderful."

The set of his jaw eases, as does the worry in his eyes. "I thought…" He takes two long breaths. "I’m glad you enjoyed yourself, sweetheart."

He must be mad. I came five times. I don’t think I was

quiet about it. I do love him calling me sweetheart. I sigh again as the knowledge that I'll have to get back to my friends soon sinks in. "I hope you enjoyed it too." My cheeks heat.

Lifting his head, he kisses my forehead. "It was perfect, Kori. You're perfect."

A nervous laugh escapes. "You are the only person who thinks so."

Blinking his golden eyes, he cocks his head and stares for a long moment. "Are you hungry?"

"Starved." And my stomach growls in agreement.

Then he smiles and my lady parts contract just as it did the first time I saw him. He's the most beautiful man I've ever seen. Giving my ass a light tap, he says, "Come on. Your clothes will be dry by now; I'll get the pasta cooked."

The insecure me, which is my normal state, thinks he's ready to do what he promised and be rid of me. At least he's a man of his word. I roll off him and when he gets up, I pull the borrowed robe from the bed and wrap it around myself. "You don't have to feed me. I'm sure you have better things to do with the rest of your day."

He stops buttoning his jeans and stands like a statue, staring at me. Blinking, he shakes his head and kneels next to me. "I have nothing in my life more important than you, Kori."

It's by far the nicest thing anyone has ever said to me and I have no response. I nod and swallow the tears trying to escape with a swarm of emotion.

Standing, he kisses the crown of my head. Then pulls on his shirt and walks out of the bedroom.

Unsure what to do or say, I stare at the hardwood floor and wonder if all of this has been a dream. The delightful soreness between my legs is welcome proof that Drayce is real and I'm not insane.

With an armload of my clothes perfectly folded, he returns and hands them to me. "Do you need anything else?"

I shake my head and a tear escapes.

Before I can dash it away, Drayce catches it on his thumb. His eyes fill with worry. "What's wrong?"

"Nothing."

He leaves no space between us as he continues to wait for the truth.

"People just aren't usually as nice as you. I'm not used to it." I want to tell him everything about myself, but I've been told all my life that no one wants to hear that sad story. First dates are for brief, light information, not deepest, darkest truths. Only this isn't a date. It's a fantasy.

His jaw ticks. "Who would be unkind to you?" Tucking my hair behind my ear, he adds, "You should be worshiped."

More tears get away and I wipe them on my shirt. "The world is full of all kinds of people, Drayce. Here on your mountain, I may seem special, but in the real world, I'm an orphan who was inconvenient. I made my own way in the world and managed to be good at cooking. Without food, I'd be nothing in most people's eyes. As it is, once the meal is done, I'm forgotten by even the patrons who raved about me."

His eyes read like an open book: rage, sorrow, pity, and something I can't identify. "You have your friends."

I smile. "Dean, Meg, and Lori are my family. They don't share blood, but they do share my life's experience. We met in a foster home when we were kids." I have no idea why I told him so much, but he hasn't run away and his eyes haven't glazed over. In fact, he's completely engaged with every word I say.

Cupping my cheek and jaw in his big hand, he presses a soft kiss on my lips. "On this mountain, you are the most important person alive, Kori Devers. That will never change."

Except that in another hour or so, I'll never be on his mountain again. I force a smile. "Thank you." Taking a breath, I hug my clothes against my chest like a shield. "I'll just get dressed and meet you in the kitchen."

After a long look where it feels as if he's reading my mind, he nods and steps away.

A moment later, I'm alone in his bedroom. I head for the bathroom and wash my face with cold water. It's how I keep those darker emotions at bay. It's been working for me all my life. Crying never helps anyone.

I return to our suite in the resort after ten, but as promised, Dean, Meg, and Lori are waiting. I tell them about my afternoon and evening, because I always tell them everything.

They all stare wide-eyed.

Finally, Dean says, "So, this gorgeous man found you in the woods and took care of you. You had sex with him, he fed you, and then he brought you back here. Now you have a date with him for tomorrow night. Did I miss anything?"

"No. That about sums it up." Except that it was the greatest day of my life.

"You're blushing." Meg narrows her gaze. Her black hair is braided and hangs over her shoulder, ending under her breasts, and she toys with the end. "You like this guy. It wasn't just a hook-up or thank-you kind of sex. I mean, he did save you from some kind of bear trap, but you like him."

"He's different." I take a deep breath and push down my feelings. It's ridiculous to have so many strong emotions attached to a man I barely know.

Lori asks, "Is there something you're not telling us?"

"Why would you ask that?" They know me too well, and I have no intention of telling them about the creature I saw or that I passed out when a giant dragon carried me over the trees. These are my best friends and my family, but if I told them that, they'd have me committed. I wouldn't blame them. I was distraught and lost. I imagined the monster.

Narrowing her gaze, Lori stares. "I'm not sure. Is there more?"

I shake my head. "Well, it was the greatest sex of my life and I did come five times."

"Five!" Meg and Dean scream at the same time.

My cheeks are on fire.

"No wonder you agreed to a date." Dean cups his own cheek then runs his finger along the rainbow shape carved into the fade at the side of his head. "I mean, any man who takes the time to give you that much pleasure when he doesn't know you is worth a second look."

"Maybe a third or fourth, if your heart can take it." Meg grips her chest and falls backward on the bed. "Draaayce."

We all dissolve into a round of laughter.

At seven the next night, I walk across the lobby of the Greentree, heading for the sliding double doors. I keep my focus straight ahead. I don't want to make Drayce wait, and I couldn't decide what to wear. I settled on a short white sundress and strappy sandals.

Movement from my left pushes me to walk faster. Someone is about to cross my path and I don't want to wait, so I speed up. My toe catches on the edge of the tile near the door. Before I tumble to the floor, a strong arm bands around my middle and presses me tight to a very large warm body.

Drayce's deep voice whispers in my ear, "Don't hurt yourself, sweetheart. I'm sure whoever you're rushing to will wait. I know I'd wait a lifetime for you."

My heart was already pounding from the near disaster, now it's hard to breathe with him so close and so male. My body is on fire with need. What the fuck is wrong with me? "You're going to have to stop rescuing me."

"Never." There's so much breathtaking truth in that one word; it stuns me to silence.

I get on my feet and face him. In gray trousers and a white button-down, he's almost as sexy dressed as he is naked. Almost. "Hi." So lame.

He releases me but keeps a hand on my waist possessively. "You look beautiful."

"Thank you." Dammit, I'm blushing again. I take deep

breaths. "We should go before my friends show up with twenty questions for you."

His gaze shifts to something behind me, and he grins. "Too late."

I turn and sure enough, here they come, with Lori leading the way in a full power walk.

Panic rises inside me and I face Drayce again. "I'm so sorry."

Running his thumb along my collarbone, he adjusts my spaghetti strap. "Don't worry. I like that they want to protect you, Kori."

It takes an hour to get away from my best friends, but in the end, they all adore Drayce. He charms them with ease and doesn't balk at a single question, not even when Meg demands to know the name of the restaurant where he's taking me. Then Lori tells him that if he doesn't bring me back by midnight, she'll have every cop in the county after him.

When we're walking away, as a final cherry on top of my mortification, Dean calls after us, "I'm expecting a full report on all your orgasms, Kori."

"Oh. My. God." I cover my face and wait at the curb. I figure after that, Drayce will get in his car and drive away, leaving me behind. A knot forms in the center of my chest.

His laughter eases the pressure. He kisses my cheek, just behind my hand. "You tell them everything, I guess."

I peek through my fingers as he opens the passenger door of a large black SUV. "Too much, it would seem."

Standing in the door, his body hovering warm and hard over me, his eyes simmer with promise. "I hope your next report won't disappoint them." His lips cover mine and he makes love to my mouth right there at the front of the resort, with guests, valets, bellhops, and of course, my friends, all watching.

Magically, I don't care that everyone can see. Within seconds, those people are not important. The only thing that matters is Drayce. I thread my fingers through his soft, dark hair and press my tongue against his.

A low growl emanates from his chest and rumbles in his throat. He breaks the kiss. Meeting my hazy gaze, he studies me. "If I don't stop, I'll need to rent us a room at the Greentree for the rest of the night."

"I'm not sure I would mind that." My voice is rough as I catch my breath, taking in the warm pine and wood scent of him.

He kisses my forehead as if I'm some cherished person in his life. "I want all of you. Don't mistake my desire to take you on a real date for not wanting to worship your perfect body. It's only that I want more."

Before I can ask what he means, he steps back and closes the door before rounding the SUV to the driver's side.

Dean, Meg, and Lori gape at me from outside the sliding doors.

"Ready?" Drayce asks.

Gathering what's left of my wits, I pull the seatbelt and clip it in. "Ready."

CHAPTER FIVE

DRAYCE

I shouldn't be nervous. I'm twice Kori's age and will likely live a few hundred years. There's nothing to worry about. Except that our connection is deeper than two people accidentally meeting. I knew from the first scent of her that she was meant for me. That's the beast in me talking. The man knows she could reject me. Once she knows the truth, that's the most likely outcome.

It's after ten when we walk out of Rialto and I take her hand in mine. "I know it's late, but I wonder if you would let me take you back to my house."

She blushes so beautifully. "If you want."

"I have something I need to tell you." There's a hesitation in my voice that reveals my anxious state.

"Oh god. You're married." She pulls her hand from mine and walks down the street away from me.

I jog a few steps to catch her and take her arm gently. "No. I'm not married nor have I ever been."

Her shoulders relax and the strain in her eyes eases. "What is it then?"

"I can't tell you here. It's something you won't believe unless you see proof, and I'm not able to give you that here." I sound like some kind of creep. It would have been smarter to just take her home, make love to her, then show her what I am.

She stares for a long moment.

My wyvern pushes forward, wanting to be seen, but I hold him inside.

Pressing the palm of her hand to my chest, she cocks her head. "Okay. I trust you."

Do I deserve her trust? Maybe not, but I want to deserve her. "Thank you." Taking her hand, I walk us to my SUV and open the door for her.

Driving us up the mountain, I keep her hand in mine on top of her soft thigh. Her short white dress leaves little to my imagination, but I already know what's beneath and long to have her under me again. The only problem is, if I take her, my nature will reveal itself. Knotting only happens when fated mates make love and it nearly took hold yesterday. I was lucky to pull free before she had the opportunity to reject me. As much as I'd love to see our child growing within her, it's not fair until she knows the entire truth.

We reach the driveway to my house and she looks across at me. "You're quiet. Am I not going to like what you have to show me?"

"I don't know." My pulse races as I stop in front of the house.

She holds my hand tighter, keeping me in the vehicle. "I

really like you more than I should in such a short time. I don't want to know anything that will change this rush of happiness I feel when I look at you."

If I could be a human man, right now, I would. I'm about to disappoint the only woman I'll ever feel total perfection with and it's killing me.

Still holding my hand at the edge of her short dress, she uses her other hand to pop open the little buttons running down the front. One by one, they separate, until only the taut peaks of her tits are keeping the fabric from full separation. She arches her back and those spectacular globes push free.

My mouth waters and I lower my head across the console to take the closer one in my mouth. I lap and suck on the tight bud, and she grips my hair and whispers my name.

Easing her hips forward pushes her dress higher until my hand and hers contact her bare wet pussy.

The wyvern roars, and I growl, slipping my fingers between her slick folds.

"Drayce, why does everything you do drive me crazy?" She spreads her knees and grips my upper arm while lifting her hips.

Slowly, I slip a finger inside her and rub my thumb over her tight clit while sucking her nipple.

She pumps against my finger, gasping and moaning as she reaches for her orgasm.

Pleasure I long to give her again and again. I love that she wore no underwear and am glad she didn't reveal the fact until now or we'd never have made it through dinner. Pulling my finger free, I taste her juices and gaze into her starlit eyes. "It's not enough." My voice is rough as I move out of the car and round to the passenger side.

She stares with wide eyes as I practically rip the door off

its hinges to get to her. Lifting her from the seat I gently place her on the hood of the car, throw her legs over my shoulders, and bury my mouth in her sweetness. Another growl escapes at the first taste of her.

Kori leans back and presses her heels into my back, fucking against my mouth.

The beast wants more and I can't deny him a taste. I let my tongue shift to the long fork of the wyvern and slide it deep inside her, teasing places only my tongue can reach.

She grips my hair, pulling me closer and screaming, "Oh. What? Oh."

My wings strain to come into the world, but I hold them inside while I feel the first of her orgasm pulse around me. Shifting back to a human tongue, I suck hard on her clit, and her juices flow on a long keen. I lap up every drop.

The beast has had enough hiding and my wings erupt from my back.

When I look up the length of her body, she has her eyes tightly closed and her fingers still grip my hair. Her white dress is belted around her waist.

Folding my wings against my back, I wrap my arms around her. "Kori, I can't make love to you as I wish until you know what I am."

Slitting her eyes open, she gazes at me, sated, and maybe loving. Or maybe that's what I want to see. "What do you mean?" She sighs. "What was that thing you did with your tongue?" She combs my hair from my face and her hand touches the arch of my wing.

"You saw me in the woods yesterday. You saw what I can become, what I am. I am both a man and a beast. I can shift from an ordinary human," I spread my wings, "to a wyvern. I have to shift every day."

Eyes wide and face white as a sheet, she pushes away and grips her dress as she scrambles down the hood of the SUV. "What is this?"

Too late to turn back, I say, "This is what I am. If we make love, my nature will come out as it tried to yesterday. Wyvern and other monsters knot when they have sex with their true mate. You have to know the truth."

She pulls on her dress, pushing it down at the bottom, and buttons the front crookedly. "What are you? What is knotting?"

I let my eyes shift to catlike slits. "You saw me, Kori. You know what I am."

Putting my truck between us, her chest rises and falls too quickly. "I didn't see anything. It was my muddled, scared, lost mind playing tricks."

"There's nothing wrong with your mind, sweetheart." I shift fast, painfully, and grow to five times the size of a man.

She stares up at me. "I think the keys are still in this thing." She pants and swallows. "I'm just going to drive myself back and you can do whatever."

My heart hurts as if it's being ripped from my chest. A roar breaks free.

Holding her ears, she crouches behind the vehicle.

I shift back to a man and shake off the change. "I can drive you back."

"No. I. I'm sorry. I'm sure that whatever you are is fine. I'm. It's. I'm not wise enough to know what this is between us. I can't..." She shakes her head. "My life has had enough drama. This," she gestures to me, "is too much."

"I'm a man and I'm in love with you. Nothing, not even you rejecting me, will change that, Kori." She should know the truth, and I pray it's enough to keep her from running away.

She opens the SUV door. "Don't say that. You can't love me. I have a job in the city and a weird little life where nothing interesting ever happens. It's enough. I'm sorry."

I want to stop her and tell her that everything is going to be alright. I long to comfort her, but she's terrified of me.

As she drives away, I shift and fly overhead to make sure she gets back to the resort safely. When she parks in the long lot to the west of the main door, I land and shift under the cover of the trees. Stepping into the light of the streetlamps, I say, "Please, Kori. I just want to say a few things before you run out of my life forever. Please."

Tears streaming down her face and makeup smeared in rivulets of black, she stops and lowers her gaze to the pavement. "I can't stay with you. Even if that was what I wanted."

Now I know what heartbreak really feels like. I suppose I never thought it would feel so literal, but my chest is on fire and so tight, it might explode. "I understand. This is a shock. I'm not human and you have other notions about what the man you'll love will be. We only met yesterday, and all of this is too much too fast."

"I'm sorry," she says for the third time.

"Please stop apologizing. None of this is your fault. I'm long past the year when my mate should have crossed my path. I thought it would never happen to me. I thought the nymph would suffice for a life partner. Nothing prepared me for you. I should have found a way to give you more time. Yesterday when we made love, the knotting almost happened and then it would have been harder to turn back. I had to show you what I am, but now you're afraid of me." My guts are in pieces. How do people survive this? "My mother tried to tell me long ago that when a monster meets his or her mate, it's like lightning come to life and striking a million times. I thought she was being dramatic. "It is me who should apologize. I didn't do any of this right. I hope you'll remember some parts of the last two days as happy memories. I know that I will always hold you in my heart, Kori."

Turning, I walk into the shadow of the woods.

Her soft crying is the last thing I hear before shifting and flying into the night sky. Once I see her hunched form enter the building, I head for my mountain.

CHAPTER SIX

KORI

*I*t's been a week since my life turned upside down. I go to work and stay past my shift. I come home so exhausted that I pass out on my couch so I don't have to think about Drayce. It's supposed to be my day off, but I can't risk the thinking time, so I walk into the restaurant.

Walley rounds the bar. He's a burly man of six feet with a heart of gold. It's rare for anyone in the New York restaurant business to continue to be kind when the world we live in is so cutthroat. He waves his hands at me and points toward the door. "No. Go home, Kori."

"I'm fine, Walley. I can help Lydia with prep for tonight." I don't like the whine creeping into my voice.

He puts a hand on each of my shoulders and looks me in the eye. "I don't know what happened while you were on vacation, but I'm here if you want to talk about it. Otherwise, you need to get out of here. You can't work doubles every day and then come in on your day off."

What would I tell him? I fell in love with a gorgeous man who seemed to adore me, but he turned out to be a wyvern shifter who thinks I'm his true mate. Um no. I can't say that to anyone. They'd throw me in Bellevue faster than I can say wyvern.

"Just let me work a few hours, please."

"What happened upstate?" His eyes are full of sympathy. "Did you fight with one of those friends of yours?"

"No. I'm fine," I lie, but I tell myself, it's only half a lie.

He nods and draws his lips into a thin line. He's not buying it. "Good. Go home or go out, but you cannot work today or tomorrow and if you keep showing up when it's not your shift, I'm going to make you take another week off."

"Ugh, why are you doing this to me?" I turn and head for the door.

"Yes, I'm the worst." He laughs.

Going back, I give the greatest boss in the world a hug.

"If you won't tell me who did this to you, go find your friend Dean and talk to him. You can't keep things all bottled up like this." He walks me to the door and shows me out.

Dean will think I'm crazy. I walk the fifteen blocks to Meg's apartment. She lives with her boyfriend, Hunter, but he's a bartender and won't be home.

The doorman knows me and waves. "Hey, Kori. How are you?"

"Fine, Nate. How about you?" I head for the elevator.

"No point complaining." He tips his black cap and answers the phone on his standing desk.

At Meg's door, I freeze. I'm about to head back to the

elevator when Meg pulls the door open. "What are you doing? Nate called me a few minutes ago."

Of course, he did. "I was deciding if I want to knock."

"What did you decide?" She crosses her arms and cocks her head. Her pigtails swing from side to side.

I walk past her into her apartment. It's a one-bedroom in a nice neighborhood. Meg makes great money as a fashion coordinator for one of the big houses. Between that and Hunter's tips from a fancy bar, they do alright. Flopping on her black leather couch, I say, "If I tell you something totally crazy, will you promise to have an open mind and not have me committed?"

She sits next to me with her legs crossed under her. "Is this about hunky Drayce who kissed you like you were the only woman he'd ever kiss again?"

"Yes." Why did she have to remind me about the kissing? Not that I need reminding. It's like he branded me with his lips. If I close my eyes, I can almost feel his lips on mine.

"Talk. No promises about the asylum, but I'll keep an open mind." She smiles and waits.

"He's a dragon. Well, a wyvern. I guess there's a difference."

"Wyverns don't have front legs, just wings. Most dragons breathe fire while wyverns often have venomous spikes on their tails." She says it as if these are just facts and I didn't just tell her Drayce is a monster.

"Did you even hear me?" I speak clearly and a little louder. "The man you met and I had fabulous sex with can change into a monster and fly through the air. He says I'm his fated mate and he couldn't have sex with me after our date because of something called knotting. I looked it up and that means—"

"I know what knotting is. I heard you." She smiles.

Sirens sound in the street and for a moment, I wonder if Meg has some secret button she just pushed to have Bellevue Hospital come and carry me away. "Why are you so calm about it? I totally freaked out. Why do you even believe me?"

She leans back on the couch. "When I was young, my parents and I went to that resort where we stayed last week. I was out playing by the lake and fell in. I couldn't swim yet, and I was drowning. Mom and Dad didn't swim either. They stood on the bank screaming for help. Dad jumped in, and he nearly drowned too."

"What happened?" I can't believe in all these years, she never mentioned she'd nearly drowned. I guess I shouldn't be surprised, she never talks about her parents even though of the four of us, she's the only one who can remember hers clearly.

"The most beautiful woman I've ever seen swam toward me and brought me to where I could stand. Then she saved my dad too. It was like she was something out of a book with her long, flowing blond hair and perfect body. She was naked save for a sheer gown. I go back and try to find her almost every year since we aged out of foster care."

"Why didn't you ever tell me this?" I thought I knew everything about Meg, Lori, and Dean.

She shrugs. "You might have brushed it off and I know what I saw. I was only four and my parents died the next year. I don't tell anyone, but it's why I always go back to those woods and the lake."

"Have you ever seen her again?"

"No. But I swear I feel her watching me when I swim in that lake and sometimes when I walk in the woods. I always feel safe knowing she's out there." Recrossing her legs, she faces me again. "Do you think Drayce is your destiny?"

My eyes prickle with tears. "I don't know, but I miss him. I feel bad for being afraid of him. He was so beautiful as a wyvern."

"And pretty spectacular as a man." Meg wiggles her eyebrows.

"He told me there are a lot of monsters living in the woods up there. I just wasn't paying attention to all the details of what he said. I was so smitten by how he made me feel. This last week, when I let myself think about those two days, bits of things he said come rushing back and make so much sense. He's a creature I can't even fathom."

"You didn't answer the question. Do you think he's your destiny, Kori? Will you be happy for the rest of your life if you never see him again?" Meg's stare is intense.

Will I? Even the idea of never seeing him again makes my stomach grip and my chest ache. "I've never believed in fate or destiny, Meg. Suddenly, I think my life is intertwined with Drayce's, and I'm miserable with how I ran away."

"I can have you in the Catskills in three hours, Kori. Just say the word." She smiles softly, and her already pretty face transforms into beautiful.

"So, I just drive up to his house and apologize for being terrified of him even though I'm still a little scared about what he can turn into, and I didn't even know about the venomous spikes." It's impossible. He'll never forgive me.

"How did you find him the first time? Because I'm betting it wasn't that he found you lost in the woods." She narrows her gaze and crosses her arms.

I tell her about being lost and getting caught up in his net. "When I was still lost, he followed, and when I fell, he carried me. I passed out and when I woke up, he was very naked and very male. We were in his beautiful cabin."

"We can leave first thing in the morning." She picks up her phone and dials.

"Who are you calling?" My excitement and relief are growing.

"Dean and Lori. I guess I should call Hunter too." Ten minutes later, we have a plan and I'm heading to my apartment to pack a bag.

$\mathcal{D}$ean called his boss and told him he had a family emergency. Lori couldn't get away, but she demanded to be videoed in.

Somehow, I figure out how to return to the place where the trap was. Now that I know it's there the net's ropes are obvious. I'm out of my mind, but I need to bring the beast to me. I know the man might be angry, but the wyvern only knows it wants me. The last time we were intimate, the need of the monster to push forward showed me that.

"Are you sure about this, Kori?" Dean grips his throat and looks at the tall trees in a wilderness a couple of miles from the road. "What if he doesn't show up? How will we get you down?"

I take a deep breath and step forward just outside the trap. "This is either the bravest or the stupidest thing I've ever done. When the trap snaps, we'll give Drayce thirty minutes to come and get me. If he doesn't, then we call 911 and I feel incredibly stupid." My voice breaks at the idea that he might not come. I may have hurt him too badly to gain forgiveness.

Meg says, "He'll come. I know he will."

Somehow, I know it too. There's a sound or a vibration inside me that came alive when I stepped back inside his woods. I take the step.

Everything turns upside down. I fly upward and am wrapped in the giant net that curls me into the air and leaves me swaying back and forth twenty feet off the ground. A scream escapes me even though I knew what was going to happen.

Dean and Meg both scream.

Recovering first, Meg says, "Holy fuck, are you alright?"

After a brief assessment, I say, "I'm fine."

"Now what?" Dean asks.

"I wait." I listen for some change in the forest. Last time, it seemed as if the world stilled when the wyvern appeared. There's no noise, but I feel him getting closer. My heart, my blood, and my flesh all tingle with his approach. "You guys can go. I'll be fine."

Dean makes a scoffing sound. "We're not going anywhere until you're either on the ground or we have proof you'll be okay."

The batting of wings through breaking the air fills me with joy. And then he lands in the tree just above me. His golden eyes are wide as he stares from his perch on a tree limb.

"Holy crap." Dean's voice is high and squeaky.

Drayce shifts his gaze to the ground.

I look down through the gap in the net. Dean clutches Meg's arm and the two gape up at the wyvern.

Drayce cranes his neck and cocks his head before returning his attention to me.

"I'm sorry," I say. My heart is pounding so hard that it takes me a few moments to calm enough to say more. "I shouldn't have freaked out and left you. I understand if you don't want me back, but you're all I can think about and I don't mind you being a bit more than human."

"A bit." Meg's voice drips with sarcasm.

The wyvern's pupils widen and warmth seeps in as if he were a man. He wraps one foot around the net and slices the rope with his other claws before easing me to the ground a few feet in front of my friends.

I guess I thought he'd carry me away, but maybe he wants me to go. My heart breaks into a million pieces.

CHAPTER SEVEN

DRAYCE

Kori is back in my woods. I never thought I'd see her again, and I've been mourning her loss for a week. I cut her down and give her the opportunity to leave. If she came to apologize, she's done that.

As a man, I can shift partially but once I'm a wyvern, it's all or nothing. I can't speak as my beast and if I shift, I'll be naked. With her friends staring at me as if they don't know if they should run or stay to protect Kori, I'm at a loss for how to best communicate.

She pushes the net aside and stands facing me. "Do you want me to go?"

I watch her and wait. I want to snatch her up and fly home with my mate. I long to never let her go, but that has to be her decision.

Stepping closer to me, she touches my wing.

Even the innocent touch fills me with a dangerous amount of hope.

"He's beautiful," Dean says. And holds his phone where Lori looks on from somewhere with a lot of noise in the background.

"What the…" Lori's voice trails off.

Kori caresses her way along the bottom of my wing. "I know you're angry with me. I don't blame you."

Angry is the last thing I am. I've never been happier to see anyone in my life. I'm stunned and confused and want to ask her how long she'll stay.

"Go home, guys. I'm going with Drayce." She presses her palm to my foot.

Turning it so that my claws face up, my heart soars when she steps into my wide paw. I ease my claws together, careful not to harm her while securing her within my grasp.

Meg says, "We'll be at Greentree. Call if you need us."

"Oh my god," Dean says.

"What's happening?" Lori shouts from the phone.

I flap my wings until we're above the trees, and fly low with the object of my every need and desire safely in my claws. I've never wanted to shift into a human more than I do right now. I have questions and even the beast wants me to rein him in. That's a first.

Landing on one foot in my yard, I open my other foot and wait until Kori steps a few feet away. Keeping my eyes focused on her wild hair and wide blue eyes, pain rips through me and I reform as a man.

"My god, does that hurt?" She rushes forward but stops a foot away.

"Yes. Did you just come to say you're sorry?" I don't know if I can take it if she's only staying a few days and leaves me again. I'm not strong enough to turn her away even for a moment, though.

She blinks. "I did owe you the apology."

"No. You didn't and don't owe me anything, Kori. You knew me for thirty-six hours, and I terrified you with what I am and how we're connected. I should have given you time." My fingers itch to touch her, but I keep them balled at my sides.

"It's kind of you to look at it that way. I've been miserable ever since I left. I never should have gone." She inches closer and presses her hand to the center of my chest.

My cock jumps to attention with a mind of its own and no idea that the conversation is vital. The wyvern only cares that our mate is touching us and we need her.

Keeping my focus on her beautiful face, I press my hand over hers. "How long can you stay?" The question of a desperate man.

She cups my cheek. Her expression is raw and vulnerable. "How long will you want me?"

I pull her into my arms. "I will want you until the end of time, sweetheart. I love you with all my being. You're my mate and nothing will change that."

She wraps her arms and legs around me and holds on with all her might. "It's impossible to love someone you barely know, but I missed you so much. I know I love you too."

The world stops and it's only Kori and me. Her body wrapped around me and my aching cock pressed between us. I want to stay in this moment, but the beast within me pushes from inside. *Mate.*

Drawing a deep breath, I kiss the shell of her ear. "Can I take you inside?"

A tiny gasp pushes from her full lips. She grinds her hips against me. "Inside or to bed?"

Fuck, I could come standing here with her fully clothed. "Whatever you want, sweetheart."

"I want you inside me. I want everything that you and the wyvern need from me. No holding back. My body yearns for it all." Using my shoulders for leverage, she rubs up and down.

Rushing into the house, I practically crash the door down, forcing it to slam open and then kicking it closed before heading to the bedroom. I lay her on the bed. "There are things I need to explain first."

She strips off her shirt and blushes. "I looked up knotting. I mean all the references are fictional or about animals, but I think I get the idea."

Gripping her heel, I pull her sneaker off and then the other. "Then you know the basics, though I'm told there's a lot of pleasure in wyvern knotting."

Unbuttoning her jeans, she pushes them down her hips. "You've never knotted with anyone?"

It's not easy to look at her naked body and keep the beast in me under control. "No, sweetheart. Knotting only happens between mates."

KORI

I love the idea that this one thing will be just for us, even if the idea of knotting seems foreign and like science fiction. Still, I'm already wet and needy for him. My breasts ache for his touch, and I yearn to have him inside me. "And you're sure I'm your mate?"

Leaning over me, he holds his weight on his hands. "I've known from the first scent that you were mine. Don't you feel the connection?"

I cup his cheek, needing some contact, and get a little frustrated that he's keeping himself on his straining arms. "I have missed you. The longer I was away, the more my mind was unsettled and my body yearned for your touch."

A low growl rumbles in his throat and he lowers his head to the crook of my neck, breathing me in. "Yes. It was devastating to think I would never see you again."

Aching with need, I wrap my legs around his hips and pull him down to me. "I need you, but there was something you said." Maybe I heard wrong. "Are you going to bite me?" It sounds crazy and painful. Also, I want that bite. I'm losing my mind.

Another growl and he licks a path from my collarbone to my ear. "If you let me, I will mark you as mine."

A desperate squeak escapes me as he licks the shell of my ear. I'm burning from the inside out. "I want everything, Drayce. I need it all." I tighten my grip on his hips and rub my dripping pussy along his thick cock.

On a deep moan, he pulls out of my embrace and kisses a path down my chest before sucking my nipple.

I cry his name and fight to catch my breath. "Where will you bite me?"

He lets me pop from his lips and braces his weight on one arm, then caresses the curve from my shoulder to my neck with his thumb. "Here, sweetheart, but not yet."

I'm about to complain that he's taking too long. I need him, but then he kneels on the floor and drags me down the mattress until my thighs cradle his head and his mouth is buried in my sex.

Thoughts and worries fly from my head as I'm inundated with pure pleasure. His tongue slips deep inside me and touches places no human tongue could reach. My body tightens, and I lift my hips, reveling in him fucking me with his mouth while gripping my hips to keep me in place.

I wrap my legs around his back and rock forward with every thrust. "Drayce. Oh, god. I can't hold off."

His tongue slips out of me, and he sucks my clit hard, pushing me over the edge as pure pleasure explodes inside me. I scream and clutch him tighter while he gently licks and teases my pussy.

I scramble back on the bed and turn to my hands and knees. Lifting my ass high, I spread my knees and lower my chest to the mattress. "Please, Drayce."

"You're everything, mate." His voice is lower and the growl of the monster is prominent. Kneeling behind me, he grips my hips. His cock notched at my entrance, he whispers my name and presses inside me with one slow, steady thrust.

Flames ignite inside me. "So good. I. You." I rock forward and back and lift my ass higher to take more of his magnificent shaft. I tremble as waves of pleasure rock me.

Drayce slides out, then presses in, moaning and growling with sounds that are more animal than man. Every sound sends my pleasure higher. Every grunt is an aphrodisiac. He slips his hand around and presses his fingers between my folds teasing my clit and spiraling me into a second orgasm.

Screaming, I jerk forward and back as the pleasure cascades and swamps me. My body quivers around his thick cock. Sweat drips down the center of my back and my skin is so sensitive, even that adds to the erotic moment.

Perfectly still, Drayce asks, "Are you alright, sweetheart?"

I rock forward and back. "So good. I need all of you. I'm on fire, Drayce."

As if it was the permission he needed, he rears back and slams into me again and again.

I meet each thrust, backing into him and reveling in the fullness and sensuality of our bodies perfectly connected.

The wyvern roars and he pulls free of me. Gripping my waist he turns me onto my back and pushes my legs apart before filling me again.

Bending my knees, I tip my pelvis to take more of his enormous shaft and scream as the beginning of another orgasm vibrates inside me. Each thrust rubs against my already super-sensitive clit. "Oh. Yes. I'm so close."

Harder and faster, he fills me. His mouth captures mine and he makes love to my lips and tongue in time with how his cock fills my pussy.

My body erupts with pleasure, and I break the kiss, my screams filling the room.

Something shifts inside me as Drayce howls and fills me with warm seed. His shaft grows, tightening the connection, and it's as if there are barbs latching into the soft tissue of my sheath. I come again immediately.

Lowering his head to the crook of my neck, I catch a glimpse of long pointed teeth before he sinks them into my flesh.

I come again and again. Screaming and calling his name, one orgasm rolls into the next and I can't catch my breath before more rapture takes me. "Oh, god."

Laving the spot where he bit me, Drayce growls against my throat and rolls us to our sides. "I'm sorry. I should have been gentler."

Still locked together, I ease one leg over his and clutch his neck. A wave of pleasure assaults me. "No. It's perfect, my wyvern. So good."

He kisses my cheek and combs my hair from my face. "You're perfect. Nothing can ever compare to this, here, with you." He jerks forward and comes again.

As his cum fills me, another orgasm rocks me. I hold onto him tighter and moan against his neck. "How long does this last? I mean, I'm not complaining. It's only, how much pleasure can one woman take?"

Adjusting to bring me closer causes him to come again and I go with him, rolling immediately into another. He roars. "I don't know." He sounds pained. "I'll try not to move. Maybe if we're still we can ease apart. I'm sorry, my love."

He's worried about me being uncomfortable. He thinks I'm unhappy. Pushing on his chest, I roll him to his back and straddle him. Pleasure swamps me. "Don't you dare apologize or think I'm not loving this." The knot is too tight to rise, but I can move my hips forward and back.

His seed fills me, and he growls and swells inside me.

"This is meant to be enjoyed, my monster." Another wave and I scream before collapsing on his chest with his arms wrapped around me.

CHAPTER EIGHT

DRAYCE

Thirty minutes later, the knot releases and neither one of us can move as exhaustion takes over. Sleeping with Kori in my arms is the second most wonderful feeling in my life. I never dreamed I would find a mate, and then when I did, I was sure she would choose her life in the city over the bucolic Catskills.

My brain has not caught up with my heart as I think about how she chose to come back on her own. After she left, I thought of running after her. A dozen times, I dreamed of searching New York City or showing up at her work. Each time, I decided to remain in my woods and let her live a normal life without me.

"Are you hungry?" I kiss her soft hair.

"No. I'm happy." She sighs and snuggles against me.

A wave of warmth flows over and through me. "I'm not sure one thing has anything to do with the other." I draw her into my arms and carry her into the living room. "I'll fix us a snack."

Heading for the kitchen, she follows and opens my tall cabinet pantry doors. She scans, then closes it. She skirts past me and looks in the refrigerator and then the freezer. "Do you have white wine?"

"I do." I study her. "What are we making?"

Her smile makes my heart beat faster. Taking a package of chicken thighs from the fridge, she puts them on the counter before grabbing an onion, garlic, and canned white beans from the pantry. Gathering some other ingredients, she adds herbs and frozen spinach with the rest. "Tuscan chicken and white beans."

"Sounds wonderful. What can I do?" I admire how she lines all the ingredients up and searches through my cupboards for her other needs. She finds a Dutch oven and knives.

Shaking her head at my knives, she continues familiarizing herself with my kitchen. "You can bring me a bottle of white wine and then chop up some garlic if you want."

Doing as I'm told, I mostly admire seeing her in her element as she cooks for us. Once the chicken is browned, she turns on my oven, then starts cooking onions and garlic.

Every once in a while, she smiles at me. "You're staring."

"I love watching you cook. I had no idea how beautiful you'd be doing what you love." I'm completely smitten, and it's not like anything I've ever felt before. Kori is everything.

Once she has seasoned all the ingredients, she layers it all back in the pot, then puts the whole thing in the oven.

I clean the dishes she's made so far and wipe down the counters while she pulls dishes from the cabinet.

"I wonder if Rialto needs a chef." She leans on the counter next to the sink.

Drying my hands, I hold my breath, wondering if I heard her correctly. "You would stay here?"

Her grin is wide. "Forgive me Drayce, but I can't picture you living in the city. I think someone might notice a wyvern flying over Manhattan."

"No. I would be uncomfortable in a city." I'm understating the issue. I have to shift or the beast in me will go mad. "I would be very happy if you would stay here."

She blushes and leans against my arm, which I wrap around her waist. "I'm happy and I'm not sure I've ever said that before in my life." She looks at me with wide surprised eyes.

Capturing her lips, I kiss her until we're both breathless.

"I could get an apartment in town if you want. I don't want to assume…"

Before she can work herself into a fret-fest, I kiss her nose. "I would love it if you would stay here with me."

"I would love that too. I packed a bag, but it's with Dean and Meg. I'll have to get the rest of my things from my apartment at some point. I can break my lease and quit my job in a few days."

"After we eat, I'll take you to the resort and we'll get your bag. I can drive you to the city for the rest." I love that we're talking about her staying here permanently.

I put the last dish from the most delicious meal I've ever eaten into the dishwasher as the doorbell rings.

Kori's eyes widen. "Are you expecting someone?"

"No." It's rare for anyone to drop by since I live so far up the mountain." I fold the towel over the handle and walk to the door.

"Hi, Drayce. I think we should talk." Astra is wearing jeans and a green blouse. I've never seen her in clothes before. Nymphs generally wear sheer dresses or nothing at all. Still, her allure is just as present as ever, though I don't feel compelled to her the way I always have in the past.

A few months ago, I was prepared to help her run away and before that, I would have told anyone that I loved Astra, though she isn't my mate. I wanted her, that much is true. "Astra, I… Why are you here?"

"May I come in?" She steps closer.

I back up to give her room.

Kori gapes from a few feet away.

"Hello," Astra says. "I'm sorry. I didn't know you had company." She smiles.

Kori blinks and offers her hand. "I'm Kori."

"Astra. I'll be Astra Barbaros soon. I'm sorry to barge in. I wanted to speak to Drayce." She looks at me. "Should I come back at another time?"

I'm about to say yes, when Kori says, "Not at all. We've just finished lunch. You two can talk and I'll take a little walk."

"You don't have to leave." I don't know why I say it, because it would probably be better if she didn't hear whatever Astra is going to say, but the thought of her walking out the door fills me with dread.

Kori's smile is magical. "I won't go far."

Astra cocks her head and looks from Kori to me, then smiles. "I'll only be five minutes."

As Kori slides into her shoes and steps outside, my heart clenches. When I look at Astra, my gut turns in knots. What had I ever seen in her? I mean, she's beautiful. No one can dispute that, but there's no comparison to the love of a true mate. I blurt out, "I'm sorry."

Her musical laugh fills the room. "That's why I'm here. I wanted to apologize for sending the bird rather than coming myself to tell you I couldn't run away with you."

"Thanks for that." Somehow, it hardly matters anymore. I don't know what else to say.

It would seem Astra feels awkward too, as she is silent and stuffs her hands in her pockets. She looks at the door. "Kori is your mate?"

"Yes." I'm embarrassed by my past behavior and ashamed that I let Kori walk out of the house in favor of privacy with Astra.

"And you're happy?" she asks.

"I am. Are you happy with the satyr?" How had I ever believed I was in love with her? I was a stupid, lonely fool.

She blushes. That's a sight I never thought I'd see. By nature, a nymph is a seductress. All those who look upon her fall under her spell, yet at the mention of Niko, she turns bright red. "I'm happier than I ever dreamed I could be. Niko is my true mate. I'm sorry I lured you into an escape plan. I knew you were smitten, and I used that to get away from my father's heavy-handed behavior. He was going to marry me off to someone I'd never met. I wanted control of my life, but it should never have been at your expense. Can you forgive me?"

"If you'd asked me that two weeks ago, I would have never forgiven you. Now, it hardly matters. I appreciate you coming here, and I accept your apology." A heavy burden lifts from my shoulders as I put the past behind me and look forward to a long, wonderful future with Kori.

Smiling, I walk Astra to the door and open it.

She stands on the threshold and looks back at me. "No more traps in the woods?"

I shake my head.

Kori steps to the doorway from the right holding a bunch of wildflowers. Her eyes are wide and full of horror. "That trap was for her? You were trying to catch a woman, or whatever she is?"

"Oh gods," Astra says.

"Kori." I brush past Astra and hold out my hand to Kori, desperate to explain.

Dropping the flowers, she backs down the steps and searches for a way down the mountain.

"I set that trap before I knew you existed, and it wasn't what you think." I have no idea how to explain the stupidity of why I wanted to humiliate Astra and Niko without making matters worse.

Stopping, Kori brushes tears from her cheeks. "You reset that trap after we met." She runs down the drive. "I'm such a fool. I thought it was an animal trap."

Heart pounding and wishing I'd told her some or all of this before Astra turned up, I run after Kori.

The steep downslope gets the best of her and she tumbles to her knees and sits with her face in her hands. "I'm an idiot. I should have known all of this was a mistake. Men don't fall head over heels in love with me. That woman in your house is the kind of woman men fall for."

Kneeling in front of her, I take her hands in mine. "I should have told you about Astra. I'm sorry. She stopped being important the moment I first saw you."

"But you reset the trap. Explain to me why you set a trap for a woman who's engaged to someone else." The pain etched on her face wrecks me.

So that she's not on the hard ground, I sit and pull her into my lap. "This is going to sound pathetic, but I'm going to tell you everything, then I'll take you to the resort. It's too far to walk and your sense of direction isn't your strong suit."

She scoffs. "That's kindly put. Tell me."

I take a deep breath and let it out. If she's going to leave me, it should be for the truth, not the small bit she overheard and speculation. "Astra is a nymph. She's beautiful and alluring because that's her nature. Like most nymphs, she's part of the nature around her. She can become part of the trees and ground, lakes and rivers. Also, like other nymphs, she can seduce all who look upon her."

"And she seduced you?" Her voice aches with desperation for that to be the case.

"No. Astra never seduced me, but she was always kind to me. I lived in these woods all my life and had long passed the age when I should have found my mate. I was lonely and she was alluring, even without intention. I pursued her for many years to no avail.

"A month ago, her father arranged a marriage for her to a satyr from Canada. It was her desire to avoid the match that drove her to come to me and ask me to fly her away from here." If I had the power to turn back time, I would live the last few years differently. I would trust that my mate would find me.

"Why did her father want her to marry against her will?" Wide-eyed, Kori is genuinely concerned for Astra.

I love how empathetic she is. Brushing her hair behind her ear, I want to kiss away all her concerns, but I continue my embarrassing story. "Her father is a bully and has the power to force others to his will. Astra came to me to take her away, and I readily agreed. I hoped I would gain a life partner and banish the never-ending loneliness of my life.

"On the day of our clandestine escape, she didn't come to the designated meeting place. I waited a long time. Finally, an owl came and delivered the message that she wasn't coming."

Kori blinks and raises her eyebrows. "I have so many questions about the owl, but maybe that's beside the point. You were hurt that she didn't come and sent only the bird."

Was I hurt? No. "I was angry and my pride was injured. So much so, that I set that trap to humiliate Astra and her mate, as I felt I had been humiliated."

CHAPTER NINE

KORI

Despite everything, sitting in his lap, leaning against his chest, is heaven. Damn, I'm one of those hopelessly in love women I always made fun of. I should be stronger than this. I should push him away and go home. But I let him hold me and relax into his embrace. "I guess I understand being angry and hurt, but why did you reset the trap?"

He lets out a long breath and his shoulders slump. "I'm not sure. You were sleeping and not available to know more about. I left you on my couch where you were safe. It felt, at the time, like a normal thing to do. I flew back to the site and reset my trap. It took only a few minutes and I rushed home before you woke up. As for why I left it set up afterward, I only know that it felt as if I should, and now I think that was for you, for us."

"Even if that's true, it doesn't change your original intent.

You loved her but you wanted to hurt her. That hadn't changed by finding me." I stand and wipe my damp cheeks. I shouldn't feel so betrayed, but my emotions are in knots. He loved someone else just a couple of weeks ago. He wanted to hurt the person he loved. Huge red flag. I need to get away from here.

Facing me, he waits until I meet his gaze. "I never loved Astra. Maybe I thought I did, but I didn't understand what love was until you crashed into my life. I wanted her because I was lonely, and when she backed out of our arrangement, I thought I would be alone forever. There is no excuse, but that is the truth."

"How do I believe you? How do I know you won't get angry with me next week and try to hurt me? You were about to run away with Astra and now you say you don't love her." I grip the sides of my head and close my eyes. I need to think clearly. I can't do that with him so close. His proximity affects my mind and my heart, not to mention my body wants him, even when I'm angry. None of this makes sense. I walk away toward the main road.

"Where are you going?" His voice is rough and full of pain.

My gut aches and my chest tightens. Tears spill down my cheeks. I have to pull myself together and figure out how to get down this mountain. "Away from you, for now, Drayce. I need to think."

The rumble of a vehicle forces me to move to the side of the drive. I wipe my face and pull my shoulders back. No man or monster or wyvern is going to wreck me like this. I should have known he was too good to be true.

Astra pulls her big pickup truck to a stop next to me and rolls down the window. "This is my fault, Kori. Drayce didn't do anything wrong. I led him to believe there could be more between us so that I could get away from my father."

"He told me," I manage to squeak out. I can see why he wanted her. It's hard to look away from her beautiful face; everything about her is alluring. I want to run away, but I stop and stare into the truck. The mythology about nymphs is somewhere in my brain, but I can't conjure it. I should have read more of the Greek classics.

She looks back at Drayce, standing with his head bowed in the spot where I left him. Returning her gaze to me, she sighs. "I want to make this right. Tell me how I can fix this."

"Can you give me a ride?" If I don't get away from here soon, I'm going to have a complete meltdown and then I won't be able to do what I must. It's already unlikely I'll find my way to civilization on my own, if I'm bawling my eyes out, I'll end up lost and dehydrated.

She nods. "I think you'd be better off staying, but I'll take you wherever you want to go."

I hop into the truck and pull on the seatbelt without looking back at Drayce. It's the hardest thing I've ever done. His eyes are on me. I can feel them, like a lifeline holding me. Even as we drive out of sight, I still feel the tug of him.

While I cry my eyes out, Astra drives me away from the only man I can ever love.

She turns on to the main road and, after a while, pulls off into a scenic view rest stop. "Where can I take you, Kori?"

Gulping for air, I don't know what to tell her. I could go to the resort where my friends are, but I can't bear to tell them it all fell apart. Seeing the pity in their faces would be too much and too familiar. Nothing ever goes the way I hope. Maybe a rental car place, if there's one in town, I could drive myself back to the city and pick up my life. More tears and gasps for air burst out of me.

I have no idea how long we sit in the overlook parking area while I sob, but Astra waits until my weeping dwindles to hiccups.

"I didn't learn to drive until recently. My mate taught me. I never wore real clothes either. I ran around my woods in nymph clothes that were sheer and magical, and talked to my trees and the water in the lakes and rivers. I spent my days frolicking. Many times, in years past, I would seduce humans who wandered off the path. It's my nature as a nymph to attract the creatures around me. I give them pleasure and that makes me feel worthwhile. It's a fair exchange." She sighs.

"A few years ago, that pattern began to feel empty and lonely. I still loved my mountains and all that thrives here, but seducing strangers had lost its appeal. I longed for something more, though I didn't know what that was. So, I stopped seducing, but the loneliness didn't go away. It became worse."

"Is that why you wanted to run away with Drayce?" I'm not jealous. It's hard to feel anything but sad at the moment.

Her luscious blond hair shifts with the shaking of her head. "No. I knew that Drayce was not the man who could assuage my emptiness. I needed an escape, and I knew he would rescue me. He's a wyvern, which is a kind of dragon. Though, don't tell him I made the comparison. Dragons like shiny things, the more rare, the more they want it. Drayce might not consciously realize it, but I think that due to his nature, I was something to be coveted and kept. Once he saved me, he wouldn't let anything harm me. That offered me a bit of safety. My father was forcing me to marry someone I'd never met or even seen."

"But it turned out the man, um... monster your father picked is your mate, right?" This world I've stumbled into is very confusing.

There's no mystery in Astra's smile though. Whatever a satyr is, she loves him. "Niko is my mate and when you meet your true mate, it's difficult to deny him. The allure of being near them is so strong that pulling away can be painful. Still, I don't want to be anywhere else but with my satyr. He and I were destined to find each other, with or without my father's interference. Though, that did complicate things."

My heart already aches for Drayce, so I know what she means. "But if I wanted to stay away, this feeling would subside, wouldn't it?"

"I don't know. Maybe after a while, if that's really what you want." She draws a deep breath. "I'm going to take you to my house. Niko will cook us some dinner and you will have all the time you need to think about what you want."

I nod in agreement. Partly because I want to meet a satyr, and partly because it's hard to deny this captivating woman anything. As we drive farther away from my monster, the ache inside me grows tighter and tighter. "Your boyfriend cooks?"

She grins wide. "He's a chef. He writes cookbooks. Maybe you've heard of him? His name is Niko Barbaros."

"Niko Barbaros lives here? Wait, Chef Barbaros is a satyr?" My mind reels at the idea. The guy has written some of my favorite cookbooks. He's a genius at mixing cooking styles and flavors.

Her laughter is perfectly harmonious. "Yes, to both." She pulls off the road and up another hilly driveway to a beautiful house. A man with broad shoulders, a chiseled face, and horns scrolling back from above his brows waits on the porch. His bottom half is covered in hair and his legs are bent like a horse's rear legs, or some other animal. He's terrifying and beautiful. I can see why Astra and he make a good match.

He rushes to the truck and opens her door. "Everything alright?" He kisses her softly on the mouth.

"We have a guest. I made a bit of a mess of things for Drayce, and this is Kori, his mate." She sighs. "She's going to stay with us until she decides what she wants to do."

Niko looks from her to me. He gives me a crooked smile. "I have a beef Wellington planned for dinner. I hope you eat meat, Kori?"

I'm almost too sad to recognize that Niko Barbaros is going to cook for me, and beef Wellington to boot. "I'm not very hungry, but I'm honored to eat at your table, chef."

He cocks his head. "Come inside and tell us about yourself, Kori."

CHAPTER TEN

KORI

After dinner, we sit on the porch and talk about cooking. I make it through an hour of a chat which should have been thrilling before sorrow and exhaustion take over.

Astra shows me to a very pretty bedroom with an en suite bath. "This was my room when I first came here. You'll be comfortable," she says as she leaves.

Alone, the tears come again. I should be stronger than this. It shouldn't hurt so much to be away from a man who, if I'm honest, I barely know. Yet, I want to go back to Drayce and tell him that I don't care about anything that happened in his past as long as he's promising me the future. He made mistakes. I've made plenty. Maybe we should talk. Maybe all of this, from the moment I got lost in the woods, is a very complex dream and I'll wake up.

Why does that idea fill me with more despair? If my

wyvern isn't real, then why does my heart feel as if it's going to explode? Dreams pale in comparison to what I'm living. Am I willing to give this up to go back to a life that wasn't very satisfying?

I stare out the window at the darkening woods. If I'd been stronger, I could have stayed with him and let him convince me that whatever he felt for Astra meant nothing. He told me as much; I was just too shocked to let his words sink in until now.

This is the second time I've run away from him and there's no trap in the woods for me to get caught up in and beg forgiveness. Thinking about it, I don't need to be forgiven, and I don't have to apologize or hear that from Drayce. I know in my heart that he's the only man who can ever make me happy.

In my entire life, I can count on one hand the memories of joy and contentment. The biggest one happened this morning, and I threw it all away because I imagined he loved someone else.

He was lonely. That's something I can relate to.

Movement in the trees catches my attention. I stare until the moon's warm glow illuminates the shape of a man standing just inside the shadow of the woods. Mostly hidden and with only dappled moonlight to see by, I know Drayce is watching me.

Quietly, I leave the safety of the bedroom and step through the house. Astra is sitting on Niko's lap out on the back porch. Neither of them looks my way as I ease out the front door and cross the yard toward where I know Drayce is waiting. I step through the tree line.

"I'm sorry." His voice is full of pain. He must have moved deeper into the woods.

I can't make out his shape. I stop before I end up face-first in the thick underbrush. "I shouldn't have run away again. It's only that I was scared of being left behind. My past pushed forward, and I wasn't thinking reasonably."

Wings beat the air and smaller branches as Drayce lowers to the ground. He's in his manly form, but his iridescent wings are fully spread behind him. The rest of him is completely and gloriously naked. Pain is etched on his brow and his eyes are hooded. "You forgive me?"

It takes all my will to keep the few feet of space between us. "I don't need your apology. I only need to know what you want from me, with me?"

He kneels in the thick leaves and looks at me with hope shining. His wings spread wide, he reaches one hand toward me. "I want to love you for all the days of my life, Kori. If you'll let me, I'll do all in my power to make you happy. I already know you are the only person who can offer me any joy."

My heart is about to burst. Taking his hand, I kneel with him. The twigs and underbrush bite into my knees and shins. I press my cheek to his chest. "I want to make you happy too."

He wraps his wings around me and slips them between me and the harsh ground. His hug is safe and warm. "I know you said you don't need my apology, but I'm so sorry for causing you pain. It will never happen again."

Thinking over the course of my life, I laugh. "That's probably not true. People who love each other always hurt them from time to time."

He cups my jaw and eases my gaze toward his. "I love you more than words will ever be adequate to describe. Hurting you will only torment me."

Monsters say the nicest things. You'd never find a human man who would pledge that. At least, none in my experience have even come close. Pressing my hand over his, I turn it and kiss his palm. "I won't run again, Drayce. Whatever happens, I'll stay and we'll work it out. I love you so much that it terrifies me. I won't let that fear drive me away ever again."

His cock presses hard and thick between us. "I would like to take you home now."

My clit aches for release just from being near him and knowing he wants me. My nipples tighten with need. "Is there someplace closer we can go?" I grip his thick cock and run my hand from base to tip.

On a long growl, he lifts me in his arms and wings us into the air. "I can't fly far with you like this, but the lake is nearby."

I hold on tight as he flies up just above the leaves and the warm summer air brushes against my cheeks. We land a minute later, on the soft slope of the lake. The moon shines down on the still water as we fumble to strip me out of my clothes.

I run my fingers over the warm, leathery expanse of his wings. Every cell in my body tingles with desire. It's as if fires burn under my skin and only his touch can feed them, as well as quell them. "So, you can change different parts without becoming the wyvern?"

Caressing my shoulder, then down along the swell of my breast, his breath shakes. "Some parts are more useful as a man than others. His long, forked tongue slides from his mouth as he kneels before me.

As he slips his tongue between my folds, pleasure ripples out from my center.

I widen my stance and moan with delight. My body shakes as he teases my clit, then enters me before repeating. My legs shake, and I grip his shoulders to keep on my feet. Again and again, the two ends of his tongue slide around my sensitive folds and rub my bud. He plunges inside me, touching deep and pushing me over the edge so hard, I wrap my arms around his and call his name. "Drayce," I say more softly as his hands cup my ass.

As I wrap my legs around him, he rolls to his back and eases me onto the tip of his cock. As he breaches my slit, I moan with the pleasure of becoming one with this magnificent creature. "I love you."

The wyvern's tongue pulls inside his full lips and when he opens his mouth, he's fully human. "I love you too."

I impale myself until we both grunt with the pleasure of joining. I lift my hips and set a fast pace as another orgasm starts to build.

Drayce grips my hips and slows me down. "Easy, love. We have a lifetime."

Every time he fills me, the base of his shaft rubs my clit and pushes me closer to the rapture I seek. Pressing my hands to his chest, I change the angle to take him a little deeper.

He growls, the wyvern close to the surface, and his eyes change, pupils narrowing to slits. "You're perfect, mate." His voice is lower than normal.

The barbs along his cock release and brush my sheath. I come in a torrent and can't stop the scream of release before collapsing onto his chest.

Gripping my hips, he lifts me enough to pound inside me from below. He grunts with pleasure once, twice, and with a third thrust, he fills me with warm cum. Wrapping his arms around me, he pulls me tight and kisses my hair. "You're everything."

When there is no knotting, I ease forward and sigh with the emptiness of his body leaving mine. With my forearms on his chest, I stare into his mostly human eyes. "Why didn't we knot again?"

Staring a moment, he brushes my hair off my cheek and tucks it behind my ear. "I don't really know. You may have conceived earlier today, or maybe that doesn't happen every time. We'll have to learn these things together, my love."

"I like that." I cuddle into his chest. "Can we go home now?"

His wings push from his back, lifting us higher off the ground and he wraps them around me in a warm cocoon. "In a little while. I have to change fully to carry you that far. As a man, my wings are only suitable for short flights. I want to hold you a bit longer."

Engulfed in his arms and wings, I know I'll always be safe here. My wild wyvern is the best man I've ever known.

EPILOGUE

KORI

It's my wedding day. I can't believe any of this has happened to me. I was lonely and unhappy for most of my life, and now I have a mate who adores me, a life where I get to co-write cookbooks with a famous chef, and a job in a local restaurant. I look in the mirror while Astra fusses over my hair and I sigh.

"I hope that's a happy sound." Astra pins the curl she just made beside the last, forming a tiara shape along my crown.

"So happy. Thank you for doing this. Meg and Lori will be here soon, and you'll be able to join the other guests." I admire the way I look on the biggest day of my life. Besides the hair and light makeup, I look happy. I hardly recognize the woman I see in the mirror today or any day in the last three months.

"I didn't think wyverns took much stock in formal

marriages." She winds another piece of my hair around a curling iron.

"Drayce is doing this for me. He even got the local judge to come and marry us. It's enough for him that we are mates and bonded for life, but I'd like the paper and customs of my human world too. Besides, who doesn't want a party?" I grin at her through the mirror and she laughs.

It's still impossible to look away from the nymph. She's like a magnet. "Well, one thing is certain, with all the food that you and Niko made over the last few days, no one will go away hungry."

The door to my bedroom flies open, and in stumble Dean, Meg, and Lori in a clatter of noise and laughter.

"We're here!" Meg's arms are full. She's carrying a dress on a hanger and rolling her suitcase. She ushers the others into the room without looking up.

Dean stares at me with wide eyes. "You look amazing." He dabs a tear from the corner of his eye.

Lori drops her things on the floor and runs across the room. "Oh my god! I can't believe you're getting married." She stops short of hugging me, as if I might break.

Standing, I pull her into my arms. "I can't believe it either."

"I'm afraid I'll wrinkle you." She laughs. "There are so many um…people outside. My head is spinning."

"It's like the monster interstellar convention or something." Dean acts as if he sees monsters every day and it's no big deal. "I'm so curious about the one with the tentacles." He pulls me out of Lori's arms and holding my shoulders, gives me a look from head to toe. "Spectacular." He hugs me.

Astra's laugh is warm and impossible to ignore, as it's like music. "Marty is a good time, but be advised, he can get attached with those tentacles and you have to wait for the suction to release. It can be…tedious."

Lori and Dean both shift their attention from me and stare wide-eyed at the nymph in her pale-blue gown that clings to every curve of her perfect body. Her blond hair streams down her back and over her shoulders like a cascade of golden waterfall.

Trying to make light of the awkward way they're staring, I say, "This is my friend, Astra. Astra, this is Dean, Lori, and that's Meg fussing over the clothes. We were all in foster care together."

Astra's hair flows to the right as she cocks her head. "Then these are your siblings. How lovely to meet you." She extends her hand to Dean first and then to Lori.

Mouths slightly agape, they each shake her hand and blink.

Finally, Dean says, "You're the first woman I've ever found attractive."

Somehow, Astra manages to look both amused and sympathetic at the same time. She grins, but her gaze is soft and full of kindness. "Don't worry. It's only because I'm a nymph. You're still gay."

Then we all laugh.

Except for Meg, who is still fussing. Finally, she turns and looks at me. "I wanted to be here to do your hair." A tear slides down her face and she rushes into my arms.

I pat her back. "It's okay. I know wrangling these two is a full-time job. Astra helped, and you can finish my hair if you want."

With a deep breath, Meg steps back and turns to look at Astra. She freezes. "It's you."

"Hello, Meg. I remember you too." Astra pulls Meg into a hug. "I was sorry to hear about your parents."

"You knew? How…" Meg pulls back and stares at Astra as if they were friends long estranged.

Cupping Meg's cheek, Astra says, "I always kept an eye on you after that day in the lake. I wish I had been watching your father too. Maybe I could have done something." She sighs, and even that sounds like the harmony of some sad song.

"Um…" Dean clears his throat. "What's happening?"

I'd actually like to know too. Then I remember the story Meg told about being rescued from drowning. "Wait, is Astra the woman who saved you when you were little?"

With a watery smile, Meg nods.

DRAYCE

The wedding was nice, but for me, Kori has been my mate from the moment I first saw her. Even though I made mistakes, she was always mine.

Still, hearing her tell the judge and witnesses that she would love me for a lifetime was satisfying. My wyvern barely contained himself.

Across the yard, she's talking to her friends, and places her hand over her abdomen. They all scream and hug her, then look over at me.

Before I know it, I'm engulfed in hugs and

congratulations. I hug them back, happy to be included in Kori's friendships with the three people she's closest to. They're her family, and I want them to like me.

Lori says, "Um, I hope this isn't rude, but will the baby be human or a mon…um…wyvern?"

Meg elbows her. "It is rude."

Dean stares with wide, expectant eyes, waiting for my answer.

Smiling, Kori puts her hand on Lori's shoulder. "The baby will be born human, though the pregnancy might be a few months longer. There are very few examples of matings between wyverns and humans, or even dragons and humans. We've been doing research, but we have a lot more to do."

"I didn't shift for the first time until I was six or seven. That's fairly normal. Though, I've heard of young shifting as early as three and as late as twelve." I'm trying to assuage their worries, but they look less comforted.

"What about a doctor?" Meg's voice is sharp with concern as she grips Kori's hand.

I listen for the strong steady heartbeat of my baby growing inside Kori. I was happy before we knew she'd conceived, and now I'm ecstatic. "There is a very fine monster doctor, as well as a human doctor living in town. We shall consult with both since Kori thinks that is best and I agree."

"The town in the valley? That's a very small hospital. What's it called?" Dean twists his mouth and narrows his eyes. It's a sure sign of a New Yorker's disappointment or judgment.

"Mountveil Hospital, the same name as the town. It might be small, but they have all the most modern equipment and doctors for all species." Kori steps to my side and presses her cheek to my chest.

I wrap an arm around her waist and admire how beautiful she looks in this wedding gown, but wish I could tear it off of her right now. The wyvern growls. "We will be prepared. You don't have to worry."

"Of course, we're going to worry." Meg props her hands on her hips. She takes a deep breath. "But we know you'll take good care of our Kori and we'll be up here to visit regularly. If we're going to be aunties and Uncle Dean, we're not missing any part of the process."

I like them, and not just because they love my mate. These are good humans who have endured much and are wonderful, either because, or in spite of their circumstances. "We wouldn't have it any other way."

The music, played by a kraken and two imps, shifts to a soft ballad. Kori sways against me.

I kiss the top of her head. "Dance with me?"

She nods, and I take her hand as we walk to the dance floor.

With her in my arms, I know my life is going to be wonderful. "You make me very happy, love."

"I'm happy too." She smiles up at me as we sway from side to side to the beat.

"Are you as worried as your friends about the baby?" I span my hand over her back and feel her warmth through the gown.

Shaking her head, she rests her cheek on me. "No. It's going to be fine. I'm not that thrilled with the prospect of being pregnant for eleven months, but I can't wait to meet our baby."

"It will go fast."

"Spoken like a man who is barely inconvenienced by pregnancy." She laughs.

"I would spare you this if it were possible, love. I would carry the baby within me and suffer all the woes of pregnancy." I tip her chin so that I can press my lips to hers.

With her eyes filled with love, she smiles. "You are the only male who I believe means that."

"I do." I would suffer any discomfort or pain to keep her happy. But this isn't possible when speaking of procreation.

"We'll endure it together, Drayce." She looks serious, but laughter lights her eyes. "I'm too happy to even fake worry. Thank you for today. I feel like a proper wife, and soon I'll be a mother. You've made all my dreams come true."

The warmth of being mated to this amazing woman floods my heart. "That is my sole purpose, mate."

She hugs me tight. "Mission accomplished."

Thank you for reading **Wild for the Wyvern**.
I hope you enjoyed Drayce and Kori's story.
They were so much fun to write.

Thank you for reading the Catskill Monsters box set.
I hope you loved these spicy/sweet stories about love
overcoming any obstacle, no matter how big.
Ready for another romantic monster adventure?
Check out *Big Enough To Bite*.

https://books2read.com/u/mZ6yKp

**In a town full of monsters,
love might be the scariest thing of all.**

SAM

Harmony Glen's been my home since the town welcomed my kind with open arms. It's a safe haven for monsters like me. It's been fun living amongst humans. Over time, all types of people have begun calling this place home. Now, there's a new vampire in town.

She walks through the park at night, sometimes singing soft, haunting melodies. Her voice hooked me from the first note. I watch from the shadows, drawn to her. So when she asks me to build a stone wall in her garden, I say yes—fast.

I lay bricks by day and try to win her over with charm, but she's slow to trust. I long to uncover the secrets of her past and be a part of her future. Maybe a giant isn't what she's looking for. But my heart's already hers, whether she wants it or not.

MARI

I was born in 1869 in a small Romanian village. My people were wanderers. After I was turned into a vampire at twenty, I left my family—but not by choice. My maker was a monster in more ways than one, and it took many decades to escape him.

The Great Revelation exposed us to the world; fear and curiosity followed. I've searched several lifetimes for a place to belong. Harmony Glen is the first town that might actually feel like home.

The creatures and humans here are kind, even when I'm not. It might have been a mistake to invite a giant into my garden, but I couldn't resist. He's steady, gentle, and strong in every way that matters. He makes my fangs ache—and he might just be big enough to bite.

ALSO BY ANDIE FENICHEL

Paranormal/Monster Romance

Dragon of My Dreams (Monster Between the Sheets)

Turnabout is Fairy Play (Monster Between the Sheets)

Soul of a Vampire (Brothers of Scrim Hall)

Soul of a Reaper (Brothers of Scrim Hall)

Soul of a Dragon (Brothers of Scrim Hall)

Soul of a Wolf (Brothers of Scrim Hall)

Soul of a Demon (Brothers of Scrim Hall)

Soul of a Phoenix (Brothers of Scrim Hall)

Soul of a Monster (Brothers of Scrim Hall)

Mantus

Riding With the Panther

The Manticore's Mate (Catskills Mountain Monsters)

Promised to the Satyr (Catskills Mountain Monsters)

Wild for the Wyvern (Catskills Mountain Monsters)

Big Enough to Bite (Harmony Glen)

Biting Bigfoot (Harmony Glen)

Bitten by Love (Harmony Glen)

Contemporary Romance

Dad Bod Handyman (Lane Family)

Carnival Lane (Lane Family)

Lane to Fame (Lane Family)

Changing Lanes (Lane Family)

Heavy Petting (Lane Family)

Summer Lane (Lane Family)

Hero's Lane (Lane Family)

Icing It (Lane Family)

Mountain Lane (Lane Family)

Christmas Lane (Lane Family)

Texas Lane (Lane Family)

Building Lane (Lane Family)

Humbug Lane (Lane Family)

High Voltage Lane (Lane Family)

For Letter or Worse (Lane Family)

Visit Andie's website for the most up to date list.

www.andiefenichel.com

Writing as **A.S. Fenichel**

HISTORICAL ROMANCE

The Wallflowers of West Lane Series

The Earl Not Taken

Misleading A Duke

Capturing the Earl

Not Even For A Duke

Visit A.S. Fenichel's website for the most up-to-date information about her books.

www.asfenichel.com

ABOUT THE AUTHOR

A.S. (Andie) Fenichel gave up a successful career in New York City to pursue her lifelong dream of being a professional writer. She's never looked back.

Andie adores writing stories filled with love, passion, desire, magic, and maybe a little mayhem tossed in for good measure. Books have always been her perfect escape, and she still relishes diving into one and staying up all night to finish a good story.

With over 60 published books, Andie Fenichel/A.S. Fenichel is multi-published in historical romance, fantasy romance, contemporary romance, and some interesting mixed-genre romances. Andie is the author of several series, including Reign of the Witch Queen, Everton Domestic Society, Witches of Windsor, and more. Strong, empowered heroines from Regency London to modern-day New York are what you'll find in all her books.

A Jersey Girl at heart, she now makes her home in Southern Missouri with her real-life hero, her wonderful husband. When not reading or writing, she enjoys cooking, traveling, history, and puttering in her garden.

Connect with Andie Fenichel
www.andiefenichel.com

Email: asfenichel@hotmail.com

facebook.com/a.s.fenichel
x.com/asfenichel
instagram.com/asfenichel
bookbub.com/authors/andie-fenichel
pinterest.com/asfenichel
tiktok.com/@asfenichel